NOTHING BUT THE TRUTH

Visit us at www.boldstrokesbooks.com

Praise for Lambda Literary Award Finalist Carsen Taite

"Law professor Morgan Bradley and her student Parker Casey are potential love interests, but throw in a high-profile murder trial, and you've got an entertaining book that can be read in one sitting. Taite also practices criminal law and she weaves her insider knowledge of the criminal justice system into the love story seamlessly and with excellent timing. I find romances lacking when the characters change completely upon falling in love, but this was not the case here. As Morgan and Parker grow closer, their relationship is portrayed faithfully and their personalities do not change dramatically. I look forward to reading more from Taite."—*Curve Magazine*

"Taite is a real-life attorney so the prose jumps off the page with authority and authenticity. ...[*It Should be a Crime*] is just Taite's second novel...but it's as if she has bookshelves full of bestsellers under her belt. In fact, she manages to make the courtroom more exciting than Judge Judy bursting into flames while delivering a verdict. Like this book, that's something we'd pay to see."—*Gay List Daily*

"Taite, a criminal defense attorney herself, has given her readers a behind the scenes look at what goes on during the days before a trial. Her descriptions of lawyer/client talks, investigations, police procedures, etc. are fascinating. Taite keeps the action moving, her characters clear, and never allows her story to get bogged down in paperwork. *It Should be a Crime* has a fast-moving plot and some extraordinarily hot sex."—*Just About Write*

"Taite's tale of sexual tension is entertaining in itself, but a number of secondary characters...add substantial color to romantic inevitability."—*Richard Labonte, Book Marks*

By the Author

truelesbianlove.com

It Should be a Crime

Do Not Disturb

Nothing But the Truth

NOTHING BUT THE TRUTH

by

Carsen Taite

2011

NOTHING BUT THE TRUTH

ISBN 10: 1-60282-198-4
ISBN 13: 978-1-60282-198-9

This Trade Paperback Original Is Published By
Bold Strokes Books, Inc.
P.O. Box 249
Valley Falls, NY 12185

First Edition: January 2011

Credits
Editor: Cindy Cresap
Production Design: Susan Ramundo
Cover Design By Sheri (graphicartist2020@hotmail.com)

Acknowledgments

In the ten years I've practiced criminal defense, I've learned nothing is ever as simple as it seems. In addition to being a love story, this story is about the art of seeing things from a different perspective.

As usual, I owe many people thanks:

Bill and Toby—thanks for all your advice from the prosecution perspective. You were both great in the law and order role, but I have to say it's fun working on the same side now.

Christie and Tom—thanks for inviting me into the world of crime.

Sandy—thanks for your patience as I sent pages flying your way up until the very last second. Your insights, as always, were invaluable.

Cindy—I love working with you. You always manage to inject just the right amount of humor into your red ink. Thanks for challenging me to be a better writer.

Stacia—thanks for always making me look good with your superb attention to detail.

Sheri—every time I think "this cover is my favorite," you totally outdo yourself on the next one. You're amazing.

Rad—thanks for taking a chance on me. I love being part of your publishing family.

To all the other authors and behind the scenes folks at BSB—you are the greatest. I can't imagine a more nurturing family.

Lainey—thanks for all the times you've listened to my real and fictional courtroom war stories. My day job may inspire some plot points, but the romance inspiration is all you.

To my readers—as always, thanks for the constant stream of encouragement, praise, and shouts for more. I save every note, every e-mail and read them whenever I need a boost.

Dedication

Lainey—I love you. And that's the truth.

CHAPTER ONE

Other people's emergencies were Brett Logan's bread and butter. Her buzzing BlackBerry signaled business was booming. *I have a legal emergency. Can you call me? Now. 911.*

"Ms. Logan, your case is next. Is your client on bond?"

Brett looked up from the tiny screen and stood. "No, Judge. He's in the holdover." She glanced once more at the e-mail message on her phone and then shoved the pesky device in her bag. Everyone who called her had an emergency. She'd return the call as soon as she finished with her current slate of crises.

Nodding to the bailiff, Brett set her bag and purse on a chair just inside the rail before making her way to stand in front of the bench. As she waited for her client to join her, she focused on drowning out the hum of activity around her. On a given morning, there were likely to be at least a dozen cases on the court's plea docket, which meant at least a dozen attorneys and clients along with a random assortment of friends, family members, and witnesses lining the rows of the gallery. All these parties conferred with each other in their various interpretations of whispers. The result was controlled commotion that courtroom veterans had learned to ignore.

Once the bailiff positioned her client beside her, Brett placed her hand on his arm. Everett Marshall was a tall, lanky, young black man, charged with two counts of possession with intent to deliver a controlled substance, crack cocaine. As the judge reviewed the plea paperwork in the file, Brett leaned over and whispered in Everett's ear. In response, he turned and gazed at the rows in the gallery, finally locking eyes with the members of his family who were there to support him.

"They're all here. You told them?" he asked.

"Of course," Brett replied. "They all wanted to be here to support you."

He nodded. Brett recognized his appreciation even in the minimal response. Up until moments ago, Everett's fate had been uncertain. He was charged with two second degree felony drug possession cases with a punishment range of two to twenty years each in the Texas Department of Corrections. Everett's first brush with the law was significant, and the prosecutor had been unsympathetic to the fact he was a first time offender. In his view, based on the quantity of drugs at issue, Everett was a drug dealer, and the best disposition was to put him away where he could do no more harm. Brett had spent all her energy finding evidence to support her contention that Everett had been drawn into his situation out of a desperate need to make money to care for his sick mother and feed and clothe his children. Along the way, he had become addicted to the currency of his drug dealing occupation. The only chance he had of breaking free was rehabilitation, not punishment. Unable to convince the prosecutor to offer anything less than ten years in the state penitentiary, she had set the case for an open plea. Everett would plead guilty, and Brett would present evidence to convince the judge to take a chance on giving her client probation with drug treatment so he could get his life back.

When Brett showed up this morning with Everett's family, friends, and employer in tow, she had a renewed discussion with the prosecutor. They reached a compromise. Everett would serve three months in the county jail and then be sent to a county-operated drug treatment facility. If he completed the drug treatment program successfully, he would be placed on probation for five years. She had explained the risk to Everett. If he messed up on even the smallest condition of his probation, he could be brought back to court and sentenced to serve anywhere up to the full twenty years. He said he understood. She hoped he did. She had long since given up trying to distinguish between clients who told her what she wanted to hear in order to move things along and those who were sincere about their commitments.

Since the terms of the plea were now agreed, the proceeding was practically rote. When the judge pronounced the sentence, Brett shook Everett's hand and wished him good luck. She gathered all the family members in the hallway and gave them an overview of how the case would proceed from that point. They had a lot of questions, many of which Brett had to answer with maybes since Everett's future was largely dependent on how he conducted himself once he got out. The Q and A ran long.

When she finally broke free, she remembered the message on her phone. She forwarded the e-mail to her assistant with a short note asking him to get whatever information he could. Crisis well in hand, she dashed off to another courtroom down the hall, completely focused on her next case of the morning.

"I hope you had a good reason for agreeing to probation for that guy." Ryan Foster made a habit of challenging the prosecutors in her division. Her philosophy was simple. If they knew they would have to answer for their decisions, they were more likely to make good ones.

The young prosecutor shrugged. Ryan imagined he was suffering under the false impression that his recent promotion to chief prosecutor in the 319th District Court would eliminate the need to explain his every action. After all, he was in charge of managing two other prosecutors and a heavy court docket. He probably believed he should be accorded a little deference in the way he chose to dispose of cases. Ryan hoped her strong stare would dispel him of any notion he was no longer accountable to her.

"Yes, I did. It's his first offense. He has lots of family support. His employer is holding his job, and he has a significant, but treatable drug problem."

"So you slap him with candy-ass jail time and feel-good drug treatment. Wow, Bill, you really taught him a lesson." Ryan paused, then swiftly changed her tone from sarcastic to sweet. "Maybe the defense attorney offered you a little something more than her persuasive legal arguments. Is that right?"

Ryan knew Bill hadn't worked under her long enough to tell if she was ragging on him in earnest or just trying to get a rise out of him. His harsh stare told her she had really pissed him off. *Hell, admit it to yourself. You wouldn't oppose an offer of special consideration from Ms. Logan.* Ryan struggled to control her features lest anything in her demeanor disclose she was projecting when she accused Bill of finding defense counsel particularly attractive. Brett Logan. Ryan knew who she was, but they had never directly crossed paths. Ryan only knew her name and her reputation as a fearless litigator. Prosecutors under Ryan's command with shit cases to try regularly sought permission to cave to Ms. Logan's mastery of the game of chicken. Brett had held out on this case, which would have been a total loser for her client, until she got a deal he could live with. Ryan was hard-pressed to admit it, but she admired Brett Logan's steel resolve. She admired her legs and her ass too, but those details she would keep to herself. Bill's voice cut into her thoughts.

"It's not weakness to give someone a chance to prove himself. I'll be watching this case. Everett Marshall makes one tiny screw-up, and I'll be in court asking for the max. You can count on that."

Ryan smiled. "Fair enough. Good job, Bill." She knew without looking he was probably shaking his head as she walked away.

As Brett waited in a long line to speak to a prosecutor about a pending case, she felt the insistent vibration of her BlackBerry again. She noted her office number on the display and stepped out of the DA workroom to take the call.

"Yes?"

"Brett, are you on your way back to the office?"

Recognizing the impatient tone of her assistant/paralegal/office manager, Anthony Panetta, Brett smiled. "Not quite, Tony. I have to make one more stop. What's up?"

"Well, Mrs. Jarvis is sitting here waiting. She brought cash. Whatever good will you're spreading around down there can wait until after you sign up this paying client, don't you think?"

Brett relied on Tony to run her business. He did a great job of keeping her on track, but he would never completely grasp her need to give each case her complete, undivided attention, no matter how much she was being paid. If Tony had his way, she wouldn't take court-appointed cases like Everett Marshall's. Unlike many attorneys, Brett spent as much time on these cases, which paid pennies on the dollar, as she did on her retained cases. She carried a heavy docket of court-appointed cases because she felt it was important to the process for everyone to have the best representation possible—no matter how much money they could afford to pay.

Tony interrupted her thoughts. "Oh, that e-mail you got? The guy wants you to call him. Only you. He wouldn't give me any hints. Promise you'll call him as soon as you get here. Maybe he has money too."

Brett silently chided herself for not responding to the message herself. "Will you call him back and set up a meeting? I'll make myself available for any time they want to meet this afternoon. And I swear I'll be there to win over Mrs. Jarvis in about thirty minutes. Okay?"

Tony's pronounced sigh conveyed his resignation to the fact he had no control over the situation. "Okay."

Brett stepped back into the district attorney's workroom. She was dismayed to see it was still crowded with lawyers jockeying for the attention of the prosecutors assigned to this particular court. Each of the twelve district courts located in the Dallas County courthouse contained one of these tiny offices located to the rear of each of courtroom. Though each prosecutor had an office on the eleventh floor of the building, these workrooms served as a war room of sorts from which they ran their morning docket. Two small desks, home to the number two and three prosecutors in the court, lined the walls of the outer section of the office. The only distinguishing characteristic between their work area and the closet-like space accorded to the court's chief prosecutor was the presence of a door. The delay this morning was due in part to the fact that the chief prosecutor in this court, Jeff Oates, was huddled in his office with his boss, Ryan Foster.

Brett, like most everyone at the courthouse, knew who Ryan Foster was, by reputation if not personal acquaintance. Ryan was a career prosecutor. Anyone who had worked in and around Dallas County was familiar with the law and order approach of the formidable woman. Brett hadn't had any direct contact with her, but she still felt her influence. It was definitely harder to work out deals with the prosecutors in the courts under Ryan's direction. She had a tendency to be more hands-on than her counterparts, which translated into according less discretion to the prosecutors she supervised.

She even looks like a hard-ass. Ryan's blond hair was pulled back into a perfect French braid and her charcoal gray silk suit was perfectly pressed. Brett looked down at her own wrinkled suit and inwardly cursed at her inability to make it through an hour at the courthouse without looking as though she had slept in her clothes. Instinctively, she knew her hair was poking out from her head in a million different directions. She shook her head in wonder of Ryan's tight braid.

As Brett looked closer, she wondered if Ryan's fierce look was a bit contrived. Her eyes were an inviting shade of bluish gray, quick and alert, and the sharp lines of her suit didn't completely conceal feminine curves. Ryan's voice was commanding, but her tone was probably an integral part of her identity as a top dog at the DA's office. Brett wondered what she sounded like at dinner with friends, whether she ever let her guard down. *I'd like to find out.*

Her thoughts were interrupted on dual fronts. Ryan's com-manding tone grew in volume as her conversation with Jeff became heated, and, further interfering with her ability to adequately eavesdrop, Brett's BlackBerry started jumping around in her purse. Cursing technology, Brett fished the beast out of her bag and read the display. Tony's growing impatience was clear: *I hope you are pulling into the parking lot. I can only restrain Mrs. Jarvis for so long!* Brett looked once again at the line of attorneys in front of her, all now actively listening in on Ryan's discourse, and she decided to abandon this quest for the money-in-the-bank case waiting at her office.

❖

"I know you're the chief, but this an important case. My personal involvement will demonstrate how seriously this office takes this case."

"Ryan, I've worked for months preparing for this trial."

Ryan knew he was right. She also knew how much she would have resented this intrusion were the roles reversed. Jeff Oates was an excellent prosecutor. He wasn't showy, but he worked hard and juries liked him. He had earned his position as chief in this court, and his position gave him the privilege of picking the best cases for himself. Ryan's announcement that she was taking over as lead attorney on the Edwards case was a blow to his authority.

Ryan flashed back to a similar conversation she'd had with her boss, the elected district attorney, earlier in the week.

"If I were him, I'd consider quitting. He's worked on this case for months and I'm supposed to walk in there and rip it out from under him?"

"Ryan, you need to get your name in the news. Unfortunately, your current position has left you with a low profile. Make a splashy headline, and the press will cover the front page with stories about this case and all your past victories. All that free press will bring the donations rolling in. Take the Edwards case. It's juicy, and the trial will last for days."

"Sir, it wasn't that long ago I had my own court. I remember what it's like to be in charge and then have someone from upstairs come yank it out from under you."

He ignored the implication. "Don't 'sir' me. If you want my job, you have to trust me."

His words were tough, but Ryan knew he sincerely cared about her future and the future of this office. Ryan did want his job. She wanted it more than anything. Leonard Duncan had already announced his plans to retire at the end of his term, and rumors were circulating as to who he would anoint as his successor. Ryan knew she was his choice. She was chomping at the bit to become the first woman elected District Attorney of Dallas County, but she hated inserting herself into a case, especially when it was a blatant grab at publicity. Ryan briefly considered telling Jeff the decision to make her lead on the case was Duncan's, but she decided hiding behind her boss would make her look weak.

"Jeff, you've done a great job on this case. I wouldn't want to try the case without you." Ryan knew he would click to the implicit threat. "I'm sure we'll make a great team, and I look forward to working closely with you on this case." Ryan forced a smile, turned, and marched out of the still packed workroom. She barely made it out of the room before Jeff muttered "bitch" for everyone in the waiting crowd to hear.

CHAPTER TWO

A bout freaking time you got here."

"Hi, Tony, it's good to see you too. Is Mrs. Jarvis in the conference room?" Brett had snuck in the back door of the office suite and was busying stowing the files from her morning cases.

"Yep. Give me those files and get up there. Now!" Tony pushed her toward the door. "Oh, and I called the number for your anonymous e-mailer again. I let it ring a thousand times, but no one answered. I hope you didn't miss another big case because you didn't take the time to call yourself."

Brett whirled on him. "Tony! Cut me some slack! I remember once upon a time when people had to wait a few hours to have their messages returned because we didn't have instant messaging, wireless e-mail, and itty bitty cell phones we could tuck in our bras. Back then the only people who had cell phones were the fabulously wealthy and people on TV like Charlie's Angels, and even they looked stupid because they were holding phones the size of bread boxes up to their ears.

"I always return my messages, even if I don't do it within nanoseconds of receiving them." She paused to catch her breath. "I'm going to meet with Mrs. Jarvis now. I promise to sign her up and get a big pile of money. In exchange, you will wait until at least four thirty before you ask me another question about who I've called or e-mailed today. Deal?"

Tony merely nodded his head. She knew he knew she was more exasperated than angry. Brett was well aware her little tirade had no effect on him and, though he might go easy on her this afternoon, he would resume his job as head nag first thing in the morning. Sighing at her lack of authority in this, her own law practice, she trudged toward the conference room to meet with her client of means.

Mrs. Jarvis owned a string of small ambulance companies in the Dallas-Fort Worth area, all of which had been raided by a federal task force the day before. Brett was familiar with the scenario. Feds, most of them desk types dressed out for the first time in flak jackets, descended on a bunch of businesses, badges in hand. The employees of the business were detained for hours while the gun-toting feds loaded up their vans with the company's computers, records, and anything else they thought looked interesting and came remotely close to matching the items identified in their search warrant that proclaimed allegations of Medicare fraud. The guns and bulletproof vests were all for show—a scare tactic designed to convince the employees that now was their chance to start spilling the beans about their employer's nefarious business practices lest they become targets of the investigation themselves.

Brett hated these cases. The next few months would be spent interviewing all the employees and reviewing box after box of records in an attempt to convince the federal investigators their allegations of fraud were baseless. She would spend hours thumbing through patient files and billing records. There was rarely ever a smoking gun for either side. Instead, shades of gray would separate her client's position from the government's allegations of fraud. But because the legal fees usually reached into the tens of thousands, Brett couldn't justify turning these paper-intensive cases away. As she watched Mrs. Jarvis sign her contract and present her hefty retainer, Brett knew Tony would be proud.

Brett walked past Tony's workspace and let the signed contract and cashier's check glide through the air to rest on top of his desk. She kept walking and merely waved over her shoulder when he called out his praise. She knew he would waste no time opening a new file, sending a letter of representation to the assistant U.S. attorney handling the case, and scheduling employee interviews, all details Brett had no patience for. If she didn't have Tony, she would never even consider taking these white collar federal cases. She preferred the relatively paper-free atmosphere of the state courthouse where deals were done with a handshake rather than multiple versions of a written agreement passed back and forth between sides.

Sliding behind her desk, Brett smiled at the fresh cup of coffee faded with heavy cream waiting next to her computer keyboard. No matter how much he fussed at her, Tony fussed over her just as much.

Brett switched on the power to her twenty-inch monitor and scanned her e-mail. She understood the necessity of having a BlackBerry, but she hated trying to read messages on the postage stamp-sized screen and her thumbed-out responses were usually unintelligible. She preferred answering her e-mails when she could actually see them on the big screen. Brett spotted the cryptic e-mail she had received earlier and typed her reply:

My office tried to call you to schedule an appointment, but no one answered. I'm in the office if you want to call me. It would help if you could tell me more about your situation so I'll be prepared when we talk. Brett.

She hit send and reached for the waiting cup of coffee. Seconds later, a pop-up announced she had new mail.

Thanks. Don't want to give more details this way. I will call you but would prefer to do it later. Cell number?

Brett read the new message and paused before answering. She used to give out her cell phone number to anyone who asked, but clients with the inability to distinguish between a true emergency and the mere need to chat had disrupted her beauty sleep on one too many occasions. Years of disrupted personal moments had driven her to use an answering service for after-hour callers. She still returned calls at all hours, but the service minimized the interruption to her evenings.

Brett reread the e-mail. Something about the enigmatic e-mailer sparked her curiosity. Against her better judgment, she typed: *Okay. Call me on cell—see number below. Brett* and hit send.

❖

No sooner had Brett drifted off to dreamland, than her infernal BlackBerry skittered across her nightstand. Brett shook herself awake and focused her sleepy eyes on the display. She didn't recognize the number. She was ready to hit the ignore button when she remembered the e-mail from earlier in the day. She punched the talk button. "Brett Logan speaking."

"I e-mailed you."

"Ah, I thought this might be you. What can I do for you?" Brett reached into the nightstand for one of the stack of small notepads she kept ready to record middle of the night thoughts and calls such as this.

"My son is in trouble. He needs a lawyer." The voice was gruff.

"Well, you called the right place. What's your name?"

"Do I have to tell you?"

"It would help if I had something to call you. How did you get my name?" Tony was forever on her to ask how her clients found her so he could keep track for marketing purposes, but Brett's question was posed purely out of curiosity.

"Friends. I don't want them to know about my son's trouble."

"Okay. What kind of trouble is he in?" Brett waited for what was sure to be a tale of a juvenile prank gone awry.

"He murdered someone and he wants to confess."

CHAPTER THREE

I must be crazy for wanting to run this office. Ryan reached into her desk drawer and felt for the bottle she kept hidden behind a sheaf of papers. County employees were not allowed to have alcohol in the building, but for years the district attorney kept his personal office stocked with a full bar complete with heavy crystal glasses. Ryan reasoned her pint-sized bottle of Scotch and paper cups were a warm-up to when she took over his position.

She would need a bigger bottle if she had more days like this one. Jeff, a prosecutor she respected, had no doubt told everyone who would listen about her power grab this morning. She could tell by the many whispered conversations that died off as she approached that her reputation as a power-hungry bitch was intact. She had no idea how she was going to be an effective leader if everyone in the office resented her. Ryan drank deeply from her paper tumbler and, as the amber liquid burned a path through her stress, she resolved to have a long talk with her boss about the method behind his plan to bring her to power.

Ryan turned to the boxes piled beside her desk and combed through the evidence in the Edwards case. No wonder Jeff was angry. He had put together a rock solid case. All she had to do was show up and win. She was relieved she wouldn't have to start from scratch, especially since she was too keyed up this night to focus on the documents in front of her. Agitation twitched through her and she recognized the source. She would need more than Scotch to take the edge off. Ryan leaned back in her chair and closed her eyes.

With the concerns of her job blocked out, she could focus on what could really relax her. An image of a tall brunette came to mind. Brett Logan. Ryan had seen her in the halls of the courthouse many times, but she hadn't connected the striking woman with the reputation of Ms. Logan. Too often, young prosecutors under her command came to Ryan wanting permission to kick a case because Brett had announced ready for trial and they knew their case was a dog. Ryan usually sent them packing. Bluffing should be a required class in law school. Obviously, Brett had the skill, but many young prosecutors were too scared of wrecking their stats to take a chance on a crappy case. Ryan found it interesting to learn the woman whose body she admired had a mind to match. She focused again on the image of Brett Logan, standing in the well of the courtroom. The image looked so real, Ryan felt as if she could reach right out and grab Brett's tight, round ass. Ryan knew what would take the edge off. She reached for the phone and dialed a number from memory.

She waited impatiently through the rings, breathing only after her call was finally answered. The voice at the other end of the phone confirmed the code word she offered and affirmed her hope that the cure she sought was available this evening. Ryan repeated the address she was given before hanging up the phone. She didn't recognize the location. She committed it to memory by repeating it silently to herself. She didn't write it down, look it up online, or plug it into the GPS in her car. Those were the rules, and she obeyed in both letter and spirit.

Ryan stopped by her North Dallas home to change clothes. Not for the first time, she wished she lived closer to the courthouse, but the constituents in North Dallas were the ones most likely to get her elected, so she purchased a modest house in the bland area of the city in order to appear to be one of them. Once she arrived at her house, she took her time selecting a suitable outfit, shedding her tight braid and sharp-lined suit as she moved through her wardrobe. Ryan tugged on a pair of designer jeans and slipped into spiked, black leather sling-backs. A snug charcoal blouse with a plunging neckline, deep burgundy lipstick, and hairspray to enhance the wave of her now free hair completed her transformation. She surveyed her image in the mirror and allowed herself a wry smile. She looked nothing like the woman pictured on her official badge.

Back in her car, Ryan pulled a map out of her glove compartment and ran her fingers along the streets, tracing her intended path. Her proclivity for following the rules mixed with the intoxicating danger of her destination to create an intense feeling of arousal. She resisted the urge to speed. She would not draw attention to herself. Not yet.

The valet was a hulking creature dressed in tight black clothes designed to make him blend into the night. He confirmed she knew the code and watched while she stowed her purse under the front seat before he drove her car to an undisclosed location. Ryan knew if anything went wrong inside, neither she nor anyone else would ever see her car again. She walked up the sidewalk, ignoring the front door, instead veering toward the side of the house. At the side entrance, she paused before raising her hand to give the requisite knock. No matter how many times she attended these events, she always experienced a twisted knot in her belly, tied with apprehension and anticipation.

As she moved slowly through the main living room, Ryan paused only to lift a flute of champagne from a passing tray. She had no trouble assessing the rest of the evening's fare while on the move. She savored a sip of the dry, piercing potion. She would have only one glass. More would be risky, and, despite her presence in this place, she was averse to risk.

Every party, no matter where it took place, was the same. Ryan always recognized at least half the guests. She took comfort in the fact there were no smiles of recognition, no snippets of conversation alluding to past connections. At these gatherings, everyone in the room was a stranger with nothing to link them here or in the real world.

The house was large with many floors, vaulted ceilings, and well-appointed furnishings. This residence was obviously owned by someone with means, as were all the venues used for these gatherings. Ryan knew a few clicks on her computer when she returned home would reveal the identity of the evening's host, but she also knew she wouldn't expend the minimal effort required. Anonymity was the price of admission as well as the benefit to be bought. Besides, she was better off not knowing.

She waited, and while she did, she couldn't help but take in the details of her surroundings. She noted hallways on the main floor leading to doors already closed. A glance up the expansive staircase confirmed available space on the second floor. She had arrived later than usual, but both company and the space to enjoy it were still on hand. Determined to take advantage, she found a vantage place and waited. She was used to exercising her preferences. It had been difficult for her to learn to be chosen. She suffered the lesson in control and struggled to embrace the waiting.

The man who approached her was young and handsome. His crisp white shirt signaled his role. It was open to his waist to reveal taut musculature that rippled as he moved toward her. Piercing blue eyes drilled desire in her direction, and Ryan shot glances around the room to escape the captivation of his steady gaze. As he drew closer, she noticed their host for the evening give the beautiful young man an almost imperceptible shake of his head. The approaching Adonis altered his path and took the arm of another woman as if she had been his original aim. After a gently whispered exchange, the two glided up the staircase into one of the rooms above. Ryan waited below.

The scent was her first clue she was under consideration. Hints of spice and earthy musk trailed behind the subtle movements of the hands gently caressing her from behind. Ryan resisted the desire to turn. Over time, she had learned not to submit to her persistent urge to see, instead allowing her other senses to have their fill. She gave in to feeling, letting her skin become her sight. Her tingling skin saw beauty and surrendered to it.

"Come upstairs with me."

Ryan nodded at the declaration, delivered in a sultry tone, and led her escort to the second floor. The hallway at the top of the staircase was long. Too long. Ryan tried to savor the wait, resisting the urge to glance over her shoulder. Rules were usually her comfort, but in this moment, she wanted to break them before she was broken. Searing heat from the hand on her arm burned deep. She clung to the warmth as if it were her only solace. She knew nothing about the stranger behind her except her touch was electric, the thick strands of her hair trailed down Ryan's shoulder and melted against her skin, and her heady scent made Ryan swoon. A door, slightly ajar, beckoned and Ryan pushed her way through as if her life depended on what waited within.

As she turned to face the woman who had chosen her, she felt the grip on her arm tighten and twist. Breathy words, warm and low, skimmed her ear. "Is this what you want?" A finger pointed to the far side of the room, and Ryan willed herself to focus. The room was occupied. The open door was an inviting signal, welcoming those who would choose to venture in. Standing just across the threshold, Ryan's first conscious thought was to leave. Arousal kept her in place.

The nude women on the chaise paused only briefly to acknowledge the arrival of Ryan and her companion before they returned to each other's pleasure. Their splendid bodies arched with each caress. The long, lithe form of the caramel-haired beauty slid along her companion, pinning her as she moved toward her center. Her blonde captive bucked against her restraint, but her resistance carried only enough force to enflame their passion. So consuming was the tableau, Ryan felt she would either melt or turn to stone if she didn't turn away. She placed one hand on the doorknob and started to back up, but the iron grasp of her attendant held her in place. Again the husky voice. "Are you sure you want to leave?"

Ryan had no words for what she wanted. In her world, to speak the desires she felt could be her destruction. She would not risk her invincibility with words this night, but she would obtain the satisfaction she sought. With a flip of her wrist, she shook off the tight grip on her arm and grasped the now idle hand. She slid her own fingers along the length of the hand and released a slow, aching breath at the simple satisfaction of the light touch. As the soft hand slipped against her own, she drew its inquisitive stroke lower. The travel of its light caress blended with the delicious pressure of generous breasts heaving against her back. Ryan's sharp intake of breath signaled her pleasure. She urged the luscious fingers in.

Ryan divided her powers of concentration between the rising tide between her legs and the cresting waves of pleasure sounding from the women on the chaise lounge across the room. As the ache of her arousal reached its apex, her concentration dimmed, and hours of waiting for blissful liberation folded neatly into seconds of release.

CHAPTER FOUR

Brett rearranged the items on her desk for the tenth time. She had to stuff most of her working files in the surrounding credenzas, but she had finally made progress on her messy workspace. She knew as soon as this meeting was over, she would drag her bulging files back out and spread them around the desktop. Tony hated her methods. He didn't even deign to call them methods. He had another name for the way she managed the filing system he struggled to maintain, something along the lines of pigpen. But Brett was one of those people who had to see things in order to be organized. If she put files in a drawer for an extended period of time, she would forget them in favor of the work that was directly in her line of sight. A messy desk was a sacrifice she was willing to make.

On most occasions, she would meet a new client in her conference room, but this case was different. Rarely did she ever get a call from someone who wanted to confess to a murder, and the intimacy of her office seemed a more appropriate setting. *You haven't actually spoken to the alleged murderer. Should I bother using the word alleged if the person who actually did the deed says he is guilty?* In a few minutes, she would figure that out, since Kenneth Phillips's parents would be in her office to discuss her representation. During the short conversation the evening before with Kenneth's dad, Brett told him it was imperative that he hire counsel for Kenneth before he could do any of the crazy things his parents said he threatened to do, like drive himself to the police station or jail, and confess. She tried to get him to put Kenneth on the phone, but she had not been successful in speaking to the young man directly.

"How old is your son?"

Hesitation. "He's in his early twenties."

"I'd like to speak with him."

"He's not here. He's staying at my brother's house in Austin."

"Can you get him on the phone?"

"I'm not sure they'll answer the phone this late. And he's shy about talking to people he doesn't know."

"I understand, but I'm used to talking to people who don't like to talk about what's bothering them."

"He's very upset. He keeps talking about the man who has been charged. He is threatening to turn himself in or maybe even harm himself."

Brett wondered what inner turmoil would be so strong as to drive a shy young man to the nearest police station to confess to a murder. She knew when to push and this wasn't the time. *"What would you like to do?"*

"I want you to help him."

"Come to my office, first thing in the morning. We'll figure this out. Do you know where it is?"

"Yes."

"His mother will bring him in the morning."

"What amount should I put in the contract?" Tony walked in and set a mug of steaming coffee on her desktop.

Brett looked up at him. "Look how clean my desk is?"

Tony rolled his eyes as if he knew where she had stashed her mess. "Beautiful. Now, what amount should I put in the contract? I have a family to feed, you know."

She knew. She also knew Tony performed financial gymnastics some months, figuring out how to pay her office bills when she was in one of her crusade phases. Even when she wasn't crusading, she couldn't help it. She didn't like to set fees in the abstract. Some attorneys charged x amount for certain types of case, no matter who hired them. Brett liked to think of her fees on a sliding scale approach. Some people shouldn't have to pay as much, whether because they didn't have the means, or they were particularly sympathetic. She needed to meet them to figure out who those people were. Tony, on the other hand, didn't think she should factor emotion into fee setting. She relied on him to keep her afloat, but she had to have the final say when it came to which clients she accepted and how.

"Leave the amount blank and I'll fill it in. I may take this one on retainer. Just depends how the meeting goes. If I do, I promise I won't get less than ten." Most attorneys of her caliber in Dallas wouldn't touch a felony case for a deposit of less than ten thousand dollars. If this murder case turned into a fight, ten grand would be a drop in the bucket. Even if her unknown client really just wanted to confess to the crime, she would spend hours negotiating a sentence. If she couldn't get an agreement from the prosecutor, she would dedicate her time to preparing for a contested sentencing hearing. Either way, she didn't know enough yet to set a flat fee, so she would collect a retainer to bill against and go from there.

"Ten's not much based on what you described."

"I said I would get at least ten. Trust me, Tony. I'll do what's right."

Tony shook his head. "I know, dear. That's what scares me." He grinned to soften his scolding. "Your office looks great. You're great. And that's why I hate to see you undersell your skills."

Brett appreciated his loyalty. "Thanks, Tony. I swear, I'll charge appropriately. Cross my heart."

❖

Ryan considered staying in bed. Her body was sore and her mind was spent. Nights spent at play drained her. She didn't understand why. She chose not to spend too much time trying to figure it out. She needed the release, and she would continue to do whatever was necessary to satisfy her needs in secret. If the well-heeled suburban backers Leonard was lining up to support her campaign learned they were working hard to place a sex-crazed lesbian in what was arguably the most powerful office in the county, they would burn their money first.

If asked directly about her sexual orientation, she wouldn't lie, but when did intimacy become the first subject people revealed about themselves? Her parents had taught her the value of discretion, and she applied their teachings to her life without exception. Whether it was Scotch in a coffee cup or secret sexual liaisons, Ryan carefully crafted her image so that her personal proclivities were well disguised behind her public persona. Image was everything.

Image was precisely the reason she would not sleep in today, or any other day when she was expected at the office. Ryan never called in sick to work. Sure, she sometimes fell ill, but she would tough it out. She wasn't one of those who would show up coughing and whining, hoping for sympathy for putting the needs of the workplace above her personal comfort. No, she was always at work early, with the appearance that she was ready to take on the world. Today would be no different.

❖

Brett was on her third cup of coffee. The thermal carafe Tony left in her office for her meeting would have to be refilled if her new client ever bothered to show up. She glanced at her watch. Ten o'clock. They were an hour late. She glanced at her cell phone. The call log showed that Kenneth's father had called from an unknown number. Brett swiveled so she was facing her computer. She pulled up the last e-mail from her mysterious caller and typed a new message.

I am at my office waiting to meet with Kenneth. I would appreciate it if you would call me and let me know when or if he is still planning on coming in.
    B. Logan

"Brett? I have Judge Langston's coordinator on two."

"Thanks, Tony." Brett punched the phone and picked up the call. "Hi, Gloria, what can I do for you?" Brett listened as Gloria ranted about how she had called another attorney to meet with a defendant on her jail chain, courthouse slang for a group of inmates brought over from the jail either to meet with counsel or to appear in court. The attorney hadn't shown up, she couldn't reach him on his cell, and the bailiffs were pissed because the inmate holdover was full. Brett tuned her out halfway through. She knew whatever lead up Gloria delivered, the end result would be a request that Brett drop by Judge Langston's court and take the appointment. She also knew Gloria probably thought of her for the appointment because she had been appearing in their court a lot lately. Even though cases were randomly assigned to courts, Brett noted that happenstance seemed to occur in cycles, and she wound up working cases in the same few courts during any given time frame. She glanced at her watch again. Ten ten. She could sit here in her office and wait, or she could occupy herself at the courthouse. She finally decided the Phillips family had her phone number. They could call and reschedule.

Gloria was still talking. Brett cut in. "Would you like me to come down and help you out?"

"Oh dear, you read my mind. I know it's late in the morning. I appreciate you coming down. I would've asked someone already down here, but—"

Brett couldn't take anymore. Gloria could go on forever. "Okay, I'll leave right now. See you in a minute." She grabbed her jacket and swallowed the last of her coffee. As she walked out of the office, she called out to Tony, "I'm headed to the courthouse. Let me know if the Phillipses call. You'll be pleased to know I'm going to earn a pittance rather than absolutely nothing waiting for new clients to show up."

Brett ducked to avoid the balled up wad of paper he slung her way. She jumped into her Prius and drove the few miles from her office in Oak Lawn to the courthouse. Three-fourths of the attorneys who had business at the courthouse that morning were long gone, meaning lots of empty parking spaces. She snagged a primo space by the sky bridge that connected the garage to the courthouse and was in the court coordinator's office in mere moments.

"Hi, Gloria, whatcha got for me?"

The frazzled coordinator spun around in her chair and promptly knocked over a mug of old coffee. As she reached for some Kleenex to wipe up the mess, she knocked over a cup of paperclips. They scattered all over the desk, half of them landing in the pool of cold liquid. Brett put a hand over her mouth to hide her grin. Gloria was in a constant state of chaos, the very antithesis to the calm and collected Judge Langston. Brett slid into a chair and gave Gloria time to collect herself. As she looked down at her suit, she detected the remains of the egg and cheese bagel she'd had for breakfast, and she instinctively knew her hair was probably doing wild things. She idly reflected that the outside observer might consider her a little frantic. She wasn't. Not really. She just spent more time caring about what had to be done rather than how she looked doing it.

"Brett, I can't thank you enough," Gloria gushed as she handed over a few sheets of paper stapled together. "I've brought this woman down on the chain twice and the attorney I appointed hasn't shown up either time. I knew I could count on you."

Brett reviewed the papers and sighed. Leave it to Gloria to think a prostitution case was worth dragging her down to the courthouse. First year lawyers cut their teeth on these kinds of cases; nothing about it could possibly require the skills of a courthouse veteran. Prostitution was only even a felony if you did it often enough. And got caught. Apparently, this defendant wasn't very good at screening her clients since she had been arrested by an undercover vice cop. Brett looked closer. The woman didn't have a prior record. The arresting officer had charged the case as compelling prostitution, a second degree felony. Compelling prostitution was a charge most often used in human trafficking cases, or cases where pimps got girls instead of women to work for them. *What the hell?* Brett glanced at the name on the paperwork: Ann Rawlings. There was no real file yet since the case hadn't been indicted by the grand jury. All Brett had was a two-paragraph summary written by the arresting officer, called a probable cause affidavit, and it was naturally designed to bolster the arrest. She wouldn't have much more to go on until the case was received by the grand jury, except the information her client could give her.

Brett gathered the papers and walked into the courtroom. Mid-morning on a Friday tended to be a quiet time at the courthouse. Many trials only lasted a few days. Texas criminal courts were generally quick to dispense justice. Jury selection on Mondays, state's case on Tuesday and Wednesday, defense case by Wednesday afternoon, and jury deliberation on Thursday, leaving Fridays for random court business and punishment hearings for those unlucky souls that lost their trials.

Brett checked the clipboard and verified Ann Rawlings was indeed in the holdover. She addressed the bailiff who was deeply embroiled in a crossword puzzle. "Sam, can I see Rawlings?"

"Windows full. Female in the chair." He didn't look up from the puzzle as he delivered his seemingly unintelligible response. Brett had no trouble interpreting his words. Each courtroom had a holdover where inmates stood in small cells waiting for hearings, trials, or one of the three cramped spots contained within where they would have the opportunity to meet with their attorney for the very first time.

Since all three spots were full, Brett slid into one of the chairs just inside the rail of the courtroom and checked her BlackBerry. No response yet from the Phillipses. Someday she might become so jaded she wouldn't let other people's emergencies dictate a sense of urgency for her, but for now the information about Kenneth Phillips's situation worried its way under her skin. The family could hire someone else for all she cared, but until she knew they did, their situation would tickle her consciousness. She just hoped he didn't do something foolish.

"Hi, Sam." Ryan had come downstairs to meet with Jeff, but when she saw Brett sitting in the courtroom, she couldn't resist the opportunity to get a closer look. Sam gave her a nod then returned to his crossword. Now that she'd exhausted her not very well thought out approach, she no longer had an excuse to continue standing next to Brett, sneaking glances at her shapely legs. She had decided she should leave, when Brett looked up from her papers and caught her eye.

Brett was surprised to see Ryan Foster standing beside her. She took the opportunity to appraise the woman known as the fiercest bitch at the courthouse. As usual, her suit was severe, with sharp lines. The cotton blend was crisp, without a wrinkle in sight. *She must not sit, eat, or drink after she gets dressed in the morning.* Ryan's hair was tucked into her usual French braid and her makeup, though light, was in perfect condition. *She might not be human. Maybe the outside is just a shell, and she's one of those lizard people underneath. What a shell, though.* Her buttoned-up appearance didn't completely contain a simmering sexuality. Brett wondered if she ever let that side of her out to play.

Sam waved a hand in Brett's direction. "Chair's ready." His way of telling her she could see her client now.

Brett stood. She was so close to Ryan Foster, she could feel the vibrations radiating from her. Brett acted on impulse and thrust out her hand. "Brett Logan. I don't believe we've ever actually met." Her hand hung in the air. Brett wondered if the rumors were true that Ryan was the anointed successor to Leonard Duncan. If so, she needed serious work on her hand-shaking skills. Finally, she felt Ryan's hand connect with hers. She had more than the basic skills in personal touch. Her soft skin belied the firm confidence of her grasp. Their clasp lingered long enough to create a vacuum when the connection was broken.

"Ryan Foster. Pleasure to meet you."

Her tone was easy and even. Had it not been for the sparks transferred in the handshake, Brett would have considered Ryan's words polite nothings. "Pleasure to meet you too."

Sam cleared his throat. Brett remembered she was here to see a client, not ogle Ryan Foster. She briefly wondered why Ryan was downstairs anyway. Except for the bailiffs, the courtroom was empty. She shrugged away the thought and walked into the holdover. Two attorneys stood at the windows. One waited patiently while his client signed the sheaf of paperwork necessary to complete a plea agreement. The other was in a heated argument with his client over why he couldn't get a better deal. Brett stood in the tiny space behind them and looked at the woman sitting in the hard plastic chair in front of her. She was shocked at her client's appearance.

Brett had been appointed to represent dozens of women charged with prostitution over the years. Sometimes she could see hints of pretty through the dull veneer that years, or sometimes only months, of selling sexual favors for hits of crack created. The women Brett encountered in the holdover were never the glamorous hookers and escorts glorified in movies like *Pretty Woman* and *Mayflower Madam*. These women couldn't afford to buy their own drugs, let alone designer clothes, fancy cars, and a high-toned loft where they could ply their trade. Selling sex wasn't a chosen career path for these women; it was a back alley detour where they did the deals that would get them through another dreary day.

Ann Rawlings wasn't one of these women. Only the hard glint in her eyes betrayed she had ever known hardship. She wore her jail-issue black and white jumpsuit and faux Crocs as though the outfit were couture. Her hair was mussy, but Brett could tell that was from having spent the last few nights in jail. The cut was stylish and her hair was shiny and healthy. Her fingernails were long and sported a deep plum polish. Her hands were well acquainted with creamy lotions. Her face was beautiful and blemish free. Brett imagined fine moisturizers lined her bathroom shelves.

Brett handed her a business card. "Ms. Rawlings, my name is Brett Logan. The court has appointed me to represent you. Do you know what you're charged with?"

Ann flicked her glance from the card to Brett and back again. Her nod was barely perceptible.

"I don't have any information other than what's in the probable cause affidavit," Brett said. She handed the paper to her and waited while she read. The detective reported he was working undercover and received an invitation to a private party at a townhome in North Dallas. He paid for the privilege of attending in exchange for the promise of his choice of sexual partners. Ann was there with two other women. She did the business end of the transaction and then instructed the other two women to provide the services the customer had paid for. Before they could begin, the detective identified himself and called for backup on his cell to assist with arrest. A search of the National Criminal Information database revealed Rawlings had no prior criminal record. Brett was puzzled. It took three misdemeanors to bump a prostitution case up to a felony. The facts she'd read so far didn't support a charge of compelling. She flipped the page. *Damn.* One of the females was sixteen. Sixteen point nine actually. She had celebrated her seventeenth birthday the day after her arrest.

Brett decided to start the process of sorting through the facts with Ann. "Compelling prostitution is a second degree felony. They're going to say that you caused this girl, Heather Daniels, to commit prostitution and because she was sixteen when the offense occurred, they don't have to prove force or threats." Brett paused. "Stop me if I'm telling you things you already know, but based on your record or lack thereof, I feel the need to be pretty detailed." At Ann's nod, Brett asked, "Why don't you tell me how you know Heather and this other woman, Ginger?"

Stony silence.

"It's kind of important that you give me whatever information you have. Whatever you tell me is confidential." Brett almost grimaced as she spoke the words. They were surrounded by four other people, at least two of whom could hear everything they were saying. Technically, there was nothing privileged about their conversation, but realistically, Brett felt confident that the other folks crowded around them were too caught up in their own troubles to worry themselves with her client's problems. Over the years, she had learned the compromises court-appointed work required.

"Your bond is set at twenty-five thousand dollars, which is high considering this is your first arrest. I can try to get it reduced if there's another amount you might be able to afford to pay."

Ann shook her head vigorously.

Brett stared down the unusual response, but she didn't argue the point. "If you change your mind, let me know. Now, I really need to hear your side of the story."

Ann shook her head again, slowly and emphatically.

"If you don't talk to me now, I don't have anything to go on other than what the police wrote here. We'll just wait until the grand jury reviews your case and it's assigned to one of the prosecutors in this court before we can try to work this out."

"That's fine." The short sentence gave Brett her first look at a hint of expression in Ann's face. Her teeth were straight and laser white. Ann Rawlings didn't sell her body for crack. She saw a dentist every six months, in addition to having a regular manicure. She took care of herself, which to Brett usually meant someone who could afford to post bond and hire counsel. Brett wanted to know more, much more, but she had done this often enough to know Ann wasn't going to talk to her until she was damn well ready. Most of the time she encountered clients in the holdover, desperate to give and receive information: how they didn't do what they were accused of; how they did do it, but shouldn't be punished for their sins; how they just needed to get out, and all they wanted Brett to do was get the bond lowered. In contrast, Ann was tight-lipped. Brett gathered the papers and stuffed them in her bag.

"I'll mail you a copy of these. You have my card if you need anything. Your case will probably be set for the grand jury in a couple of weeks. If you are indicted, I'll come to court on your case, but you won't be brought down again until we're ready to resolve your case, one way or another. I'll come see you when we get an offer for you to consider. In the meantime, call or write if you want to fill me in." Brett started toward the door, but paused before leaving. "Is there anyone you'd like me to call?"

Finally, the woman's face displayed emotion. She turned pale and stark fear filled every feature. Brett started to walk back over, hold Rawlings's hand, and assure her everything would be okay. Even as she took the first step, she realized Rawlings wasn't looking for comfort. She was looking for safety, and she had found it within the confines of the county jail. *Who am I to take that from her?* Brett acknowledged the silent answer. "All right then. I'll talk to you soon."

❖

"Give me the highlights of the case." Ryan only wanted the information to assure herself Jeff's strategy was sound. Despite the way she had spent her evening, Ryan knew the Edwards file as if she had worked it from the day it was indicted. She had returned to her house at four a.m., showered, changed, and driven directly to the office. Her body was still sore from her workout the night before, but she forced herself to huddle over the box of evidence until she could recite the salient facts off the top of her head. She knew her command of the details of the case would draw annoyance rather than admiration from Jeff, but she was determined to show him and everyone else that the years she'd spent upstairs hadn't dulled her sharp litigator instincts.

"Ross Edwards. White male, fifty-five years old. Widow. No kids. He befriends Mary Dinelli, a disabled vet. Gulf War. Fifty-two years old. Maybe they have an affair, maybe not, but in any event, she tells her family she has a love interest and suddenly she drops out of sight. She gets a regular dole from the government, and someone is cashing those checks. Also, her family gets regular text messages with vague descriptions of what she's doing."

Ryan interjected. "What's the first clue things are not as they seem?"

"Hard to say. She wasn't close to her family, so the fact that she sent them text messages at all is kind of weird. I mean, you text people you're close to, right? Texting isn't something you do with distant relatives."

Ryan nodded as if in agreement, but she couldn't relate. She didn't have anyone in the circle of closeness Jeff referred to. She didn't text at all, but even if she did, she didn't think she knew anyone she would choose to receive the quick, casual updates associated with the medium. "Go on."

"Dinelli's house catches fire. Supposedly, she makes an insurance claim. Fills out the paperwork, mails it in. Even shows up at the insurance office with her new boyfriend, Ross Edwards, to make the claim. She gives a sworn statement, then gets pissed off when the insurance company tells her they are investigating whether or not there's coverage for the fire."

"Wasn't the policy good?"

"Policy was solid, but like most, it specifically excludes arson. The insurance investigator thought the story about how the fire started was fishy. Something about how they thought they might have left an iron on in the house, but the initial responders found evidence of accelerants. Anyway, this woman who showed up as Dinelli, goes ballistic, saying how she paid good money for that insurance policy, and she doesn't understand how they can rip her off. Threatens to go to the state department of insurance with a complaint. She stomps out with Edwards in tow."

Ryan fought the urge to tell Jeff to cut to the chase. He was obviously enjoying the telling of the story, carefully working his way up to the revelation that would be the lynchpin of their case. As much as she wanted him to get to it, she realized his story-telling efforts now were practice for spinning the tale into a guilty beyond a reasonable doubt verdict in front of a jury. She settled for making a few gentle prods here and there.

"So they determined the fire was the result of arson."

"Yes, but at that point, they were concerned with other evidence they found at the scene. The arson investigator found human bone fragments in fairly close proximity to several bullet casings in the debris from the fire. He contacted Richardson PD, and they started digging deeper. At first figuratively, then literally. When they couldn't find the rest of the body, they brought in a cadaver dog who led them to a dead body buried in the ground where the living room had been, with what appeared to be a gunshot wound to the head. Sent the remains off to SWIFS." He referred to the Southwest Institute of Forensic Science, the lab that performed most of the forensic analysis for law enforcement in the North Texas area.

Ryan knew the punch line, but she didn't steal it.

"The body was formally identified as Mary Dinelli. Exact time of death was hard to pinpoint, but she definitely hadn't suffered any fire-related injuries. Anyway, the medical examiner was certain the cause of death was the bullet in the head and that the shooting occurred prior to the fire. DFD contacted her family and verified that while someone was sending texts to her family and making fire insurance claims on her behalf, Mary Dinelli was dead and buried underneath the rubble of her own house."

"I didn't see any information in the file about how they made the initial connection to Edwards." Ryan was grateful for the chance to ask a real question.

"Sorry." Jeff's expression was sheepish as he handed over a copy of the search warrant affidavit for Ross Edwards's apartment. Ryan took a few minutes to review the document, which was itself a classic example of story weaving. In order to obtain a search warrant, the arson investigator had to convince a judge that the place he wanted to search contained evidence of a specific crime. He would submit a carefully crafted affidavit outlining the type of crime he was investigating along with the specific evidence he expected to find at the place to be searched. Many times, these affidavits were written on the fly, while law enforcement personnel staked out the residence to be searched. On those occasions, the document would contain nothing more than a bare bones recitation of only the essential facts.

The affidavit in support of the search warrant for Ross Edwards's apartment was an epic novel. The specific crimes enumerated were arson, insurance fraud, identity theft, and the biggie, murder. With that grab bag of offenses, the list of specific items was easily expanded to include just about anything. All the investigator had to do was connect whatever he was looking for to its use as an instrument of one of the many crimes he believed Edwards had committed. Ryan viewed the connections as tenuous, but the investigator had done a convincing job of spinning a tale that placed Edwards at the center of full-scale fraud perpetrated on disabled veteran, Mary Dinelli. Surveillance cameras at banks around the metroplex had recorded Ross Edwards in the company of a woman who, in the grainy camera footage, vaguely resembled Mary Dinelli at a time when Ms. Dinelli was cold, dead, and probably buried on her own property. Once the judge signed off on the warrant, pretty much anything in the place was fair game.

What they found in Edwards's apartment was a goldmine. Sitting in a nightstand drawer was Mary Dinelli's cell phone with Ross Edwards's fingerprints all over it and the cryptic texts to her family still in the log. Based on the medical examiner's estimated date of death, Mary Dinelli was long dead when texts were sent from her phone telling her family not to worry, that she was fine. No smoking gun, to be sure, but when combined with the find of a few of Dinelli's benefit check stubs, and Edwards's appearance with a woman posing as Dinelli at the insurance company, they had enough to bring him in for questioning.

Ultimately, a grand jury, hearing only evidence in support of an indictment, true billed his case, and Edwards was charged with multiple crimes—theft and capital murder topping the list. Bond was set at five hundred thousand dollars. Within days, Edwards was back on the street. Jeff and his investigator had gone crazy trying to figure out how he came up with the cash to pay the bondsman the ten percent fee. If they could prove the money was from ill-gotten gains, they might have been able to get the bond held insufficient, but for now they had to settle for the stringent pretrial reporting instructions the judge had imposed. In addition to whatever his bondsman asked him to do, Edwards had to check in with the court once a week. He was forbidden from opening or closing any monetary accounts, and, just for inconvenience sake, had to undergo a weekly piss test.

Ryan tossed the search warrant affidavit back onto Jeff's desk. "You realize you don't have any hard evidence."

"We'll line up the evidence we've got. The jury will go in the direction we lead them."

"You hope." Ryan knew the circumstantial evidence all pointed squarely at Edwards. At least for the theft/fraud. The murder was a different story. Mary Dinelli had been shot point-blank in the back of the head, but exhaustive searches for the weapon that killed her turned up nothing. There was no physical evidence to tie Edwards to the shooting or even the house where Mary had lived. But he had opportunity and motive to kill her. Their job would be to convince the jury to link the hard evidence on the theft case to the murder, and Ryan's political future hung in the balance.

The United States Attorney's office had made a strong play early on to try the case in federal court. Insurance fraud and arson were both solidly within their jurisdiction. Leonard Duncan had taken the case directly to the court of public opinion to win his bid to keep the case in his courthouse. It turned out to be a life or death decision. The U.S. Attorney had to get permission from main justice in DC before they could seek the death penalty. In contrast, the Dallas County District Attorney merely had to get an indictment for capital murder to get the death penalty on the table. Since the case stayed here, Ryan was under pressure to deliver the ultimate result.

"So do you want to bail now that you know it's not a slam dunk?" Jeff delivered the challenge with a heavy dose of sarcasm. Ryan wasn't biting.

"No, but now I understand why Mr. Duncan thought you would need my help."

"Look, I worked this case up myself. I presented to the grand jury, I—"

Jeff stopped abruptly, and Ryan heard motion behind her. She had chosen this time to meet with Jeff, hoping most of the morning docket would have cleared out. "We're busy here." Ryan didn't look up and her tone was dismissive.

"I know, I know, dispensing justice. Well, I have a bit of justice I'd love for you to dispense."

Ryan instantly recognized the voice. She could tell the person who spoke was smiling, but her voice was strong and commanding. Friendly tones mixed with firm resolve. She looked up into kind eyes, eyes that betrayed the voice. *She comes across all tough, but she's a softie underneath. Compassion.* Ryan was at once pleased and dismayed to have discovered Brett's primary weakness. She knew how to cure it. "What do you need?"

Brett handed her a single sheet of paper. Ryan skimmed the contents and handed it back. "And?"

"I don't have enough info to fully evaluate the case, but I thought I'd check and see if you might be open to a waiver?"

"We don't usually do waivers on second degree felonies." Ryan ignored Jeff's stare. Brett was asking for a sweet deal in exchange for her client waiving the right to have her case heard by the grand jury. Waivers were popular with lower level felonies, especially drug cases. Those inmates would crowd the county jail while waiting for the drugs they were caught with to be tested by a lab before their cases would ever be formally charged. Brett's request was perfectly reasonable for a prostitution case, but this wasn't a run-of-the-mill prostitution case. Compelling prostitution wasn't run-of-the-mill.

Ryan finally faced Jeff. She knew she was tramping all over his territory. She couldn't help herself. What she couldn't figure out was whether her action was a power play or merely a desire to interact with Logan. Ryan decided not to examine her motivation.

Brett shot an imploring look in Jeff's direction. He answered with a shrug. She directed her pitch at Ryan, sure she'd detected a hint of humanity in their brief interaction outside the holdover. "This is a prostitution case, plain and simple. The only reason the officer charged it as compelling was the statutory age component. Seriously, there's no evidence my client compelled Daniels to do anything or that she was aware of her age."

Ryan looked at the report. "Math isn't my strong suit, but it looks like the arresting officer was correct in determining Daniels was under seventeen. He doesn't have to prove your client used force or threat."

"Agreed. But you do have to prove my client *caused* Daniels to commit the act."

"I'm certain that issue will be fully explored."

"Why waste the time?" Brett was done trying to appeal to Ryan's seemingly nonexistent good sense. She wanted to get to the bottom line, a plea offer. "What's the going rec for prostitutes right now? Thirty days, county jail? At three for one, by the time this case is heard by the grand jury, she'll have more than enough time in to satisfy that. Let her waive indictment, and you save everyone a lot of time and trouble."

"Why, Ms. Logan, how kind of you to be so concerned about our resources. Our little old office truly appreciates your compassion." Ryan didn't care that her sarcasm wasn't winning points. She didn't need leverage. The DA's office boasted over a hundred prosecutors. They had the power to bring charges against whomever they wanted. Sure, that kind of power had to be balanced with discretion, but Ryan didn't need some hotshot defense attorney telling her how to run her division. Besides, the best way to teach the prosecutors under her command how to have a backbone was to show her own strength. She pulled a pen from her jacket pocket and wrote down the case number from the police report Brett had handed to her. "I'll run this through the grand jury myself. It's time we stopped prostitution at the source." Ryan felt a faint prick at her own hypocrisy, but she stuffed any rising internal debate.

"What the hell?" Brett snatched her paperwork from Ryan's grasp. "I came in here to talk to Jeff."

"So you could try and intimidate him into offering your client a cush deal?"

"My client hasn't even said she's guilty. I just wanted to explore all her options. Seemed like it was a cush deal for you. You get to wipe a case off your docket with very little trouble."

"Human trafficking merits all the trouble it takes to bring the perpetrators to justice." Ryan knew she was exaggerating the significance of the case, but she wasn't going to back down now, despite a nagging feeling she was overcompensating for her attraction to Brett.

"You have got to be kidding me. Three women selling their bodies do not equal a white slave trade. I came to Jeff because he has some sense of perspective. You, on the other hand, have spent too much time in your office upstairs to appreciate the nuances of the real world."

Brett was flushed. Ryan noted her adversary's other weakness. She expressed emotion about her cases. *I bet she keeps tissue in her purse,* Ryan thought with disdain. She didn't have time to think about it more since Brett turned and headed for the door. "I'll see you at grand jury." Brett shot the words over her shoulder.

CHAPTER FIVE

Brett wished she had kept her mouth shut. She never should have tried to talk to Jeff Oates with his boss sitting right there. Not only had she alienated the woman who would probably be the next elected district attorney, she'd put Jeff in an impossible position. He would've had an easier time asking for forgiveness than permission. Now that Ryan Foster had her hands all over the case, she'd never be able to work out a deal. Not that Ann Rawlings had even asked her to work anything out. She hadn't told her word one about the allegation. Something about the glamorous woman dressed in jail stripes intrigued Brett.

She shrugged out of her shoes, leaned back in her chair, and placed her stocking feet on her desk. It was highly unlikely Ryan would have the time or inclination to actually shepherd a low-level felony case through the grand jury herself. She'd check the docket later and find out which prosecutor was assigned and talk to him or her directly.

The morning in court had eaten into the noon hour, so Tony had picked up a chicken Caesar wrap from Eatzi's, part of which she was already wearing. She had blocked out her afternoon to meet with Ms. Jarvis's office manager who would arrive any minute. Since she was in charge of all the ambulance companies' files, Brett considered interviewing her a top priority. She stifled a yawn in expectation of a very boring afternoon. Her dread was interrupted by the ding signaling receipt of a new e-mail on her desktop computer.

Sorry he didn't make the meeting at your office. Couldn't get off work.

I have a few questions about how all this will work. Will he be arrested right away? How long will he be in jail?

Brett didn't need to read the e-mail address to know her mysterious, non-appointment-keeping client had resurfaced. E-mail was perfect for quick and easy communication, but it wasn't great for detailed explanations requiring lots of back and forth. Mr. Phillip's questions were better answered in person, or on the phone at the very least.

I'm happy to answer your questions, but it would be much easier in person. Shall we reschedule your appointment?

Brett leafed through some paperwork Tony had left on her desk. She finally admitted she was stalling. She slipped on her heels and made her way to the conference room to listen to hours of droning about numbers. What she really needed was a juicy murder case.

"Leonard, I think I should spend more time in the courts."

Ryan loved her office on the eleventh floor. In turn, she hated the cramped working quarters of the courtroom prosecutors. But her morning encounter with Brett Logan was a wake-up call. Beyond a tinge of remorse for the walls she'd thrown up between herself and Brett, Ryan had no regrets about the way she handled the situation, but she felt out of practice. She spent her days reviewing files and advising the prosecutors under her direction, but except for high profile cases, she hadn't handled direct negotiations in years. It was way past time.

Leonard had a different view of the best way to use her. "Nonsense. I need you up here."

"No, you don't. I was down in Langston's court today. I miss the direct negotiating. Don't you think I'd get better visibility down in the courts?"

"Sure you would. You'd have more liabilities too." Leonard held out a hand, palm up. "Now before you get all worked up, hear me out." Ryan nodded. "You hang out down there too much and every close call you make will be a headline. Odds are at least half will be negative. You want to be in the paper? Then you show up at every local function you can find, commenting about the importance of being tough on crime. That's going to get you consistently good press. Trying to show you're tough on crime in the courtroom? That's a crapshoot. Go for the sure thing, Ryan."

Ryan didn't take his advice lightly. She was a veteran prosecutor, but a political novice. She'd worked in this office since before she graduated from law school. After spending two summers as an intern, she was a shoe-in for an entry-level spot in one of the misdemeanor courts. In the intervening years, she had worked every position at the courthouse except that of her boss and his first assistant. Normally, the first assistant would be the natural choice for successor, but Braden Marcus loved the administration side of the office and had absolutely no interest in subjecting his life to political scrutiny. Ryan didn't crave the public eye, but she wasn't about to live out her career without ascending to the top spot. If she didn't, she would be a failure. Ryan Foster didn't fail.

"What about the Edwards case?"

"Edwards? That's a slam-dunk. No liabilities there. You focus your efforts on managing your prosecutors and show up to try that case. I'll handle the rest."

Ryan nodded assent but crossed her fingers behind her back. She would do more than just show up. She would star in the stage production of *Ross Edwards Gets the Needle*. The case might be a slam-dunk, but with some special effects, it could also be her ticket to becoming the next District Attorney of Dallas County.

❖

"If I never hear the words 'necessary and reasonable' again, I'll be happy as a clam." Brett would never understand how any lawyer could enjoy working document-intensive white-collar cases. She grinned when she thought of her mother, the CPA. Joan Logan would regale her family over the dinner table with tales of credits and debits gone astray and beautifully crafted journal entries. While Brett's brothers leaned forward with eager interest, Brett rearranged peas on her plate, wishing she were in her room reading a mystery. If she'd taken more interest in her mother's discussions when she was younger, she might be like her brothers. Both of them were successful, rich, and married. Ostensibly, they were happy.

Brett was successful. She had awards and accolades to prove it. Rich and married she had yet to cross off the to-do list she'd been issued when she became an adult. Happy? She didn't give happiness a lot of consideration. She did the work she did because it felt right. Rich might feel right too, she thought. And married? She had written that particular venture off her list. Marriage and work were a combination she couldn't seem to make work. Her happily married, successful parents and brothers couldn't wrap their minds around Brett's resignation to a solitary existence.

"Brett, are you dreaming about what you're going to buy me for Christmas with all the money Ms. Jarvis and her many ambulance companies are going to funnel into the firm?" Tony slid into the seat across from her desk. He waved a hand in the air as if to waken her from her trance.

Brett knew she did well in spite of herself. Tony managed the purse strings of her firm with a tight grip. If it weren't for him, she would be both single and destitute. Brett had stolen Tony from the federal public defender's office where he had worked as a paralegal for a number of years. She recognized that his strong work ethic and ability to manage a daunting caseload would translate into the kind of manager she needed for her business. She had never made a better decision. Tony was motivated not only by his own desire for success, but by the fact he had a wife and two teenagers relying on him for support. She often wondered how he made a home life work since he spent so much time invested in the success of her firm. Why was everyone else able to achieve a perfect blend of personal and professional life?

"You know, Tony, I don't thank you enough for taking such good care of me."

"No sentimentality, Logan. I'm just doing my job, and I do it out of a strong sense of self-interest."

"Whatever. I swear I will dedicate the next week to work on the Jarvis case. I'm going to see my folks this weekend. I'll get a referral from Mom for a new forensic accountant. I knew more about debits and credits than that last bozo we consulted. Ms. Jarvis wants to go full guns on a defense, so we'll want also want a billing consultant. Frankly, I'm sick of the government using their hazy Medicare regs to send honest-minded, hard-working business people to prison."

"Atta girl. I'll make some calls and we'll get started on Monday." He stood. "It's four o'clock. Let's shut down for the day. You'll need a weekend to relax if you're going to hit the ground running next week."

Brett agreed. She reached over to shut off her computer but paused to open Outlook one last time. No word from the Phillips family. Oh well, she would have to find a way to make Medicare billing seem juicy since she didn't seem destined to be working on a new murder case anytime soon.

CHAPTER SIX

R yan swore she would swallow a bottle of pills before she would ever resign herself to living in a place like the one looming before her. She forced herself to open the creaky front door. The assault on her senses nearly sent her running. Sour, musty odors gagged her and the muted color of the dingy carpet and out-of-date wallpaper combined to create a dull, dusty impression. The effect was like looking through a haze. She imagined that was how the residents of Pine Grove Nursing Home saw the world every day.

"Hello, Ms. Foster. Your aunt will be so happy to see you."

Ryan offered a forced smile. She didn't agree. Eunice Foster didn't do happy, and she didn't tolerate happy in others. And that, Ryan thought, is why this godforsaken place is perfect for her. Only a strong sense of duty forced Ryan to make these regular Saturday visits. Besides, Eunice was the only family she had. Leonard would be proud of her fostering that connection in the months running up to the election.

Many of the rooms she passed were decorated with various knickknacks, designed to minimize the institutional feel. Eunice's room was stark in comparison. Ryan bet her aunt reveled in the institutional feel. It was orderly. It was consistent. It was impersonal. It fit Eunice to a tee.

When she arrived at the door, she saw her aunt sitting in a stiff-backed chair, a Bible resting open in her lap.

"Hello, Aunt Eunice." A slight nod was Ryan's only hint her presence was acknowledged. At least she was consistent. Ryan pulled up a chair and took a modicum of pleasure at the flick of annoyance in her aunt's eyes. "How was your week?"

Eunice made a show of closing the Bible and setting it on the small table beside her bed. Every tiny motion was designed to show Ryan her visit was an intrusion. Ryan knew she would never win. If she didn't show up every Saturday, at exactly the same time, her aunt would be angry, and Ryan would never find forgiveness.

These visits were painful, but Ryan didn't dare cut them short. She wasn't sure what would happen if she did, but irrational childhood fears snagged her in their grasp. She and her parents hadn't reconciled before they died. Although her aunt didn't really know her at all, without her, she was all alone. An hour of painful silence in this room was worth the comfort of knowing she wasn't completely on her own.

❖

"Hey, Brett, can you pick Lori up from work and bring her to Mom and Dad's? I had to drop her off this morning, and I'm stuck at Stacy's volleyball tournament. If they keep winning, I'm never going to get out of here."

Brett laughed. Despite his pretend tone of annoyance, she knew her brother John was in heaven. His oldest daughter Stacy was the star setter on the Highland Park High School volleyball team. John was her biggest fan. "Sure, what time? And you and Stacy better show up at the house eventually, or Mom will bring dinner to the sidelines."

"We'll be there, but we might be a little worn out. We've been here since the crack of dawn. Lori should be done by five. She brought a change of clothes, so you gals can head straight over. We'll be there as soon as we kick everyone else's a—I mean butt."

Brett hung up the phone and glanced at the clock. Four o'clock. Lori Logan, her sister-in-law, was the director of nursing at Pine

Grove Nursing Home. Brett had just enough time to change before heading across town to pick her up.

When she arrived, Lori met her at the front desk. "John said you were my taxi for the evening. Here you are, right on time."

Brett read from Lori's harried expression and urgent tone that right on time wasn't necessarily helpful. "Need a few minutes?"

"More like half an hour. I have a little issue. Wanna head on without me?"

"Not a chance. I love my parents, but I don't need to brave a round of defending my chosen occupation all on my own." Lori's career choice drew even more skepticism than her own, and she and Lori had formed a strong alliance.

"Fair enough. There's a Starbucks next door. Grab a jolt of caffeinated courage. I'll meet you over there in thirty."

Brett nodded. As she turned away, she spotted a familiar face across the nursing home lobby. She grabbed Lori's arm and subtlety pointed. "Do you know her?"

"Sure. That's Ryan Foster. Her aunt's a resident. She's here every Saturday, like clockwork." Lori cocked her head, her puzzled expression melting into a knowing smile. "She's beautiful. Want me to introduce you?"

Brett shuddered. "No thanks. Ms. Foster and I have met. Over the course of a few short moments, we managed to become bitter enemies."

"Too bad. Beneath her staid exterior, I imagine she's a wildcat. Look at how buttoned up she is. All that control has to be holding something at bay."

"Lori dear, your imagination has gotten the best of you. Did you sneak in my house and raid my lesbian fiction collection? Now you're romanticizing visitors to the nursing home."

"Ryan Foster has been here every Saturday afternoon for the last three years, without fail. No one, I mean no one, is that consistent. Consistency equals a need for control. Anyone who needs that much control has a wild side they're working hard to cover up. Mark my words."

"You're crazy. I'm going to get coffee. You get back to work. Meet me at Starbucks when you're done." Brett shook her head as she walked back toward the doors. Lori didn't have a clue about Ryan Foster. She was probably a control freak because she couldn't stand to think of a world with chaos in it. She was the embodiment of law and order, unable to see shades of gray in her black-and-white existence. Even as she felt disdain, Brett's curiosity was sparked. Ryan must have some redeeming qualities if she was so dedicated to a family member as to make regular visitation part of her routine. She must love her aunt very much.

"Excuse me."

Brett looked up then quickly down again. The door handle did seem strangely soft, perhaps because she was grasping Ryan's hand and not the handle itself. *Oh, shit.* "I'm sorry; I was lost in thought and didn't see you standing there." *Well, not right there. Actually, I was thinking about you, but not that way.* Brett's prior knowledge of Ryan's presence did nothing to dispel her surprise at literally running into her while leaving. She judged by Ryan's expression that the surprise was mutual.

"I didn't see you either." Surprise was replaced by something else, but Brett couldn't place it.

"Odd, isn't it? Us running into each other here?" Brett didn't know why, but she felt compelled to strike up a conversation.

Ryan arched her eyebrows. "What are you doing here?"

"Giving my sister-in-law a lift. She works here." Brett suddenly had a crazy idea. She tried to stop herself from saying it out loud, but she heard her voice before she could squelch it. "She's running a bit late. If you don't have somewhere you need to be, why don't you join me for coffee?"

Ryan glanced at her watch as if buying time to make an excuse. Although she still considered the idea hare-brained, Brett pushed the point. "Come on, thirty minutes tops. We got off on the wrong foot. Let me make it up to you with a latte."

Ryan offered a hint of a smile and gestured to Brett to lead the way. Moments later, they were settled at a tiny table in the Starbucks next to Pine Grove. The contents of the paper cups in front of them symbolized the stark differences between them. Brett sipped from her four-pump mocha topped with double whip, while Ryan drank a cup of regular drip coffee. Black.

Ryan wished she had ordered decaf. One cup of regular coffee first thing in the morning was all the caffeine she usually allowed herself. Somehow the idea of ordering a cup of decaf in front of Brett Logan made her feel like a wimp, so she capitulated. Why she cared what Brett thought, and why she was even here was a mystery.

"So do you have a relative at Pine Grove?"

"What makes you ask?"

"Idle conversation." Brett raised her cup. "You know, what people have over coffee? Besides, that would explain why you were there this afternoon."

Ryan started to tell Brett her reasons for being at Pine Grove were none of Brett's business, but an inner voice reasoned Brett wasn't necessarily being invasive with her questions. Ryan knew she sucked at idle chitchat. She also knew she needed to remedy her deficiency if she planned to enter the political arena. Besides, Brett's friendly manner made her want to open up. At least a little bit.

Only one way to get started. Disclose a little something. "My aunt is a resident. Has been for a few years. I see her on Saturdays." Ryan sighed. She had only offered three bits of information, but she felt worn out from the effort.

"Every Saturday? Sweet of you to visit so regularly."

Ryan was puzzled by Brett's assumption. She didn't consider her regular visits optional. Or sweet. She did what was expected. Nothing less. "She's my aunt."

Brett nodded and waited, as if Ryan's statement was just the beginning. Ryan took the opportunity to change the subject back to more familiar territory. "How long have you been in private practice?"

If Brett was puzzled by the change in topic, she didn't show it. "About six years. I worked as a public defender for Tarrant County and then the Feds before I opened my own shop. I definitely prefer working for myself. I started out taking a lot of court-appointed work. Guess that's what I was used to. Wound up handling more than my fair share of capital cases. Had to learn how to market to get more retained cases. Most of my cases are full fee now. About fifty percent federal and the other half in Dallas and surrounding counties. I still do court-appointed work, but mostly out of a sense of obligation. Plus some of the most interesting cases have defendants who can't afford counsel." Brett abruptly stopped talking and took a long sip of coffee.

Ryan didn't even remember her initial question. When she asked it, she had had no idea it would elicit such a detailed response. While she enjoyed learning more about Brett, Ryan wondered, with a sense of dread, if Brett expected her to share a similarly long tale of her career escalation. She snuck a look at her watch. Only ten minutes had passed since they had entered the coffee shop. She looked up to find Brett had caught her checking the time. Ryan wished she could take back her action. Surprisingly, she didn't mind being here with Brett. She found Brett extremely attractive and personable. Ryan may not ever agree with her in the professional arena, but on a personal level, she enjoyed her affability and warmth. Ryan had many acquaintances, but if someone asked her to name a true friend, she wouldn't have a name to give.

"You'll come home immediately after school. Everyday. Don't think you can dally. I know what time classes let out, and I've walked the route. I know how long it takes."

"But, Aunt Eunice, the debate club meets on Tuesdays after school."

"Don't care. You'll be here. You don't need clubs to get good grades. Besides, they travel, right?" At Ryan's nod, Eunice continued her litany. "You won't be doing any traveling. You'll be staying right here in this house working on your basic schoolwork. If you have time left over, you can read the Good Book out loud to me. You do have a fine voice. You don't need to be wasting it arguing in some club."

When she first arrived at her aunt's house, Ryan was relieved to be far away from her arguing parents. They hadn't been able to decide if they should skin her alive or send her to an exorcist. Aunt

Eunice's house of stern was their compromise. Within hours, Ryan realized life wasn't going to be any easier with her stoic aunt than it was with her volatile parents. At least at home she could shout and wail about the injustice of her parents forbidding her to have any contact with Julia. Eunice forbade her to even speak Julia's name out loud. She commanded Ryan to produce all the notes and tiny trinkets of her ill-fated high school romance and watch as all evidence of her relationship with Julia burned into ash.

"You've always been a prosecutor haven't you?"

Ryan shuddered at the interruption. She realized she was sitting at a Starbucks, not in front of a roaring fire, and instead of her strict aunt, she was looking into the smiling eyes of Brett Logan. "I have."

"Have you always been so talkative?" Brett immediately wished she'd asked an open-ended question.

Ryan wasn't totally bereft of social grace. She smiled at the joke. "Yes," she said, then promptly joined Brett in laughter. "Seriously, you could say I save myself for the courtroom."

"Do you miss it?" The minute the more intimate question left her lips, Brett felt the air between them cool.

Ryan felt the conversation shift to less comfortable ground. She didn't want anyone focusing on her several-year absence from the courtroom. She steered the topic in the direction she wanted it to go. "You'll see me there soon."

"Really?"

"I'm trying the Ross Edwards case."

Brett, like everyone else within a three hundred mile radius of Dallas County, was familiar with the Edwards case. The press painted Edwards as a cold-blooded sociopath. Allegedly, he had murdered at least three women in various parts of the country, then collected their various government benefits. Women whose trust and devotion he had won. The crime reporter from the *Dallas Morning News* had dubbed him the Benefit Killer.

"I thought that was Jeff's case." The moment the words left her lips, Brett could see Ryan's back arch as she puffed up.

"The case belongs to the District Attorney of Dallas County."

Well, la-di-da. Who the hell talks like that? Brett couldn't resist the urge to push the point. "Well, duh. I mean Jeff's been working on Edwards for months. Is he quitting?" Cases belonged to the court they were assigned to and were randomly assigned to a prosecutor in that particular court. Since Jeff was the chief in Langston's court, he would naturally reserve the high profile cases assigned to that court. Even if he were transferred to another court, he would usually get to decide if he wanted to take the case with him. Logic dictated the only thing that would keep Jeff from working the Edwards case would be if he quit the office altogether.

Ryan didn't like Brett's implication. She considered saying Leonard had ordered her to work on the case, but abandoned the idea because that explanation would beg the question of why. Actually, it wasn't uncommon for a super chief to try a high profile case. Less common, though, was a division chief taking over weeks before trial. Ryan had to admit that if she were Jeff she would have been floored to have the lead spot on the case ripped from her. She didn't have an explanation she cared to share, but she realized she needed to work on one. Surely, Brett wouldn't be the only one asking. Ryan opened her mouth to respond, still not quite sure what she was going to say. Brett's vibrating BlackBerry saved her the trouble.

"Sorry, I need to take this." Brett walked a few feet away and whispered into her phone. Ryan pretended to read the specials board, while surreptitiously glancing in Brett's direction. Brett might be infuriating, but she was damn attractive. At five-ten, Ryan was used to being the tallest woman in the room, but Brett was just as tall or taller. Today she wore jeans, black leather boots, and a sea-green sweater that accentuated the emerald flecks in her hazel eyes. The jeans and sweater hugged her slender form, and Ryan felt herself wanting to hug her body along Brett's form as well. Her desire to be close to Brett wasn't limited to a physical urge.

She forced herself to look away. Years of discipline would not be undone today. She would make a call later to deal with her corporeal cravings. Her emotional hunger would keep

Ryan stood as Brett hung up the phone. "I need to go."

"I'm sorry." Brett held up her phone. "Wrong number. I was expecting a call or I wouldn't have answered."

"Not a problem. I need to go anyway." Ryan hoped by repeating the statement she might begin to believe it was true. Brett looked disappointed. Was she? A few moments ago, she'd seemed annoyed at Ryan, let down by her new role in the Edwards case. Now she looked sad to see her go. Brett was complicated.

Time to go. Ryan pushed in her chair. "Thanks for the coffee." She strode out the door without waiting for Brett's response.

Brett watched as Ryan almost ran into Lori in her haste to leave.

"She sure was in a hurry to leave," Lori said. "Something you said?"

Brett watched Ryan cross the parking lot until she disappeared from sight. "I guess. We were talking, then my phone rang and I took a call. When I came back to the table, she was up and out of here like she couldn't get away fast enough."

"You've got to stop letting work interfere with your social life, dear." Lori's smile softened the admonishment.

Brett nodded. Lori was right, but she sensed the interruption of her ringing phone wasn't the real reason for Ryan's exit. She was sorry their time together had ended so awkwardly. Beneath her prickly veneer, Brett sensed Ryan possessed a shy sensitivity only a few ever managed to see. Brett wanted to be one of those who got a glimpse.

❖

"Dinner's almost ready." Brett watched her mom, Joan Logan, duck under the large platter of steaks her dad carried from the grill. "Let's eat outside and enjoy this beautiful weather. Everyone grab a plate and pick out your steak. Brett and John, will you help me carry the salads outside?"

"No problem, Mom." Brett grabbed the enormous salad bowl and a set of tongs and, along with her brother, helped set up the patio table. The Logan family jostled their way around the kitchen, handing plates back and forth as they selected their main course. Once they were all gathered, her dad, seated at the head of the table, spoke the words he did at the beginning of every meal.

"Let's all hold hands and pray."

Brett was used to these moments. She wasn't a religious person. Brett believed in the power of prayer, but she called it positive thinking. When she made silent requests for intervention, she was reaching out to the universe, not a particular entity. If there was a God, she didn't have a problem with him granting her requests, but she didn't focus exclusively on him. Her thoughts were interrupted by the infernal ringing of the BlackBerry.

"Sorry, everyone." Brett broke the circle and scooted out of the room with her purse in tow. She connected to the call. "Hello?" She sighed. Finally, the mysterious Mr. Phillips. She hoped she could make more headway in this call than e-mail had allowed. "Yes, I got your e-mail. I'm happy to answer your questions, but I don't have simple answers. I think it would be best if we met in person."

Brett listened as Mr. Phillips told her he had traveled to Austin himself to help his brother manage young Kenneth.

"He is eaten up with guilt about the man who is in jail. The one the police think committed this murder."

Brett was done with abstract references. "Do you know the name of the man in jail?"

"Kenneth cut out some newspaper stories about him. I think his name is Ross Edwards."

Brett gasped.

"Did I say something wrong?"

"No." Brett struggled to compose herself. What a bizarre coincidence to learn she had a potential client who wanted to confess to Ryan Foster's headline murder case. She squelched the nip of pleasure that came from knowing she would have an opportunity to run into Ryan again. "I've heard of the case."

"I just need to know a few things to be able to set my son's mind at ease."

Brett struck a balance between comforting and firm. "Totally understandable. I'm happy to answer your questions, but I want to do it in person. We can all sit down and take whatever time is necessary to formulate a strategy."

Mr. Phillips didn't respond. Brett waited through the silence. She may need to pay her bills, but she didn't need to beg for clients. Either Daddy brought his baby boy in for a meeting or not. Either way, this was the last time Brett was going to talk to this man without a retainer.

"I don't know how much we can afford to pay you."

There it was. The motive for all the hesitation. Mystery dispelled. She could hear Tony's voice now: "Tell him to call legal aid. Tell him the court will appoint an attorney if he can't afford to hire one for his son. Tell him you can't eat gratitude." In response she thought: *The court won't appoint counsel until the kid is already under arrest. Legal aid isn't going to know how to deal with this kind of case. I don't eat much.* Finally, Brett found her voice.

"Come into the office, and we'll figure something out."

❖

"Dinner's great." Brett scooped another forkful of her mother's famous garlic mashed potatoes. She was on her third helping. *I guess I do eat a lot.* "It's so nice to get a home-cooked meal."

Her brother John chimed in. "If you'd ever settle down, you could make your own."

"Better yet, if you got a real job, you could hire someone to make dinner every night and then tell people it's your own," her brother Brian added.

Brett punched him in the arm. "Oh, aren't you all funny?" Brett knew her brothers were teasing. Mostly. "Like you two ever have to think about where your next meal is coming from." She directed her comments at their wives. "Seriously, do they even know how to turn on the oven or even order from a take-out menu?"

Brian was the first to speak up. "Precisely my point, dear sister. Marry well and all your troubles will be gone."

"Yep, Brian's life is perfect since he met me," his wife Ashley said.

"And I've already asked if you have a sister, right?" Brett batted her eyelashes. Despite all the teasing, Brett knew there was an undercurrent of seriousness in their words that needled her even though she had long ago decided to stop using their yardsticks to measure her success. They both knew she was fully capable of doing anything she put her mind to, but they couldn't comprehend her choice to do more work for less money. Both brothers followed in their father's footsteps, launching their careers at the same venerable Dallas law firm where their dad was a senior partner. Tax advice, unwinding derivatives, mineral rights. All three males in the Logan family were happily engaged in the practice of transactional law. Brett could not imagine a more boring existence. Right now all she could think about was sneaking upstairs and Googling everything she could about the Edwards case. If she took Kenneth Phillips's case, she might fill up the first page of results herself. She knew a whole page of Internet hits wouldn't impress the males in her family, but it might soften the blow for Tony who was expecting her to collect a decent fee. Publicity was golden.

❖

Ryan was amazed at the number of search results on her screen. A persistent curiosity had driven her to the Internet after her encounter with Brett earlier that day. Simply typing her name into the Google search engine yielded a wealth of information. The results ranged from information about Brett's legal career to her involvement in local organizations and social issues. Brett Logan graduated from law school in 1994 from the University of Texas at Austin. If she hadn't taken any breaks between undergrad and law school, Ryan calculated she and Brett were probably close to the same age. She was a member of the local GLBT Chamber of Commerce and the Dallas Gay and Lesbian Bar Association. She volunteered at the local GLBT Resource Center and she regularly donated her time to legal clinics in the Oak Lawn community. She cosponsored a booth at the Gay and Lesbian Pride festival. The evidence all pointed to one revealing conclusion. Brett was a lesbian. She had to be.

And, in every online photo, she was as gorgeous as she appeared in person.

Ryan had desperately sought the information, but wasn't sure what to do with it now. After she read everything she could find, she cleared the search history on her Internet browser and dialed a familiar number. After a brief conversation, she hung up the phone and repeated the address out loud several times as if the sound of her voice would etch the location in her mind. She gazed at the bottle of Scotch across the room longingly. She was edgy tonight, but she worried she wouldn't be able to stop at one or two shots of the golden liquid to calm her nerves. She could indulge in whatever she wanted once she reached the house, but she wouldn't risk driving intoxicated. She needed the salve that waited for her more than she needed to quiet her jittery nerves in this moment.

The drive was long. She had not been to this area of town in quite some time. Decidedly suburban, this area was populated by hard-working dads, mall-going moms, and their two point five children. She drove the speed limit and signaled all turns. Full stops at signs and careful entry into intersections. At a flash of her badge, any patrol cop would close his ticket book, but her badge couldn't erase memories. Her ability to be invisible would reap the rewards she sought this evening.

She almost laughed at the unexpected surprise. A house party down the street from the largest Baptist church in Dallas. What would the parishioners say if they knew? Would they proselytize to the partygoers or would they merely lament their quick descent to hell, while enjoying a burger at the food court under the church's spacious dome? Ryan didn't know the answer, but she did know discovery tonight would keep her from winning an election for anything.

When Ryan arrived at her destination, she pulled in behind the other cars waiting at the valet stand. Ryan wondered if the neighbors wondered why they weren't invited to the party. Were they jealous not to be included in the assemblage of expensive cars and well dressed visitors? She shrugged away the question. These gatherings were carefully crafted to deflect attention from their real purpose. Ryan knew nothing about the elaborate details contrived to disguise each event. She didn't want to know. Her ignorance kept her safe.

Once inside, she struggled to maintain her usual self-control. She would adhere to the rules, but she had dressed to attract. Tonight, she was determined to draw attention quickly. Tight designer jeans hugged her thighs before fanning out slightly over spike-heeled red leather lace up boots. Her snug black silk sweater accentuated her breasts. She moved through the partygoers. She was keyed up, and she attributed it to the caffeine from earlier. Flashes of Brett kept invading her thoughts. She pushed away the obvious conclusion that the edge she felt had anything to do with the conflicting emotions she experienced in Brett's presence.

The solution to take the edge off approached her from behind.

"You have a delicious ass."

The voice was honey smooth and the hands grazing her jeans teased her arousal. Ryan relished the attention for a moment before turning toward her admirer. The woman facing her was riveting. For the second time that day, Ryan was face-to-face with a beauty whose height allowed her to look her in the eye without having to tilt her head. Visions of the lengths of their naked bodies fully aligned, lying side by side, made Ryan wet.

The woman was dressed in white leather. A tight bodice, laced in front, pushed her breasts to full attention. Snug pants hugged slender hips and encased the woman's very long legs. Ryan's mind wandered to another tall drink of water, and she imagined Brett Logan standing before her, masterful in leather. She resisted the urge to smile at the image in her mind considering she had last seen Brett dressed in faded jeans, well-worn Nikes, and a University of Texas sweatshirt. She pushed away the tickling notion that Brett in her jeans was considerably sexier than the luscious leather clad brunette standing before her. She found her voice.

"I do? How can you tell?"

"My hands tell me everything I need to know. They are always right."

"Your hands can taste?"

"All my senses rely on whatever my hands tell them. They're always right."

"They are, are they?" Her fantasies fought to come to life. She couldn't have the woman she was thinking about, but she could have the one who was here for no other purpose than to please the guests of the house. Ryan may not break the rules of the house, but she was already breaking her personal code. Don't flirt. No unnecessary conversation. Don't beg. If she didn't get to a room with this woman soon, that last tenet was in serious danger.

"Follow me?"

Ryan took the woman's hand and followed.

CHAPTER SEVEN

B rett studied the woman in her office doorway. Her clothes hugged her body like a sausage. Her tight red curls were at odds with her olive skin. Her coral colored lipstick ran outside the lines and her blue eye shadow was a throwback to the eighties. She talked like a person hopped up on caffeine, and although she was petite, she managed to maneuver her body so that she blocked the person Brett really wanted to see.

Brett asked Mrs. Phillips to take a seat on the couch to the side of her desk, and she focused her attention on Kenneth. She placed his age at around twenty. He was rail thin. His clothes hung on his body like those of a hastily dressed scarecrow.

"Kenneth, before we get into the facts of why you are here, I need to let you know some ground rules." He nodded. "I need you to be able to tell me everything about this case and I need to be able to ask you questions. Frank and personal questions about what you tell me." Brett shot a look at Mrs. Phillips. She was perched on the edge of the sofa, barely sitting. Brett wanted her out of the room. "I am bound by law and the rules of my profession to keep everything you tell me confidential. However, in order for attorney-client privilege to apply, the information you share with me has to be shared in private."

Kenneth nodded. His mother didn't move. Brett wondered if she was talking into the wind. Time to be perfectly clear. "Mrs. Phillips, I'm happy to talk to the two of you together about the procedural aspects of this case, but I need to talk to Kenneth privately about the facts of the case itself."

Clients liked the comfort of family and friends. Their presence fortified them for the things they planned to say and the admonitions they expected to hear. But Brett preferred these sessions be one-on-one. She would spend ample time explaining the nuts and bolts of the criminal justice system to both mother and son once she had the facts she needed to evaluate how much trouble her client faced. The presence of friends and family at this stage threw a wrench in the works. People didn't like to confess, even to minor indiscretions, in front of their parents, spouses, or best friends. Their physical presence often equated to minimizing.

Mrs. Phillips didn't budge, so Brett tried a more direct approach. She stood and walked toward her office door, motioning for Mrs. Phillips to follow her.

"I want to be here when you talk to my son." Her tone was firm and resolute. Brett paused, searching for soft words in which to couch her dismissal of the woman.

"And I want you to be. When we start to talk about the many things you need to know in order to help your son through this process, but right now I need to talk to him alone."

Kenneth pointed to his mother. "She knows everything." He delivered the simple sentence with what seemed maximum effort. Since he had entered her office, Brett suspected the young man was hopped up on something. He was too skinny, for one thing. For another, his arms and legs jittered with the intensity of craving most junkies couldn't keep hidden. His eyes darted all over the room, rarely settling on a single object for more than a few brief seconds.

"Everything?" Brett asked. Kenneth nodded. "Let me make sure I understand. Your mother told me you want to confess to a murder that you were directly involved in. Is there anything about the facts of that crime that you haven't already shared with her?"

Kenneth shook his head from side to side. Brett held up her hand. "I need to you answer out loud."

"She knows everything."

Brett doubted Mrs. Phillips knew everything. She doubted any of them, Kenneth included, ever would. Motivation and remorse were components of criminal activity often discovered after exhaustive soul-searching. Her concern today though was the details of the murder itself, and her concern for confidentiality was moot if Kenneth had already spilled his guts to his mom. If that was the case and Kenneth consented to having her present, then Brett wasn't going to put up a fuss. Especially since it didn't seem like young Kenneth planned to do any talking without his mommy in the room. Brett made a mental note to explore the dynamic between the two when she could get Kenneth alone. In the meantime, she offered one last caveat to her potential client.

"If, during our discussion today, you think of anything you haven't already told your mom, we'll need to ask her to leave the room while you tell me. She can be compelled to testify about anything you tell her whether I'm present when you tell her or not. You only get to stand behind attorney-client confidentiality when the communication you have with me is made in private. Understood?"

"Understood."

"Your mom tells me this has something to do with the Ross Edwards case. Do you know Ross Edwards?"

"No."

Brett quickly realized getting information out of Kenneth was going to be a slow and arduous process, which was no different than most clients. "Okay, why don't you start talking? I'll save my questions until you're done." Brett sat back in her chair and watched as Kenneth shifted in his seat. At first, she thought he was trying to gear up for the telling, but she was confused when he pulled a wadded up piece of paper from his back pocket and began smoothing it out on his lap.

"What's that?" So much for saving my questions, she thought.

"He wrote down what he wants to tell you," Mrs. Phillips answered.

Brett tried not to show her annoyance. She turned so she was facing Kenneth and directed her next question to him. "Have you shown what's on that paper to anyone else?"

"Just me."

Time to nip this in the bud. "Mrs. Phillips, I appreciate you being here with your son." Brett paused to let her kind words sink in before she became forceful. "This process requires that Kenneth and I communicate directly. I have to be able to rely on whatever Kenneth tells me as being the truth according to him. The best way for that to happen is for me to hear whatever he has to say, spoken by him. Does that make sense?" Though the last question was clearly rhetorical, Mrs. Phillips nodded.

"I wrote it." The sound of Kenneth's voice was a welcome relief. He held up the paper. "Do you want me to read it to you?" Brett wanted no such thing. She wanted Kenneth to tell her about the murder. Something was off, but she couldn't quite put her finger on it.

"Is that how you would like to tell me what you have to tell me?" In response to his nod, she said, "Why don't we start that way?"

Brett watched Kenneth carefully as he read. His mother watched closely as well, hovering on the edge of the sofa as if hanging on his every word. His method of telling his story would work for now, but Brett planned to make it perfectly clear he had to be prepared to answer her questions if they were going to have any kind of long-term working relationship.

I was hanging out with my homeboy, John. We wanted to get some T-bars, but we didn't have any money. John said he knew where we could do a lick. I thought we were going to a DART station, but he took us to a house over in Richardson. We climbed the fence and he jimmied the sliding glass door. When we got inside, John and I grabbed a laptop in the living room and John went to another part of the house. I heard a woman cry out and went to see what happened. John was standing over this lady. He said she came up on him, so he hit her in the head. She was just lying there, but she looked like she was breathing. I said we need to get out of here. We grabbed what we already had and ran. We took the stuff to John's place.

The next day, John said he had gone back over there and the lady was still in the floor where we left her. I went back over there with him and we took some more stuff. She was dead. John had the idea to bury her. We didn't want to get caught digging in the yard, so we pried up some floorboards and dug a grave under the house. We couldn't get the floor to look right again, so John said we should set fire to the house. He said if we did, they would think she died in the fire and it would cover up any evidence that we'd been there. He found some lighter fluid in the garage and poured it around the house, lit it, and we took off. We pawned the stuff we took and bought some T-bars and weed.

When he finally lowered the papers, he looked shyly at Brett as if seeking approval. She struggled for an expression that would achieve balance between praise for the telling without endorsing the actions he had detailed. She had no idea if she pulled it off. She wanted to grab him by the shoulders and shake the stupid out of him. Instead, she launched into interrogation mode.

"I'm going to ask you a few details to fill in my notes." She waited for his nod. "Did you have any idea anyone was in the house when you got there?"

He shook his head, but Brett wasn't satisfied. He'd never make it through a police interview if he couldn't even get the words out with her. "Out loud."

"No."

"Did either you or John have a weapon when you entered the house?"

"I didn't. I don't know about John. I don't think so."

"What did John use to hit the woman?"

"Some metal thing. Like a tool by the fireplace."

"A poker?"

"I guess, yeah. He used it to pry up the floor too."

Brilliant plan. Brett didn't speak the sarcastic comment, but she wanted to. Burglary of a home was bad enough, but to compound the offense by not only killing the homeowner, but burying her body and setting her house on fire was classic idiocy.

Kenneth's mother interrupted her thoughts. "What happens next?"

"Well, we need to talk about that." Brett took a breath and while she did, Mrs. Phillips jumped into the gap in discussion.

"When you take him in, will he go to jail right away? Will you get some kind of agreement with the prosecutor first?"

Brett formed a T with her hands. "Time out. You're getting ahead of the game. I don't take on capital murder cases."

"Sure you do. You have a very good reputation for success."

Brett wondered if Mrs. Phillips realized how relative success was in the arena of capital murder cases. "I used to. I don't do that work anymore."

"Why did you even agree to meet with us?"

Fair question. Brett didn't have an answer that didn't sound lame. The mere mention of the Ross Edwards case had intrigued her, and she hadn't realized the state was seeking the death penalty until she read the press release online. Just because a case was eligible, didn't mean the district attorney would go for the full deal. Despite Texas's reputation as a hang 'em high state, efficiency called for many death penalty eligible cases to be prosecuted as a mini-caps, reducing the punishment exposure to life with no eligibility of parole. A capital case took considerable county resources including individualized jury selection as well as the years of appeals that would surely come after a guilty verdict.

Brett also had to admit she had become interested when she first heard the man's voice on the phone saying his son wanted to confess to a murder. She knew if he turned himself in, he risked being eaten alive by law enforcement officials who wouldn't look further than a young man's simple story. Now that she had heard the story for herself, she realized the case against Kenneth Phillips was indeed a capital case. Both arson and burglary were felonies, and the resulting death of the woman in the house, probably Mary Dinelli, could make this case death penalty eligible. She was torn. She didn't want to work on a death penalty case, but if she got involved early, maybe she could get the state to take the death penalty off the table. Intrigued by the case, not to mention Ryan Foster's role as the lead prosecutor, Brett knew what she was going to do.

"Then we have to talk about an agreement. Between us. If you want me to represent Kenneth, I will. We'll talk about whether he wants to turn himself in—"

"Oh, he definitely wants to do that."

Brett didn't try to hide her frustration at the interruption. She kept talking. "And we'll also talk about his options. The prosecutor won't negotiate with us in the abstract. In other words, he'll want to know exactly what Kenneth has to say before he will offer anything." Brett knew Ryan Foster herself would be the one to sign off on any plea offers on this case, but she still referred to the prosecutor as a "he" out of habit. She didn't like to let clients know the prosecutor might be a woman unless it was necessary. Defendants had a tendency to assume a woman would either cut them a better deal out of sympathy or, if the offer was unreasonable, it was because the female prosecuting the case was a bitch. Either situation was possible, but she didn't like to deal with preconceptions.

"Can't you just talk to this prosecutor and work something out before Kenneth goes to jail?" Kenneth's mother asked.

Brett decided to cut to the chase. "We'll have a lot of details to work out if Kenneth wants to turn himself in. I will be happy to talk to you about all of them, but before we get to that, we need to enter into an agreement." She paused to make sure she had their attention. "I have a contract prepared. I'll need an initial deposit of ten thousand dollars to bill against."

Mrs. Phillips looked like she was going to pass out. "I don't understand. All we want you to do is turn Kenneth in and make sure he doesn't get the death penalty."

"This is a very serious matter. You may think what you're asking for is simple, but it's not. It's going to require a lot of time and effort on my part to negotiate a deal on Kenneth's behalf, and ultimately the district attorney's office doesn't have to make any deals. The initial retainer I quoted is actually quite small, considering the possibilities." Brett sat back in her chair thinking Tony would be very proud of her for addressing the formalities so directly.

"We don't have that kind of money."

"What can you afford to pay?"

"What would you accept?"

Brett may be a bleeding heart, but she didn't play this game. The majority of her time as a lawyer was spent negotiating. First rule: don't negotiate against yourself. She may cut a potential client a lot of slack when it came to their ability to afford her fees, but she never broke this rule. People needed to feel invested in the process and if she bid herself down to a fee she couldn't live with, she risked resenting her client and her client wouldn't respect either her or the process.

"Not much less, I'm afraid." Brett asked again, "What can you afford?"

"We don't have much. A few hundred dollars. Maybe a thousand."

Brett shook her head. She wanted to help, she really did, but she couldn't take on a capital murder case for a thousand dollars. She'd already expended almost that amount in time at her standard hourly rate. This case could move rapidly or not. She couldn't predict. Either way, taking tiny payments would mean it could be years before the Phillips ever had even the initial retainer paid off. Taking payments usually meant Brett and Tony would spend more time working as bill collectors than as legal representatives. Brett didn't like to run her business that way, so she encouraged potential clients to find other sources of funding their legal defense. She gestured around her office. "I understand you may not have more, but I can't afford to take Kenneth's case for that small a fee. I have bills to pay and an employee who relies on me to keep the business afloat. Kenneth would certainly qualify for court-appointed counsel."

"Can he get that now?"

He couldn't. Kenneth wasn't charged with anything. For all Brett knew, no one even suspected him of a crime. If he was arrested and signed an affidavit of indigence, then an attorney would be appointed, but not before, no matter how serious the crime. Even as she pondered the dilemma, Brett was struck by the inherent unfairness, at least in Kenneth's situation. To Brett, the problem was a challenge, and an idea was already forming that might solve both the problem of providing Kenneth with a lawyer and extricating herself from the situation.

"Kenneth, if I promise to do everything I can to get you help, can you promise me something in return?"

He cast a look at his mother before nodding assent.

"Don't talk to anyone else about this. Don't do anything about this. For twenty-four hours. Promise?"

Chapter Eight

R yan reviewed her notes. There were a number of pretrial motions filed by the defense in the Edwards case, and Jeff had apparently put off responding. She would do them herself, but in the meantime, she had a list of things to take care of with regard to the other prosecutors under her command. Ryan picked up her notes and headed to the bank of elevators.

She glanced at her to-do list. At a staff meeting earlier in the week, Sheri Archer, a prosecutor under her supervision, had mentioned she was arguing a motion to suppress this morning. Sheri was assigned to Judge Langston's court and Jeff, as her direct supervisor, would be the one writing her annual review, but Ryan decided to take the opportunity to try to catch Sheri in action since ultimately she would be the one to decide if and when Sheri were promoted.

Ryan skimmed the text of the motion Sheri was defending. As usual, the defense motion was sparse, alleging only that the police search of the defendant's vehicle was done in violation of his constitutional rights. Since the search was done without a warrant, the burden was on the state to establish legal grounds for the search.

When Ryan entered the courtroom, Sheri was lobbing gentle questions to a Garland police officer. Ryan's glance at the defense table delivered a jolt. Brett Logan was the defense attorney on the case. Ryan congratulated herself on her good fortune.

Sheri handled her part deftly, laying the basic foundation to justify the warrantless search. The officer pulled the defendant's vehicle over for a traffic violation. When he performed a check on the defendant's identification, the officer discovered what he thought was an outstanding warrant. While his partner checked for more detail, the officer ordered the defendant out of the car, handcuffed him, and then placed him in the back of his squad car. Then he conducted a search of the defendant's vehicle and located a small vial containing traces of cocaine.

Sheri's part was done for now. She imagined Brett would press the point that the defendant hadn't consented to the search, but it was well settled law that the police department was authorized to conduct a search of a vehicle following an arrest, for both safety reasons and to take inventory of the contents of the vehicle that was being towed away. Ryan anxiously awaited Brett's strategy.

"Good morning, Officer Stanton. My name is Brett Logan and I represent Mr. Jones, the defendant in this case. I'm going to ask you some questions. If you don't understand my questions, please let me know and I will rephrase them until you do." Brett searched through some paperwork on the table until she found a bound notebook that she placed near the edge. She looked the officer directly in the eye for several seconds before she began.

"You asked my client for permission to search his vehicle?"

"Yes."

"During Ms. Archer's direct exam, I didn't hear you articulate any particular reason for that request. That's because you didn't have any reasonable suspicion to expect you might find contraband in Mr. Jones's vehicle, correct?"

"We often find contraband in vehicles, ma'am." The usually respectful title was marred by a smirk.

Brett wasn't deterred. "I suppose you didn't understand my question, officer. I'll break it into smaller parts. You pulled Mr. Jones over for failing to signal a right turn, correct?"

"Yes."

"He immediately responded to your lights and siren by safely pulling off the main road into a parking lot?"

"He did."

"He complied with all your instructions regarding producing his driver's license and proof of insurance?"

"Yes."

"Nothing about his demeanor indicated suspicious activity?" Inflection was the only indication Brett's bullet statements were actually questions. Ryan admired the technique. Essentially, Brett was testifying. The officer, apparently weary of the exchange, decided to vary his responses.

"I don't understand what you mean."

"He didn't fidget?"

"No."

"He didn't have any difficulty understanding your instructions?"

"He didn't appear to."

"He did what you asked?"

"Yes."

Brett wasn't giving an inch. "So your answer to my original question is no?"

"Correct."

Ryan knew Brett had just narrowed the issue. Sheri could no longer argue the officer had a reasonable suspicion about the presence of contraband in the vehicle since nothing about the defendant's actions led to that conclusion.

"Let's talk about the search you performed on Mr. Jones's vehicle. He did not give you permission to search his car, correct?"

"No, but—"

Brett held up her hand. "You answered my question, thank you." She paused and consulted a sheet of paper. "And I believe you testified that when you performed the search, Mr. Jones was handcuffed and seated in the back of your squad car."

"That's correct."

"You handcuffed him because you believed an active warrant called for his arrest?"

"Yes."

"Yet, while you were still at the scene of the traffic stop, you learned differently."

"That's correct. We learned an individual with the same name and date of birth had an active warrant. Further investigation into the individual's description led us to conclude that individual was not this defendant."

"So, officer, if you had not found illegal drugs in my client's vehicle, he would have been free to go."

"We would have written him a ticket for the traffic violation, but yes, he would have been free to go."

Brett caught the judge's eye. "Permission to approach the witness, Your Honor?" Judge Langston nodded. Brett stood and strode over to the officer. She placed a notebook on the railing of the witness stand. "Officer, do you know what this is?"

He took a moment to thumb through the contents. "Yes. These are the inventory procedures for evidence and other belongings seized in conjunction with an arrest."

"And this manual represents the current procedures that are in effect for the Garland Police Department?"

"Yes."

"Your Honor, I'd like to offer this notebook into evidence as defendant's exhibit number one."

Judge Langston inclined her head to the prosecution table. "Any objection from the State?"

Sheri looked puzzled. Ryan didn't know all the facts of the case, but she could see the possible path Brett was following. Sheri struggled and finally came up with an objection of sorts. "I'm not sure why these procedures are relevant, Judge."

Brett was quick to respond. "I would be happy to ask a couple more questions which I think will establish relevance." At the judge's nod, she faced Officer Stanton.

"You called a towing service to remove my client's vehicle?"

"My partner did, yes."

"The truck wasn't on scene when you conducted your initial search, correct?"

"No."

"Therefore, the tow truck driver didn't witness the search of the vehicle. Correct?"

Officer Stanton didn't try to hide his impatience. "Obviously, if the truck wasn't there, the driver wasn't either."

Brett held up the notebook. "Would you turn to page forty in the manual and read the first paragraph out loud?" She waited while he read the listed procedure that specified inventory searches were required to take place in the presence of the personnel who would take possession of the vehicle. "So we can conclude that because you didn't follow the procedures listed in this manual regarding an inventory search following arrest, your search was based on some other exception to the defendant's constitutional right to be free from unlawful searches and seizures?"

Officer Stanton shifted in his seat. Ryan knew he was feeling boxed in. Now that he admitted he didn't have evidence of drugs prior to the search, and hadn't followed the procedure to inventory the vehicle, which would have revealed the presence of drugs, there was only one argument left. Ryan hoped Sheri had prepped him on the recent change in the law.

"We have a right to search the car to make sure no contraband is destroyed, and ensure our safety."

"Sure you do, officer. I apologize. I should have asked this before. Were there any other passengers in the car?"

Ryan could tell Brett already knew the answer to the question. She could also tell Officer Stanton hadn't received proper training regarding the recent Supreme Court's opinion in *Arizona v. Gant*, issued several months earlier. For decades, police had been able to search vehicles they'd stopped for just about any reason, especially the contention that the defendant might either pull out a weapon or loose powdered drugs into the atmosphere to avoid detection. A recent challenge to that aspect of the law had won on the grounds that a defendant, already removed from the vehicle, especially one in handcuffs seated in a patrol car, was not in a position to brandish weapons or destroy anything. Now that Brett had eliminated all the exceptions that might be advanced by the police, the judge was likely to rule the evidence be tossed on the grounds the police had violated his constitutional rights. Ryan watched while the judge heard each side's arguments, promising to issue a decision by the next day.

Ryan approached the rail to shake Brett's hand. She craved the contact and welcomed the opportunity to disguise her motive behind simple professional courtesy, but before Ryan could reach her, Brett dashed off toward the rear door of the courtroom that led to the judge's chambers. Ryan watched her go. She felt strangely blue about the missed opportunity for a connection with Brett, but she didn't allow her attention to linger on the unfamiliar sentiment. Instead, she shrugged and turned to deliver a lecture about proper preparation to her subordinate.

❖

Judge Langston made a quick exit through the door behind her bench. Brett grabbed the papers off her table, jammed them in her briefcase, and made a beeline through the clerk's office so she could catch the judge in chambers before she shut her office door. Brett slipped into her office as the judge was hanging up her robe. Beneath the robe, she wore a smart tailored suit in deep crimson.

"Judge, may I talk to you for a moment?"

"Do we need Ms. Archer?" The judge referred to the prosecutor. Brett realized the judge thought she wanted to talk about the case she had just argued. She quickly assured her she wasn't trying for an *ex parte* communication. "No, ma'am. I have a question about an altogether different matter."

"All right then." Judge Langston reached behind her desk for a tray containing a dainty china tea set. "Cup of tea?"

Brett smiled and nodded. She knew she was invading the judge's standard morning break. Every day, no matter what was going on in the courtroom, she broke at ten thirty and retired to her chamber for a twenty-minute tea break. No one, including the judge's coordinator, dared interrupt once the tea pouring began, but if you could catch her before she got started, you were likely to be invited to join. Tea with the judge was an invitation not to be declined.

Brett waited until the tea was poured and prepared. Finally, the judge took a deep sip, set her cup down, and leaned toward Brett. "What can I do for you, Ms. Logan?"

"Judge, if an individual was arrested for a serious crime and qualified as indigent, you would appoint counsel, correct?"

"I think you know the answer to that."

"I do. Here's a question I don't know the answer to. If an individual committed a serious crime, but no one suspected them, yet they wanted to turn themselves in, would you appoint counsel before they had their first contact with anyone from law enforcement or the district's attorney's office?"

"This individual is indigent?"

"Yes."

The judge revisited her teacup. Brett waited. She was well acquainted with Judge Langston's habits. Thinking while drinking was one of her calling cards.

"How serious is this crime?"

"Capital murder."

Langston didn't flinch, but Brett caught a glint in her eye and realized the judge understood this whole line of questioning was not hypothetical.

"A logical course of action might be to talk to someone in the public defender's office. They might be able to facilitate whatever this individual needs."

The judge was right, and Brett had considered that option after Kenneth left her office the previous afternoon. A few clicks of her mouse later she learned the public defender's office couldn't help Kenneth Phillips. The Dallas County PD's office had at least one attorney assigned to each court, but that wasn't enough personnel to cover all the cases where defendants qualified for appointed counsel. To supplement the roster of public defenders, the county judges had a list of attorneys who voluntarily agreed to take cases for much less than they could charge in their private practice. Brett was on the wheel, as it was called, as were most of her colleagues. Many of the most interesting felony cases had at their center defendants who couldn't afford to hire what they not so affectionately called a free world lawyer.

There were generally two reasons judges reached for a name on the wheel of court-appointed attorneys: the public defender's caseload was too high or the public defender's office had a conflict. Conflict was the reason Kenneth Phillips couldn't get assistance from the PD's office. Although Ross Edwards was currently represented by an attorney in private practice, his first counsel had been an attorney employed by the public defender's office. Since all the attorneys employed by the PD's office were technically part of the same firm, they couldn't represent two defendants whose interests were opposed to each other. Kenneth's confession was certainly in Ross Edwards's best interests, but their prior representation of Edwards could come into conflict with Kenneth's. It was too soon to tell and too much to risk.

Judge Langston greeted the news that the PD's office was conflicted out by pouring herself a second cup of tea. Once she prepared it to her satisfaction, she ventured a question that had obviously been nagging at her.

"I assume you are talking to me because this case is pending in my court?"

Brett nodded. She knew it wouldn't take the judge long to sort through the possibilities of which pending case Brett's not so hypothetical questions were about. At this point, she just wanted to get to the point. She wanted the judge to appoint someone to represent Kenneth. Then she could wash her hands of the affair. The young man and his confession would be in capable hands, and she could go back to her moneymaking health care fraud cases. The last thing she needed was to get bogged down in a capital murder case for a pittance of a fee.

"Yes, Judge. I was hoping—"

Judge Langston interrupted her. "Don't tell me anything else about it. I trust your judgment that this individual of which you speak would qualify for appointed counsel. Just do whatever you need to do to provide quality representation and submit a bill when you're done. Understood?"

"Judge, I don't think I was clear. I'm not trying to get appointed to the case. In fact, I'm not on the death penalty certified list anymore."

"Well, you used to be, right?"

Brett nodded, but rushed to add, "I chose to take myself off the list. I didn't come here bargaining for this case. I just want this person to have good legal representation at the earliest possible stage."

Brett had stopped taking capital cases when she came home one day to find that her last girlfriend, Stephanie, had quickly and quietly moved every one of her belongings out of the townhome they shared. Stephanie Whistler had a demanding job as a doctor at Parkland, the bustling Dallas county hospital. As busy as she was, Stephanie had been able to shed the emotional aspects of her caseload when she crossed the threshold of their cozy home. Brett, on the other hand, had scattered the detritus of her clients' troubles throughout their house, and their desperation eclipsed her happiness. Brett often thought it ironic. They were both trying to save lives, but Brett's methods were the death knell of her own relationship. With Stephanie's departure, Brett swore off putting others' lives before her own. Her oath was of little consequence. She hadn't wanted for female company, but she hadn't dated anyone she would consider cohabiting with either. It wasn't long before she fell back into her old ways. She may not work on death penalty cases anymore, but she did throw herself completely into the cases she did work, cutting herself off from the possibility of lasting relationships. So far, no one had tempted her from that path. The sad thought was accompanied by a flash of a memory. Ryan Foster was similarly focused on work and appeared to be similarly alone.

"I have no doubt you'll provide him with the best representation," the judge said. "I can get you back on the list, but frankly, if your client wants to confess, a fine attorney like yourself should be able to negotiate the death penalty off the table." The judge started to clear up the evidence of their tea party as if the subject were concluded. Brett knew the judge expected her to leave now, but she couldn't resist one more shot.

"I appreciate the vote of confidence, but I've taken on a pretty heavy federal caseload lately. I think there are lawyers whose certification is current who would be in a better position to handle this case."

Judge Langston finished replacing her tea tray exactly as it had been when she had started her break. When she finished, she turned and fixed Brett with a penetrating stare. "This individual found his or her way to you. Unless you have a conflict yourself, I don't see any reason you wouldn't be the best person to handle this case. I'll look forward to seeing even more of you in my courtroom." She reached for her robe, slipped it on, and made her way back to the bench. Brett followed. She had no response to the judge's assessment. No acceptable one anyway. To keep protesting would make her seem like a whiner. Besides, it wasn't like the distraction of a capital case would be an imposition on her personal life, such as it was. She didn't want to admit, even to herself, that the only true conflict she had was the combination of attraction and challenge she felt for the new lead prosecutor on the case.

Ryan knew Brett hadn't left the courtroom yet, but she nevertheless felt a tingle of surprise when she saw Brett walking toward her. Their brief coffee meeting, date…Ryan wasn't sure what to call it, but it had been strange. She suspected Brett was reaching out to her that day, but the time they spent together was too short for her to assess the motive. Ryan wanted Brett's objective to be a desire to get to know her personally, but she reasoned it was more likely Brett was jockeying for a good position with the next district attorney.

Ryan had certainly experienced plenty of similar attention lately even though she had not officially announced her candidacy. The past month had been full of what Leonard liked to call fishing trips. He had squired her around the county like a matchmaker looking for the perfect spouse, except she was the suitor, pledging her faith to multiple partners. She had stopped protesting. Leonard waved off all her protests that she wasn't cut out for politics. "Politics isn't something you choose. It chooses you," he said. He insisted that Dallas County was poised to host its first female elected DA, and Ryan was perfect for the position. Whatever she lacked in terms of politicking prowess, he was happy to provide. After eighteen years in office, Leonard Duncan knew all the available sources of support, legitimate and otherwise. Ryan imagined there wasn't much Leonard didn't know about what went on in Dallas County, and his knowledge of where the powerful people kept their skeletons hidden only fueled his own power. Not for the first time, Ryan speculated that Leonard certainly must know about the parties some of his most select constituents attended. She pushed the thought away, unwilling to acknowledge how it made her feel to consider the possibility her mentor might know her secret. Surely he didn't.

"Can I talk to you? Privately?"

Ryan noted again the undercurrent of command present in Brett's soft tones. The result was a gentle authority she wanted to obey. Brett probably won many hearings like the one she had just witnessed.

"Sure. Shall we go upstairs?" At Brett's nod, she led the way out of the courtroom. While they waited at the bank of elevators, Ryan watched Brett stare intently through the wall of glass that fronted the Frank Crowley court building. Local magazines rated the view from the criminal court building as the number one way to see the magnificent Dallas skyline. Positioned on the western border of downtown, the criminal court building offered an excellent view of not only the striking skyline, but some of Dallas's most notorious landmarks, including the grassy knoll and the Texas School Book Depository. The irony of the view wasn't lost on Ryan. Her goal was to put away the accused individuals that either walked these halls or were in residence across the street at the Lew Sterrett Justice Center, aka the Dallas County jail. If their last view of freedom was one of the best, then they would just regret their loss all the more.

Normally visitors had to sign in and obtain a badge before being admitted to the offices of the district attorney, but Ryan took Brett the opposite direction of the reception area. She punched her code into the keypad and held the door open for her. Ryan chose not to examine why she was not observing protocol. She walked through the narrow hallways, past the tiny offices that lined the corridor, nodding to the few prosecutors who happened to be upstairs during morning docket. Once they reached her office, she ushered Brett in and shut the door behind them. As Brett looked around, Ryan recognized she was proud to have Brett witness the level of power she possessed, symbolized by the well-appointed corner office. She may never garner the kind of dollars a private practice attorney could command, but a flash of her badge would bring to bear the might of all the police power available in a large city. Money wasn't everything.

Brett cleared her throat, and Ryan nodded for her to speak. "Thanks for talking to me. I'm not sure we needed this much privacy, but it's nice to see where you work. You certainly have an amazing view."

Ryan shrugged and made an attempt at modesty. "I don't get a lot of opportunity to enjoy the view, but I have to agree, it's amazing." She stared at Brett seated across from her. She didn't seem sure how to begin whatever it was she wanted to discuss. Even seated, it was apparent Brett Logan was a tall woman. Her torso was as long and lean as the rest of her body. Today she was wearing trial clothes, a black suit with crisp lines. Her only nod to fashion over function was a soft white silk shirt with an oversized collar and a freshwater pearl necklace. Not a stain in sight. Ryan couldn't resist a comment. "You look very polished today."

Brett glanced down and pointed at her blouse. "Give me a few minutes and a cup of coffee. You'll be certain to change your mind. My clothes and my meals have a magnetic attraction to each other. I'm helpless to resist."

Ryan smiled. She couldn't help herself. Brett's self-deprecating humor was only one of her attractive qualities. Brett matched her smile with a huge grin. Perfect teeth, twinkling eyes. She didn't look like someone with something pressing to discuss. Ryan wondered what this meeting was about, so she decided to restore formality and get to the point. "Okay, Ms. Logan, what do you need today?"

Brett seemed to ignore the change in tone, her smile still showing. "Call me Brett. And thanks for taking the time. I know you're busy. I want to talk to you about the Edwards case."

Ryan's smile disappeared. She was instantly suspicious, though she couldn't pinpoint the exact reason. But the hair on the back of her neck stood at attention and her stomach started to churn. Was Ross Edwards changing attorneys? He had already been represented by the public defender's office before mysteriously coming into the funds to post bond and hire Luke Tyson, a standard around the courthouse. Ryan had no fear of Tyson. He represented a ton of defendants with no regard or worry for the varying degrees of difficulty required by each individual case. He had a reputation as a winner, but the reputation was bigger than the man. He would do a good enough job to foreclose any claims of ineffective assistance, but he wouldn't mount a stellar defense.

Brett Logan, on the other hand, was a different story. Based on what Ryan had witnessed that morning, she was concerned. Brett was well prepared and quick on her feet. Jurors would love her easy smile and good looks. Ryan was confident justice would prevail, but taking Brett down would have to be part of the strategy. She usually relished such a prospect, but she found herself dreading it already. She decided to meet the challenge head-on.

"Talk away."

"I may represent a person of interest in the case."

Ryan paused to consider what she decided was Brett's purposely vague choice of words. Did she represent Ross or not? Ross Edwards was certainly a person of interest, but Brett used the term like the feds did, referring to someone who might be a conspirator, but not the center of the action. She wanted to ask her questions directly, but she wasn't ready to cede her power away, so she merely nodded to indicate Brett should continue.

"Before I talk to you more about this person, I wanted to know if you would let me review the police report or at least fill me in on some of the pertinent facts." Brett knew her request was unusual, but it wasn't unheard of. She wasn't asking for state secrets, after all. She knew plenty of other prosecutors who would have no problem sharing this bare bones information with her. Brett had carefully cultivated a reputation for honor and integrity, and she enjoyed the benefits of information that came with it. Obviously, the DA's office was holding back details about this case or Brett would have read more during her online searches than the mere facts that Mary

Dinelli was dead and Ross Edwards had been arrested and charged with theft and murder. She figured if she could at least get a glimpse at the official report, she might be able to figure out how Kenneth fit in and why his involvement had been missed.

Ryan's first instinct was to escort Brett to the door. She didn't have any obligation to share information about their investigation with an attorney who wasn't officially on the case. She didn't even have to share all of it with Luke Tyson until certain statutorily required deadlines were in play. She hesitated. "Are you signing on this case?"

Brett hedged. "Maybe."

"If you're replacing Tyson, I'm going to need to see an order substituting counsel before I'll talk to you about the case." Ryan pulled a stack of files on her desk closer as if that concluded the matter. She barely gave the papers a glance while she waited for Brett's response.

"I'm not representing Ross Edwards."

"Then you don't have any grounds to request discovery."

Brett shook her head. "Ryan, I'm not asking for formal discovery here. I may have an interest in this case, and I'll be happy to share specifics at the appropriate time. You can help me determine the appropriate time more easily by sharing the police report with me." She offered a conciliatory tone. "Come on. I give you my word. I won't share any information you give me with anyone."

"Do the prosecutors in my division usually give you what you want?" Ryan tried not to make the question sound accusatory, but she feared it did. Apparently, Brett Logan was used to getting what she wanted, despite policies Ryan herself had set in place. She watched the pieces of realization shuffle into place on Brett's face. If she said no, then how could she expect to get the information she requested now? If Brett said yes, then she risked getting those very prosecutors that helped her out in trouble, thereby drying up her sources. Ryan wanted to know which path she would choose.

"I don't make it a habit to take advantage of favors."

Diplomatic. Ryan liked Brett's response. "A bit odd seeking favors from me, don't you think?" Brett cocked a questioning eyebrow to which Ryan responded. "We hardly know each other. I don't owe you anything."

"Nor I you." Brett thought she detected a slightly flirtatious tone. She wondered about the source. She was at a loss as to how to respond, and she finally settled on the idea of floating an offer with a slight flirt of her own. "But you never know when the situation might change."

Ryan shifted in her seat. The undercurrent between them was making her feel uncomfortable even as she was drawn toward Brett. Time to change the subject. "Who's the person of interest?"

It was Brett's turn to shift in her seat. "I'm not prepared to say."

"Yet you expect me to hand over evidence. Evidence we haven't shared with anyone outside of the lawyers who have actually entered an appearance on this case."

Brett offered one last overture in her attempt to get a glimpse at the police report. "I understand why you haven't shared any information. Nothing you show me will go any further. I realize you don't know me, but you can check around. My reputation is solid."

"No need. When you're ready to tell me about your person of interest, I'll make a decision about what, if anything, I'll share with you."

Brett stood, signaling she was done trying. Ryan felt the chill of her absence before Brett crossed the threshold. She knew her lack of cooperation hastened Brett's departure, but she couldn't see her way clear to giving her what she wanted. Her attraction to Brett gnawed at the edges of her professional demeanor, but she had given in as much as she would. Attraction wasn't an appropriate motive for breaking rules.

CHAPTER NINE

Hey, T, what time are the Phillipses coming in?" Brett breezed by Tony's desk, grabbing a handful of French fries from the lunch spread out on wax paper on his credenza. "Yum, these are good. Where did you get them?"

"I haven't a clue and Hunky's."

"They're pretty good for to-go fries." Brett stopped mid-fry. "Did you call the Phillipses?" Brett had called Tony before she left the courthouse and left him a cryptic voice mail. She asked him to call the Phillipses and arrange another meeting with Kenneth. She didn't take the time to explain that Judge Langston had appointed her to the case, and she worried he might have conveniently ignored her request without that knowledge.

"What do you mean, did I call Mr. Phillips?" Tony's indignant tone told her she had misread the situation. "I called, he didn't answer. I left a message. He hasn't called back. Would you like to check the rest of my work from this morning?"

"Mea culpa." Brett grabbed another fistful of fries. "Forgive me?" Between bites of crispy goodness, she explained. "I talked to Judge Langston about Kenneth's situation, and she appointed me to represent him. Well, not him exactly, but she appointed me to represent the hypothetical person I talked to her about. We'll just keep a running bill and submit it when the case is over."

"Will do."

Tony's tone was chipper, not at all what Brett had expected when she told him they would be paid pennies on the dollar for a capital case she hadn't had any desire to take in the first place. "You're in an awfully good mood." She polished off the rest of his fries to fortify herself for whatever he had up his sleeve.

Tony handed her a napkin and a slip of paper with a name and phone number. "Mrs. Ambulance Company referred a friend."

"Not another Medicare case."

"Yes, another Medicare case. Those cases pay the bills, you know."

"I may have to cut back on some of these paper intensive cases while I gear up for the Phillips case." Brett braced herself for the fallout.

"Excuse me, miss. Is there something you're not telling me? I thought this was an open and shut, confess and work out a deal kind of case."

"Maybe. Ryan Foster is taking lead on the case."

"Oh. I see."

Brett knew she didn't need to elaborate. The feelers about Ryan's run for the district attorney's office were out in force, and her office had received no less than a half dozen invitations to meet and greets with the potential candidate. Ryan could view the publicity of a trial as more valuable than an open and shut plea deal. Brett wondered what Tony would think if he knew how she got hot just sitting across from Ryan and her power desk in her large top floor office. She shrugged away the memory.

Brett dreaded election season. Every yahoo with political aspirations threw their hat in the ring, and they spent their first dollars purchasing the mailing list of the Dallas Bar Association where they would begin begging for dollars to support their campaigns. She, like every other attorney who litigated, felt the need to cough up at least a minimal contribution to the judges and other officials she regularly encountered. Brett never felt like she was gaining an advantage with her contributions, but she did view the act as a type of talisman to ward off the ill will of those who might recall the absence of her name from their donor lists.

"I'm a little worried she may not deal."

"Can you talk to her?"

"I did talk to her this morning, though I left out the fact I might be representing one of the real killers. She might be under the impression I'm signing on to represent Edwards. She wouldn't really tell me anything about the case, so I was pretty cagey with her." Brett couldn't quite put her finger on it, but it bothered her that all she had was Kenneth's side of the story. She wasn't comfortable starting plea negotiations without knowing more about what kind of case the state had, not to mention the fact that in her experience, her clients didn't always provide the complete picture in the first round of talks. Getting to the bare bones of the matter was usually a process requiring several circles around the facts, before she and her client could zero in on a version of the truth. Brett suddenly had an idea that might help eliminate some of the circling.

"Will you see if you can get Jake Simmons to come in this afternoon?"

"Pretty short notice."

"If he has the time, I think he'll do it for me." Jake Simmons was the best private investigator she knew, and he owed her a favor. She left Tony with the debris from his lunch and went to the tiny kitchenette down the hall to forage for something to supplement the greasy carbs she had filched from him. She settled on a Yoplait, but she wasn't happy about it. Moments later, Tony buzzed her desk phone.

"Jake's coming by at three."

"Thanks."

"That leaves you plenty of time to make calls on the new case. I scheduled them in first thing in the morning."

Brett groaned her response. She dug deep in the plastic yogurt container as if it might contain a treasure in the bottom. Something like a cheeseburger with bacon, extra mayo, and another side of fries. No such luck. She tossed the empty container in the trash and focused on her desk, even straightening it a bit.

❖

Ryan finished eating her sandwich and tossed the brown paper bag into the trash can beneath her desk. High fiber wheat bread, turkey, lettuce. No mayo. She saved the apple for an afternoon snack. She grabbed a gym bag from the corner of her office, tossed the apple inside, and made her way back downstairs. Jeff, finishing off the last of a greasy slice of pizza at his desk, looked surprised to see her.

"Hey, Ryan, what's up?"

She contemplated telling him about Brett Logan's visit. He had a right to know about a potential development on the case. She considered for a moment before deciding she would tell him when or if she had something specific to say. Instead, she focused on the original purpose of her trip downstairs.

"No trial today?"

Jeff shook his head. "Most of our docket shook out. We're starting a TBC in the morning." He referred to a trial before the judge, rather than a jury.

"Do you have a change of clothes?" Ryan knew he would. No one got to be in the kind of shape he was in without daily workouts, especially if they put foul stuff in their bodies like the lunch he was devouring. Since she knew he arrived at the office as early as she did, she surmised he was a workout on the way home kind of person, meaning he would have a gym bag either here in the office or in his car. Just like her.

He glanced at the bag in her hand and nodded.

"Well, grab it and let's go." Ryan decided they could change in the restrooms downstairs and sneak out Leonard's private access to the building. This afternoon's field trip was on a whim, meaning she hadn't brought a suitable change of clothes. She didn't want to be seen walking through the halls in the rough sweats she wore to the boxing gym downtown.

To his credit, Jeff didn't ask any questions. He hefted a well-worn Adidas bag from under his desk and followed her out of the room.

After they changed, Ryan led the way to the parking garage next to the courthouse. She bypassed her reserved parking space and walked to the row of white sedans that represented the district attorney's fleet. She would much rather drive her Lexus sedan. She would have if she were by herself, but she didn't want to invite Jeff into her personal life in any way, even if it were something as simple as him riding along in her only true self indulgence.

Richardson was a quiet suburb just north of Dallas with a population of just over a hundred thousand. The city was home to a number of the world's largest computer and networking companies. As a result, many of its residents were upper middle class. All the major growth was on the west side, and the east side of the city remained singularly unchanged except for an explosion of Asian-owned businesses. Rows of 1920s bungalow houses lined aging streets. Large pecans and oaks, whose limbs touched worn rooftops and left huge piles of leaves on lawns, stood in the yards of houses neglected for reasons of old age, disability, and fixed income.

Before the fire, Mary Dinelli's house had been a pristine contrast to the rest of the neighborhood. Photos from a recent appraisal file showed a well-maintained dwelling with pale yellow siding, shiny black shutters, and a cherry red front door. Now only a detached garage and garden shed remained standing, and both buildings looked out of place next to the charred patch of ground in the middle of the lot. Before being trampled by teams of firefighters, dragging yards of thick hose, the landscaping had been thriving and colorful. Now the yard was dead and brown.

"I could have told you the house is gone. Whatever was left after the fire was torn down and removed by the city."

Ryan ignored Jeff's comment and got out of the car. She walked to the center of the lot. Jeff stood at the edge of the lot for a moment before he followed her. Ryan didn't say anything as she paced the perimeter of the space where Mary Dinelli had met her end. Jeff stood off to one side, barely hiding his impatience at this exercise. She would get back to him when she was done. Right now, her singular focus was the scene of the crime, what it could tell her, and what she would tell the jury about the scene and the victim.

She tugged on the door to the garden shed. As she expected, the interior was neat and clean. All of the contents had long since been removed. She pulled several photographs from the envelope and held them up against the shelves. Squinting, she could imagine the rows of tools depicted in the pictures nestled into their individual nooks and cubbies in the shed. Disability notwithstanding, Mary Dinelli was a meticulous, tidy gardener.

Jeff was still standing where she left him.

"What's the matter, Oates, don't like the down and dirty?" Ryan purposely chided him.

His response was defensive. "I've seen plenty of dirt. Way messier than this. I can flash through autopsy photos without a flinch," he bragged. "This patch of grass? It's nothing."

"That's where you're wrong. This patch of grass symbolizes what Ross Edwards did to Mary Dinelli in a way the jury can stomach. Autopsy photos will make them uncomfortable. A couple of shots of a dead body, and they'll want you to put those pictures away, but you can leave a picture of this decimated lot up on the screen during the investigator's entire testimony, and they won't squirm. What they will do is see the scorched earth approach Ross took to his victims. He wiped her out. Her bank accounts, her property, her life. All that's left is a burned patch of grass."

Ryan didn't wait for a response. She put the photos back in the envelope and got into the car. Jeff slid into his seat. His silence was tense, as if he were pissed off at having been schooled about relating to a jury. Ryan could imagine the fast flickering thoughts in his head. *What does she know about juries? She hasn't tried a case in who knows when?*

If those were indeed his thoughts, Ryan had to give him credit. At least part of the reason for this afternoon's field trip was to allow her to answer those questions for herself. She hadn't tried a high profile, emotional case in years. The last case she had been directly involved in was all about numbers, mortgage fraud, and her presence in the courtroom had been for the sole purpose of displaying to the jury that the district attorney was so dedicated to the heinous crime of financial fraud, he was sending his top lieutenant to find justice for the citizens of Dallas County. Ryan needed to know if she still had the touch, the magical weave-a-story, paint-a-picture touch that had gotten her noticed in the first place. She had spent so much time on the eleventh floor, far from the people part of the job, she wasn't sure she could summon the fierce emotion of vengeance and retribution she would need to convince a jury to order Ross Edwards to his death.

Until now. Standing in Mary Dinelli's burned patch of everything she owned, Ryan summoned all the emotion she needed to exact vengeance. This woman, who gave her service to her country, had been robbed of the only reward she sought: to live her days in quiet peace, a modest pension to keep her in potting soil and garden tools. Ryan wanted to plunge the needle into Edwards's arm herself.

CHAPTER TEN

Jake's here."

Brett placed her hand over the phone. "Great. Thanks. Tell him to come on in." She turned her attention back to her call. "Kenneth, I'm going to get hold of the police report, and then I'll call you to make arrangements to meet again." She had already explained to him that the judge had appointed her to represent him, and he wouldn't have to worry about payment. Frankly, she was glad to finally be talking to him, rather than his pushy mother. Which reminded her to ask, "Do you have your own phone? Seems like I should call you directly rather than through your parents'."

He ignored the question. "Why do you need the police report? Don't you believe what I told you?" His voice started to squeak. "I'm going to go to the police. I can't stand the pressure anymore."

Brett took a deep breath, but the act didn't completely dissipate her impatience. "No, you're not. Not if you want to live. The cops will have you for lunch. I need to know more objective information before I can give you solid advice. This is a high profile case, and the prosecutor wants to put a needle in someone's arm for the death of Mary Dinelli. You want me to represent you? Then you trust my advice. Understood?"

Kenneth sobbed. "Yes."

"Okay. I'm sorry to be harsh." She wasn't sorry, but she did recognize the need to soften her tone in response to his emotional reaction. She was surprised to hear his voice quiver since he had delivered the tale of the crime with so little affect. "Now, hole up somewhere. I'll call you. Soon." She hung up the phone before he could say another word.

"Difficult client?"

Brett was startled but recovered quickly. She stood up to hug her visitor. Jake Simmons didn't dole out hugs to just anyone, but Brett knew she would receive a firm embrace. She hadn't seen him in years, but he hadn't changed one bit.

Jake was a retired Dallas cop and now worked full time for the law firm of Ramirez & Dearning. He wasn't an employee of the firm though, and would occasionally take on other work if he didn't have a conflict, and if he found it interesting. What Brett was going to ask him to do probably wasn't going to be interesting, but she knew she could count on him to give it a shot.

Jake wasn't prone to idle chitchat. He pulled out a pad, similar to the whip out notebooks he would have used when he was a beat cop. Pen poised over paper, he waited for Brett to outline the assignment.

"I need to get hold of a police report."

He visibly relaxed. "That should be easy. What agency?"

"Richardson PD, and it may not be as easy as you think. It's on the Ross Edwards case. Ryan Foster is lead on the case, and she's guarding her case file like a mother protecting her young."

Jake laughed. "Not a role I'd normally cast that woman in."

At that opening, Brett decided to veer off course. "To tell you the truth, I don't know her very well. Actually, I don't know her at all."

"Yeah, she's been upstairs since you went into private practice."

"She a good litigator?" Brett urged Jake to share. She did want to know about Ryan's trial skills, but that hadn't been the primary purpose of her fishing expedition. What she was really after was insight into Ryan's well-hidden personality. Jake had done a stint as an investigator with the DA's office after his retirement from the Dallas Police Department. Maybe he had gotten a glimpse of the woman concealed behind the lawyer persona.

"She's solid. Law-and-order, through and through. But sometimes seeing things as only black or white can be a handicap."

Brett could tell by Jake's tone he was referring to both the professional and personal sides of Ryan Foster. "Good to know." She switched gears. "Here's the deal. I'm representing someone who may be heavily involved in the case they've built against Ross Edwards. He wants to confess his involvement, but I don't feel comfortable bringing him in until I know more about the State's case. Ryan's stonewalling me."

"She won't show hers unless you show yours." Jake succinctly summarized her position.

"Exactly."

"Give me a rundown, and I'll see what I can find out."

Jake left a few minutes later, armed with all the details Kenneth had provided. Brett was confident Jake would find out whatever he could. In the meantime, she planned to do some digging of her own.

❖

Ryan learned to keep a glass in her hand for the duration of these interminably long functions. This evening the glass was filled with tonic and a wedge of lime. Empty-handed, she would have no control over the well-meaning hosts who hated to see the guest of honor lacking in any way. As it was, they concentrated on introducing her to all the well-heeled guests capable of funding her campaign. She had only been at this particular gathering for half an hour, but she couldn't wait to leave.

Across the room, Leonard cleared his throat with a hearty rumble and clapped his hands for attention. "Ladies and gentleman, thanks to all of you for being here tonight. We appreciate the hospitality of the Fraziers." He paused to allow the crowd to applaud the millionaire host couple who had opened their historic home for this occasion. Ryan cringed as the applause died down. She dreaded what was coming next.

"And now I'd like to introduce the woman we're all here to support. She's achieved success both in and out of the courtroom as a superior litigator and an accomplished leader among the prosecutors in my office. I've known her for years, and I've never seen anyone work harder. I know that as the next elected District Attorney of Dallas County, she will continue to work hard for all of you. Please join me in a big round of applause for your future DA, Ryan Foster." He waved a hand in Ryan's direction and the crowd opened up to allow her to make it to his side.

Ryan approached on autopilot, a script of appropriate well-memorized election year platitudes on the tip of her tongue. As she reached Leonard's side, she nodded at the crowd, but just as she was about to speak, she spotted a face in the crowd that seemed strangely out of place.

❖

Even though she knew Ryan was the guest of honor, Brett wasn't prepared for the rush of electricity surging across the room when their eyes met. The pull was so strong, she couldn't look away. Was it just her imagination, or did Ryan seem to stumble through her first words as she also seemed unable to break the line of sight between them? Brett grabbed a glass of champagne from a passing waiter to redirect her focus. She sipped the bubbly and spent the next few minutes adding to her distraction with some of the scrumptious appetizers being passed through the room.

"A Republican? Well, what a surprise."

Brett swallowed the canapé she'd just shoved in her mouth. Ryan was standing beside her and her magnetism was full strength. "That certainly would be a surprise. A pleasant one for my family, but one they will have to continue to hold their breath for."

Ryan smiled. The smile was tentative. Endearing. "So you're the black sheep of the family?"

"The blue sheep, actually."

"I take it I won't be getting your vote?"

Brett gestured at the crowded room and dodged the question. "Doesn't look like you need it."

"I don't know about that. The campaign's just getting started. I can use all the help I can get."

The room was full of old money Republicans, influential and well connected. Even at this early stage, Ryan was assured her party's nomination, and winning the general election would be a breeze. Yet, Brett heard notes of sincerity in Ryan's tone. *She doesn't take success for granted. Mark one in the plus column.*

"Are you here for the free food or cocktails?"

Brett stopped her mental tally of Ryan's qualities. "I'm meeting someone."

"I didn't realize campaign events could morph into date nights." Ryan's delivery was deadpan, but Brett flashed back to the hint of flirtation she felt in Ryan's office at the courthouse. Surely this staunch Republican heir to the conservative district attorney wasn't baiting her with innuendo? Before she could fashion a response, Brett felt herself engulfed into someone's arms. She knew by the scent exactly who it was.

"Brian! Let me go. This isn't a touch football game. You're wrinkling my jacket." She detangled herself from her brother's arms and held him at arm's length. "Don't you ever get tired of wearing Polo?" Brett saw the hurt flash in his eyes and she instantly regretted her playful remark. She hugged him close and kissed him on the forehead. He responded by tickling her sides and their embrace devolved into child play.

Watching their interaction, Ryan was beyond confused. The man's name tag bore the same last name as Brett's, and these two were obviously well acquainted. Were her Internet research conclusions that faulty? She had been certain Brett was a lesbian, but maybe she was just, what was the word the community used? An ally. That's right, ally.

"Are you going to introduce me?" The man looked back and forth between Brett and Ryan. Brett complied. "Ryan Foster, meet Brian Logan. Wealthy Republican donor. Civil lawyer extraordinaire." She slid her arm around his waist. "And my brother."

Thank god. Ryan didn't pause to wonder about the strong sense of relief she experienced upon learning Brian didn't have any romantic connection to Brett. She was still curious about why Brett was at this event. *Only one way to find out.* "And you? Are you here to steer your brother's vote in the right direction?"

"I'm fairly certain we have very different perceptions as to what constitutes the right direction. I'm here in part to demonstrate tolerance, but mostly to hook up with a wealthy dinner date. Brian's taking me to dinner after he's done schmoozing with all you starched shirt types."

Ryan wondered why Brett hadn't just met Brian at the restaurant instead of here at this conservative love fest. Her reflection was interrupted by a question from Brian.

"I suppose you can't ditch the other guests and join us for dinner? We're going to Five Sixty." He referred to Wolfgang Puck's Dallas venture. Surely he was kidding. She couldn't leave a room full of supporters with bottomless checkbooks, not even if it meant she got to have good face time with potential donors. She was torn. The invitation was tempting. And not because of any money Brian Logan might have at his disposal. She glanced at Brett who offered a smile before punching him in the arm. Brett's words decided her fate for the evening.

"Brian, don't be a goof. Ryan can't leave. You're not the only one here with funds for her campaign. She's got some schmoozing to do." Brett cast a sympathetic look in her direction. "We should get out of her hair."

Ryan didn't agree, but she nodded in contravention of her desire. She would love nothing more than to escape from the throngs of well-wishers staking their claims to her future administration. "She's right. I'd love to join you, but I need to make the rounds. Rain check?" She faced Brian, but her words were directed at Brett.

As if she could read Ryan's mind, Brett answered. "Absolutely."

❖

"She'll make a fantastic district attorney. When's the last time we had someone in that office fresh out of the courtroom?"

"She's not fresh out of the courtroom, Brian. She works out of an office upstairs. Right next to Leonard Duncan's. She hasn't tried a case since I've been in that courthouse."

"I thought I heard someone say she was getting ready for trial in a few weeks."

Brett shrugged. "She is, but it's the first one in a while. I'm not saying she doesn't have skills. I would have no way of knowing whether she does or not. I'm just saying her skills might be a bit rusty."

"Well, she's devoted her whole life to prosecuting crime. I'd be happy to have her protecting our community."

"Since when did you become so interested in the DA's race?"

Brian leaned in. "This is top secret, okay?" Brett nodded. "Our firm is negotiating with Leonard to come on board and head up a white collar crime section."

"And it wouldn't hurt your future clients if the next elected DA was indebted to you and your new law partner?"

"You make it sound so sinister."

"It is a little bit, don't you think?" She didn't like the thought of Ryan as a professional commodity.

"Come on, Brett. This is how business is done. Don't tell me you haven't picked up a thing or two about networking since you've been in private practice."

Brett didn't want to admit it, but she had. As much as she loathed attending pseudo social events, a few months into private practice she'd learned how necessary it was to professional survival. She had started out by placing a few ads in local publications and waited for the business to roll in. She quickly found that she was spending most of her time on the phone weeding through people who either had no money to pay her or didn't even have a criminal law problem, but just wanted to talk to her about their various other woes. As a public defender, she had no need to solicit new business and even less concern about her client's ability to pay for her services. Now that she had her own rent and salary to pay, in addition to Tony's salary, she carefully cultivated networking relationships since personal referrals generated the most reliable source of income.

"Yes, dear brother. I know plenty about networking, but there's a difference between developing relationships and paying for them."

Brian shrugged. "Nothing illegal going on here. Just planting seeds. How they grow is out of my control."

Brett didn't agree, but she didn't want to spoil dinner by engaging in an argument. Too much like work. She changed the subject. "Know anything about Ryan Foster besides her legal prowess?"

"Like what?"

"Like does she have family? Where did she grow up? What's her favorite color?" She threw in the last for levity, but she found herself desperately wanting to know the answers to her other questions. What other family besides an aging aunt did Ryan have to rely on? Was she married, engaged? Was she a Dallas girl? The only question Brett didn't ask herself was why she cared so much.

"I don't know much. I think she grew up in Rockwall. Went to Harvard. Graduated top of her class. She probably had her choice of any cush job she wanted, but she took a position at the DA's office and has worked there ever since."

Brett nodded. No doubt Ryan had received offers from many top firms after graduation, all paying at least three times the starting salary for an assistant district attorney. While it wasn't unusual for top grads to accept the lower paying positions to get trial experience, they tended to move on to higher paying careers within a few years. Ryan had not.

But Brian hadn't answered the question she was most curious about. She gave up subtlety in favor of information. "So is she married?"

"No. Don't think she ever has been. She's pretty dedicated to her work. Not a lot of time for a personal life."

Brett didn't respond that he and John both worked demanding jobs but still found time for spouses and children. She hadn't been able to make a personal relationship mesh with her dedication to her work. Interesting that Ryan appeared to have the same issue. Brett filed this fact away for future reference.

❖

They might still be at the restaurant. Ryan shoved the thought away and forced herself to steer her car directly home. The glad-handing at the fundraiser had zapped every last bit of her energy. She didn't have the wherewithal to be social one minute longer. At least not if being social meant making idle chatter over food and cocktails, and she knew that was exactly what Brian Logan expected. She was well aware Brian was a partner at Logan, Lambert, and Johnson, and they were foaming in anticipation of Leonard joining their firm. They would support Leonard's heir apparent even if it were Mickey Mouse.

Brett had plenty of reasons to kiss her ass too, but she'd already made it clear that wasn't her style. Ryan found her approach refreshing. If Brett were at the restaurant alone she would join her without hesitation. But she wasn't. Ryan was both relieved and disappointed.

CHAPTER ELEVEN

Brett yawned. Dinner with Brian the night before had been a mistake. Tony rang her cell at six a.m. to remind her about the new client meeting, and it took every ounce of energy she had to resist falling back into the pillows. She had managed to drag her weary self into the office for the seven thirty meeting, charm the new clients, collect a healthy retainer, and now she was at the courthouse taking care of her morning docket. Days like today she wished she had a young associate she could send to take care of minor matters.

She filed the thought away and glanced at the task list on her BlackBerry. Most of her docket today consisted of announcement settings on misdemeanor cases, announcement being a misnomer. If she chose, all she had to do was show up, sign a pass slip, place in it in the court file, and she was done for the day. These settings were intended to be designated times for defense attorneys to discuss the cases set that day with the prosecutors in the court where the cases were assigned. Brett took advantage of this opportunity on most of her pending cases, but sometimes she was just buying time to allow her clients to decide if they wanted to set the case for trial or accept a plea agreement. Misdemeanor defendants generally didn't have to appear until their case was set for some kind of disposition, so Brett didn't have to rush from court to court to appease her various clients.

Today she was especially grateful for the slow pace. She managed to sign off on her cases by ten a.m. and decided to see if she could catch the grand jury prosecutor handling Ann Rawlings's case. She didn't hold out much hope of being able to dissuade whoever it was from presenting a charge at the grand jury setting scheduled for early the next week, but perhaps she could convince him or her to influence the grand jurors to consider a lesser charge.

Brett pushed the button for the eleventh floor and flashed back to her last trip to the top floor of the courthouse, the day before. She needed to talk to Ryan about Kenneth, but she really wanted to find out what Jake had managed to unearth before she did so. Hopefully, he would have some information later this afternoon. Kenneth's mother had called her again this morning wanting to know when they could turn him in. Mrs. Phillips had even suggested taking Kenneth to the jail herself if he promised not to talk to the police before Brett could be present. Brett had given up trying to explain why that wouldn't work. Kenneth could stand outside the jail confessing crimes all day long, but unless there was an active warrant directing the Dallas County Sheriff to take him into custody, he would remain a free man. She urged Mrs. Phillips to be patient and promised to call her later in the day with more information.

As Brett approached the intake desk, the grand jury secretary greeted her. "Hi, Brett, need to look at a file?" Joyce Grandon was the unrelenting gatekeeper of the files waiting to be heard by the grand jury. She received the reports from the various law enforcement agencies, made the files, and assigned the cases to the prosecutors in the intake division according to protocol. Defense attorneys were allowed limited access to the information in those files, and though the extent of the access was determined by the individual prosecutors, access to the prosecutors went through Joyce. If you treated her with respect, she would track down prosecutors and their files with dogged determination, but if you didn't then you weren't likely to know much about the facts of the case until after it was indicted. Brett accorded Joyce with the appropriate deference and enjoyed the rewards.

"Thanks, Joyce. It's set next week. Defendant's name is Ann Rawlings. Compelling prostitution."

Joyce stood and made her way over to one of the many tall filing cabinets housing pending files. "Lady pimp, huh? Sounds like an interesting case."

"I'm hoping to find out how interesting. Who's presenting?"

"Let me see, looks like this one's changed hands a couple of times." Joyce glanced through the file. "Now that's strange."

Brett found herself leaning closer, over the counter. "What is it?"

Joyce hesitated as if she weren't sure how much to reveal. "The presenting prosecutor is Cindy Laramie, but there's a note on here that says for us to check with Ms. Foster before taking any action on the case."

Brett pondered the meaning of the note. "Any action? Like even whether or not to present?"

Joyce looked over her shoulder before replying with a whisper, "That's how I read it." She read the note again. "Cindy has a standing order to let the defense attorney of record read the police reports in her files."

"I suppose this note trumps that?"

Joyce slid a few pieces of paper across the counter. "I don't really see how you reading something can constitute 'action' on my part. Especially not if you read it quickly."

Brett complied, relying on her memory to capture anything of consequence. She skimmed the three stapled pages quickly then nodded to Joyce who slipped the report back in the file and into the filing cabinet before anyone else could notice. The only additional clue she'd gleaned from the full report versus the probable cause affidavit she read a few days before was the fact that the investigation began with a tip from an anonymous caller reporting prostitution of a different kind than was found when Ann was arrested. According to the caller, the location where Ann was arrested was hosting a wild sex party, not prostitution per se. Brett filed the piece of information away, certain it had some significance.

"Hey, girl, I was hoping I would find you here."

Brett nearly jumped out of her skin, but quickly recovered and gave Jake Simmons a hug. She mouthed a quick thanks to Joyce then steered Jake out of the intake office and into the central area of the eleventh floor. Once they were standing close to the windows that faced downtown Dallas, she finally asked him what he had managed to find out about the Edwards case.

"I hate to disappoint you, but not much." Jake shook his head. "I reached out to an old buddy of mine with a solid contact on the Richardson PD. They're buttoned up like a virgin's wedding dress on this one. Apparently, Mr. Duncan himself warned them he would crucify them in the press if they had any leaks. What's in the papers is carefully crafted to reveal all they want to let out pretrial."

"Shit."

"I'm sorry, Brett. It's obvious Duncan wants this case sewn up tight. The guy at Richardson made some comment to my buddy about how he wasn't going to risk his job to keep the DA's office from acting hastily. There may be something exculpatory there, but you're going to need to get to someone closer to the case to get your hands on it."

Brett grabbed his arm and squeezed. "Jake, I think that was exactly what I was hoping to hear."

Jake looked puzzled, but returned her smile. "I don't see how it's much help, but let me know if I can do anything else."

"I will." As he walked toward the elevators, she had a sudden thought. "Hey, wait up!" Brett pulled him to the side. "I do want something else." She tore a scrap of paper from a notebook and scrawled out the address she'd memorized from the grand jury notes she'd just reviewed. "Here, can you check out this address? Talk to any witnesses about a prostitution ring that might be operating there?" At his puzzled look, she realized he thought they were still talking about the Edwards case. "Sorry, different case entirely. Oh, and keep track of your time so you can bill me. Case reference: Rawlings." He nodded and promised to call her with whatever information he found.

As Brett watched him walk toward the elevators, she had already shifted gears back to the Edwards case, and she was considering the logistics of setting up a meeting with the police and Kenneth Phillips. As if on cue, Ryan Foster appeared.

"Did you and Brian enjoy dinner at Five Sixty?"

The question was such a non sequitur to the thoughts of murder and punishment floating around in her head, Brett stumbled her response. "What? Huh? Dinner? Oh yeah, dinner was great. Too bad you couldn't join us." *Us? You mean you.* No way would she have wanted to share a meal with Ryan only to have her brother drooling over her ascent to a powerful office.

"I wish I could have," Ryan replied and the emphasis on each word signaled she meant it. Brett wondered what a quiet dinner with Ryan would be like. She didn't look like the type to enjoy the decadence of an expensive restaurant. She didn't look like she enjoyed much at all beyond the thrill she seemed to get from working harder than anyone else in the office. Brett wanted to find out for herself if she could witness Ryan in a pleasurable moment and spontaneously decided to seize the opportunity. "Care to join me for dinner, maybe this Friday? I can't promise Five Sixty on short notice, but I know a bunch of good places."

Did she just ask me out? On a date? Ryan was tempted to run full tilt back to her office to avoid having to figure out what just happened, let alone figure out how to respond. In her panic, she nearly missed Brett's next words.

"Just two attorneys swapping war stories and fundamental ideas about our system of justice. You could look at it as a great opportunity for opposition research."

Ryan let out her pent up breath. Not a date after all. Kind of a pseudo business dinner. She could do that. Couldn't she? "Friday sounds great."

Brett handed her a card. "Here's my e-mail. Shoot me your address and I'll pick you up. I'll make a reservation, but nothing too dressy."

Ryan shook her head. For some reason she couldn't articulate, she didn't want Brett to see her drab house. Nor did she want to cede control of the evening by not having her own transportation. "Since dinner's your treat, I'll pick you up. I'll e-mail you, and you can reply with your address."

"Deal." Brett started to walk toward the elevators, then she realized she should take advantage of this friendly moment to talk to Ryan about Kenneth Phillips. Since Jake hadn't been able to turn up any more information on the Edwards case, she may as well go ahead and confront the situation. She turned back. "Ryan?"

"Yes?"

"Turns out I do have some information on the Edwards case. Do you want me to talk to you or Jeff about it?"

What the hell? Ryan didn't know what to say in response. Did Brett just ask her out to pave the way toward a good deal for her new client, Ross Edwards? Ryan had talked to Edwards's current attorney, Luke Tyson just yesterday and didn't get a whiff from him that he was about to be fired. Maybe he didn't have a clue. Trial was just a couple of weeks away. Ryan doubted Judge Langston would take kindly to a motion to substitute counsel. Those usually came with a request for continuance, which was even more unwelcome in Langston's court.

Ryan wanted the dinner with Brett, but she wanted straight answers more. If Brett were playing her, she could save them both some trouble. *Only one way to find out.* "Are you signing on to represent Ross Edwards?"

Brett was surprised by the question, but quickly realized she shouldn't be. Her sniffing around could definitely be construed as a stealthy takeover approach. She usually did like to do some checking around when a potential client who was already represented contacted her about representation. Potential clients who wanted to shed their current counsel often painted their lawyers as incompetent fools. Sometimes they were right, but more often a mix of unrealistic expectations and differing communication styles was the real problem. So Ryan thought she was after Edwards as a client. Brett could only imagine she was freaking out at the thought of having her nice neat trial timeline disrupted by the introduction of a new defense attorney. *Well, she's in for a surprise.*

"No. I'm not representing Edwards. But I do represent a person of interest."

"A person of interest?"

"You're probably going to want to sit down for this."

CHAPTER TWELVE

She shouldn't have made a date she knew she would have to break. Brett shook her head at her lapse in judgment. Inviting Ryan to dinner was a stupid move, even if a Friday dinner would have held a lot more promise than lunch in a busy diner. The rear table at this greasy spoon was not at all what she had envisioned when she first asked Ryan to join her for a meal, but it was where they ended up after Brett revealed the reason she needed to talk to Ryan in private about the Edwards case. She knew as soon as she told Ryan all about Kenneth Phillips, there would be absolutely no chance they would be having a nice romantic dinner anywhere.

Ryan pushed her fork around a plate of fruit and cottage cheese. Not very appetizing, in Brett's opinion, and based on the amount left on Ryan's plate, she felt the same. Brett couldn't blame her for losing the desire to eat. If she were on the other side, finding out her rock solid case was falling apart, she might have left some fries uneaten. As it was, all that was left on her plate was a small dab of ketchup.

"I don't know why you didn't just tell me this the other day in my office."

Ryan's annoyance was palpable, further ruining any of Brett's imaginings about what a real date with her would be like.

"You've never done any defense work, have you?"

"What are you implying?"

"I'm not implying anything. I was merely checking in with you about your perspective. I have a duty to my client to make sure that I don't reveal their confidences before I have their permission and before it's appropriate to do so. You're not bound by those same restrictions. I'm guessing you never have been."

Ryan appeared to relax, but only slightly. "I did my first internship at this office and I've been here ever since." She shrugged. "I don't think I could do what you do. Don't think I would care to."

As much as she wanted to discuss how they were going to deal with Kenneth, Brett couldn't resist following the thread of philosophical difference. "What if someone you loved was accused of a crime? Would you want them to hire an advocate, or just show up at the nearest police station and hope for fairness and mercy?"

Ryan considered Brett's question. It wasn't a fresh hypothetical. All criminal law attorneys had considered what they would do themselves if the cops came knocking, but any thoughts Ryan had ever had on the issue were fleeting. The only relative of hers that would even think to contact her if in trouble was her aunt, and Aunt Eunice was tucked away from all such troubles at the Pine Grove Nursing Home. The very idea of Aunt Eunice violating the law was laughable.

"My aunt is my only living relative, and it's pretty unlikely she'll ever need counsel."

"What about you?"

Ryan stiffened. "What about me?"

"What if you found yourself in trouble?"

"Are you implying something?" Ryan punctuated her remark with a slight smile she didn't feel and forced her tone to remain even. What was Brett implying? Ryan had only one secret, and it was so neatly tucked away in its own compartment of her being that she didn't even consider it a part of the professional self she regarded as the whole of who she was.

"Don't be silly." Brett laughed. "I doubt we'll ever see you, Miss Law and Order, on trial, but don't tell me you've never considered what you might do if you were ever, let's say, mistakenly arrested."

"I haven't. I suppose if such an unfortunate event ever occurs, I'll figure out what to do. Now, can we resume discussing what to do about your client?"

"Sure. As I said, I represent someone who wants to come forward with information about the death of Mary Dinelli. I believe the information this person has may change your view of the individual who is currently charged."

"Name?"

"I'll let them tell you themselves, but before I bring this individual in, I need to know if you might be willing to take the death penalty off the table."

"You know I can't answer that."

"I know you're not likely to, but I know that you can."

Ryan's curiosity took hold, but she peppered her response with contingencies. "If your client has solid information that leads to a conviction without putting the taxpayers through the expense of a trial then I will consider a sentence that is something less than the death penalty. Just consider, not promise."

Brett knew Ryan had just made a big concession. She thought about Kenneth's whipped demeanor, so out of place for someone so young. Since she didn't know much about the evidence to begin with, Brett found it difficult to assess whether Kenneth's version of the crime was more egregious than whatever Ryan already thought. Taking him in, rather than having him show up at police headquarters, was certainly the better option. At least if she was there, she could stop the interview if things got nasty.

"Fair enough. I'll call you this afternoon to arrange a meeting."

"Actually, you should just come in this afternoon. I'm deep into trial prep. The faster you bring whoever this is in, the more likely I am to throw you a bone for saving me some time."

Brett shook her head. She had to have a long and detailed conversation with Kenneth about his rights before she brought him in to face Ryan. "Tomorrow. We'll be in tomorrow."

"Nine a.m. Meet me at the DA workroom." Ryan stood and grabbed her separate check. "See you then." She stalked off and their "date" ended as abruptly as it had begun.

❖

Ryan engaged every ounce of restraint she had to walk slowly away from Brett. She wanted to run back to the courthouse, away from the distraction of Brett's vivacious charm and beauty, to think through the revelation Brett had shared. At the same time, she wanted to forget the case and enjoy sharing a meal with Brett. The latter wish might have been possible an hour ago, when they weren't working in direct opposition, but now even an innocent dinner would have the appearance of impropriety.

She shrugged away the thought. She had no business socializing with Brett or anyone else for that matter. Not only did she have full slate at the office, she had a heavy schedule of pre-campaign appearances, and now her slam dunk, high profile case was about to be riddled with holes. She needed to focus on damage control.

Ryan didn't bother checking in with the receptionist when she returned to the courthouse, instead heading directly for the workroom outside of Langston's courtroom. Jeff was having a late lunch, a working one, consisting of a sloppy burger and a giant order of fries. Was she the only one who assigned any value to eating right?

"If that's the Edwards's file you're looking at, you should get ready to take some notes."

Jeff wiped his chin. "Huh?"

"Brett Logan is bringing in a witness tomorrow morning."

"On this case?"

Ryan shook her head. "Yes. Try and keep up."

"What kind of a witness?"

"I don't know."

"What do you mean, you don't know?"

"We'll find out for sure in the morning, but I think this individual may be involved in Mary Dinelli's murder."

"You *think*?"

"Watch your tone. We may be working on this case together, but I'm still your boss."

"Sure, *boss*, no problem. I just wonder why you decided to have this little conversation with Logan on your own. It's not like you're known for your ability to charm information out of opposing counsel."

"I guess your relationship with her isn't as great as you think since she came to me not you." Jeff looked sheepish, signaling Ryan's words had the intended effect. "Get the case detectives in here this afternoon. I want to go over every detail of the case as we know it before Brett brings whoever this is in."

"Do we know anything at all about the 'witness'?" Jeff's tone was deferential this time.

"No."

"Maybe we should stake out Brett's office?" His suggestion was offered tentatively, but just the same, Ryan couldn't believe he said it out loud.

"Seriously, Jeff? What the hell are you thinking?"

"What?" He looked genuinely puzzled. In response to Ryan's probing stare, he said, "Don't tell me you've never employed a little ingenuity preparing for a trial."

Ryan didn't respond. She didn't have to. Her exploits were legendary around the office. She was known for getting information when no one else could, often by treading the fine line between ethics and the end result. Her dogged pursuit of evidence and witnesses was the quality that got her noticed by her boss Leonard Duncan, and launched her up the career ladder. She didn't have much direct use for those skills in her administrative capacity as super chief, but she encouraged the prosecutors under her supervision to be creative when it came to moving cases along.

Yet Ryan hadn't even considered using some of her infamous methods on Brett Logan, and she didn't want Jeff to either. Ryan flashed to her earlier excitement at the prospect of an evening alone with Brett. That wasn't possible now, but she had no desire to burn the bridge she had stepped out onto.

She averted her eyes from his expectant gaze. "Here's how we're going to prepare. We're going to review this file with the detectives until we can recite every detail from memory. Tomorrow morning, we're going to meet with this 'witness' and then we'll deal with the fallout, whatever that may be."

As she buried herself in the reams of paper spread out on the desk, Ryan contemplated her own personal fallout: facing Brett Logan in the courtroom. On opposite sides.

CHAPTER THIRTEEN

Privacy was a relative concept at the courthouse. As Brett paced the front steps, she pondered where she could have a conversation alone with Kenneth Phillips. Before she took him in to meet with Ryan and the detectives assigned to the case, she planned to have a thorough discussion of his rights. She'd even prepared a written release of sorts, detailing the fact he wasn't a suspect, the police weren't looking for him, the crime he planned to confess to could carry the death penalty, and she couldn't make any guarantees about the outcome. The release had no real legal value, but it might cover her ass if Kenneth suffered confessor's remorse at some point in the future and decided to blame her for her role in what was sure to be a lengthy term in prison.

Brett glanced at her watch. None of this mattered if he didn't show up. Her original plan had been to meet Kenneth and his mother at her office. After her lunchtime revelation to Ryan yesterday, she told Tony to get Kenneth and his mother back in her office so she could prepare them for this meeting. Tony had a lot of probing questions before he made that call.

"Are you sure you're doing the right thing here?"

"What do you mean?" Brett's response hadn't been defensive. She was used to Tony digging deeper into the reasons behind her decisions. He had always been a valuable sounding board, never just an office manager.

"Well, no one suspects this kid was involved do they?"

"As far as I know, that's correct. All signs point to Ross Edwards as the only suspect. Of course, I can't get my hands on any discovery, including the police report, so for all I know they have a list of other suspects lined up to prosecute as conspirators once the Edwards prosecution is over."

"And you don't think it would be better to ride it out, just in case Kenneth never pops up on anyone's radar?"

"Me, personally? Maybe so, but it's not my choice. I'm not the one with guilt eating away at me and a cloud of uncertainty hanging over my head. Besides, he might enjoy some leniency by coming in before they come looking for him."

"Yeah, but isn't it your job to make sure he knows all his options?"

Any other lawyer might have bitten Tony's head off for his challenging remarks, but Brett appreciated his frankness. She hit the send key on her computer and turned to face him. "You are absolutely right. I just forwarded you a draft of a release for Kenneth to sign. Look it over and let me know if you see any areas that need revision. I'll go over it with him this afternoon."

Tony hadn't been able to reach Kenneth or his parents yesterday afternoon, despite numerous calls. Finally, this morning, she received a voice mail from Kenneth's father, letting her know that they had received Tony's messages about the meeting at the district attorney's office, and they would meet her in front of the courthouse at eight. Brett had called back immediately, but despite her attempts to convey her preference for meeting at her office, she was unsuccessful at making contact.

So here she was, standing on the courthouse steps, people watching until Kenneth arrived. She rarely entered the building through the front entrance, choosing instead to walk through the lesser-known tunnel from the parking garage. Brett wondered, not for the first time, about what went through people's minds when they selected clothes to wear to the courthouse. Once, early in her career, she told a female client to dress for trial like she was going to church. She was flabbergasted when the woman showed up in a skintight, backless dress and five-inch spiked heels. She no longer relied on her client's judgment about appropriate attire, instead she offered very specific direction.

Brett glanced at her watch again. It was ten minutes till nine. Even if Kenneth showed up right now, she wouldn't have time to talk to him before their scheduled meeting. She would have to call Ryan, but she didn't have a clue whether to postpone the meeting or call it off altogether. She reached for her BlackBerry and dialed the number, deciding the right words would come once she heard Ryan's voice. Before she hit send, she heard a timid voice behind her.

"Ms. Logan?"

Kenneth Phillips looked as lost as he did the day she met him. The only difference was that today he was alone.

"Hi, Kenneth. Where are your folks?"

He gave her a strange look. "My mom couldn't take off work. Are we going to do this or what?" He sounded anxious.

Brett had been hoping to finally meet the elusive Mr. Phillips, but apparently, neither of Kenneth's parents cared enough about his fate to make the trip to the courthouse. Even though Kenneth was an adult, she had hoped to have the frank discussion about his rights and options in the presence of his parents, if for no other reason than to have witnesses. She briefly contemplated making a call to encourage them to show up, but she was already going to have to tell Ryan they would be late. She sighed and reached for her BlackBerry once again.

"Ryan, it's Brett Logan. I had something come up at the office so I'm going to be about half an hour late. No, no problems, just running a bit behind. See you at nine thirty. Yes, yes, we'll be there."

❖

"Let me guess; they're not coming"

Ryan put the phone down and faced Detective Kim Paulson. They were in the cramped DA workroom, waiting on Brett and her client to show up. Judge Langston had graciously offered the use of the jury room for their meeting, and Jeff reassigned his morning docket so he would be free for the meeting. Ryan had spent the entire afternoon the day before with Kim and her partner Mike Harwell going over every detail of the Edwards case. She hadn't worked with either detective before, which wasn't surprising since the suburb of Richardson had a fairly low murder rate compared to other areas of the county. Ryan had been impressed with Paulson's commanding knowledge of the case, especially since Jeff informed her she had been assigned to work with Harwell just the week before, but Ryan had a hard time with Paulson's steady stream of sarcastic remarks.

"They're coming. They'll just be a few minutes late."

"You sure about that? I wouldn't be surprised if they no show." Detective Paulson rocked back and forth on her heels and stared at Ryan's phone as if she could intuit Brett's true intent.

"They'll be here." Ryan hoped she was right, but she had no desire to dwell on other possibilities. "You can cool your heels in the cafeteria downstairs if you want." She opened a file folder and pretended to concentrate on the notes within, effectively dismissing the anxious detective.

Her ploy didn't work. "That's okay. I think I'll stick around." Paulson pulled up a chair and leaned in over Ryan's shoulder. "What's that you're looking at?"

Ryan closed the file. She hadn't been able to focus on the contents anyway. "I'm done. I'm going to head upstairs to take care of a few things before they get here." She started toward the door and almost collided with Jeff and Paulson's partner, Mike, as they entered the room. Ryan regarded Jeff. "You look out of breath."

"They were outside, on the front steps. Now they're in the law library." Jeff delivered the proclamations between heavy breaths.

"They who?" Ryan was pretty sure she knew, but she wanted to hear it. While she waited for Jeff to respond, she grew annoyed at Kim Paulson who once again hovered over her shoulder, as if she were hanging on Jeff's next words.

"Brett Logan and her client. Some young guy," Mike Harwell answered for Jeff. They went into one of those tiny rooms in the law library downstairs.

Ryan was torn between being pissed at Jeff and relieved that Brett was at least on the premises, presumably with her client. Obviously, Jeff had honored only the letter of her words from the day before. He may not have staked out Brett at her office, but he was obviously watching her every move here at the courthouse this morning, with the assistance of Detective Harwell no doubt. If she found out it was more than that, she was going to tear him limb from limb.

"Tell me you didn't try to listen in."

"Gimme a break."

"Tell me." Ryan needed the words.

"We didn't listen in."

Ryan made her way to the door. "They'll be here at nine thirty. No one, I mean no one, talks to them until I get back. Understood?" She waited till Jeff and the detectives nodded in assent, and then she left the room. She didn't have anything to do while she waited, but she didn't want to be trapped in that tiny room with them all frothing at the mouth. She felt oddly protective of Brett and her young client, no matter what he might have to say to her about his involvement in the case.

Ryan walked to the lobby area on the fifth floor and leaned over the railing. From here she would have a perfect view of anyone ascending the floors via the escalator. She hoped Brett wouldn't think she was stalking her, but she wanted to catch her before they went into full on interview mode. She didn't have a clue what she planned to say, but whatever it was, she didn't want to say it in front of her team.

❖

The tiny room in the law library was designed for one person. There were two such rooms; one held a video phone for conferencing with inmates at the jail, the other had only a regular phone. Brett drug an extra chair into the room with the regular phone, and she and Kenneth squeezed into place.

"I thought we were going to talk to the prosecutor."

"We are. If that's what you want to do, but before you make your decision, I want to talk to you about your rights and your options." Brett pulled the paper she had prepared from her briefcase. She was partly relieved Kenneth was alone. It would give her an opportunity to assess whether the idea about turning himself in was his or his parents'. "I'm going to read this to you, then let you read it yourself. Then we can talk about it. Okay?" Kenneth nodded and Brett began to read the release she had drafted. When she finished, she handed the paper to him and watched while he read.

"Let's talk about this."

"I get it." He picked up a pen from the desk, scrawled his name on the paper, and shoved it back toward Brett.

She shoved it back. "You may get it, but I need to be sure. What's the worst thing that can happen if you choose to confess your involvement in Mary Dinelli's death?"

He shrugged.

"Kenneth, I understand that you want to do this, and you need an attorney with you when you do, but I'm not going to be that attorney if I don't feel like you know what you're getting yourself into." She paused. "Now, let's start with something different. As far as I know, no one suspects you were involved in Dinelli's death. If you choose to confess, you will probably be taken into custody. What's the worst thing that can happen to you if you are charged with this murder?"

"The death penalty."

"That's correct. I'll do everything in my power to get you a lesser sentence, and the fact that you are willing to cooperate in the investigation could go a long way to us working out some kind of deal, but the prosecutors are not going to make any offers until they hear what you have to say. Do you understand that even if you cooperate, you could be looking at a life sentence?"

"Yes."

"You'll have to answer all of their questions. If they feel like you're holding something back, they may end the interview and any chance you have of getting credit for cooperating will be gone."

"Can't I just read them what I wrote?" Kenneth pulled the folded, worn paper out of his pocket. Brett recognized it from the first time they had met at her office.

"You may be able to read your statement, but you'll also have to answer any follow-up questions they want to ask. If you want to talk to me before you answer, you just let me know, and I'll ask for a break. I know it seems like we're playing this by ear, but I know what I'm doing. If you want to go this route, this is the way it's done. We can't work out any deals in the abstract. We have to give them something solid first. Understood?"

Kenneth nodded. Then, in response to Brett's penetrating stare, he articulated his answer. "Yes, I understand."

"Okay, let's go do this." Brett stood, picked up the release, and they squeezed their way back out of the small space. She had no real idea if Kenneth understood the enormity of what was about to happen. Kenneth would tell his story, then the prosecutors and most likely the case detectives would ask penetrating questions to determine if he was telling the truth. They would try to trip him up with details, wanting to rule out any inconsistencies that might be exploited later by a good defense lawyer. Brett was used to the freewheeling nature of debriefing sessions, but it was still rare to be taking in a client who was not already in custody or at least charged with something. She hoped she was doing the right thing, but ultimately it wasn't her decision. She could only provide advice about potential outcomes, offer counsel, and hope her clients knew what they were doing when they ultimately decided on a path to follow. Though it wasn't in her nature, she trusted Ryan Foster to do that right thing.

❖

Ryan turned just in time to see Brett and a young man emerge from the stairwell, and she mentally kicked herself. She had been keeping one eye on the elevator and the other trained on the escalator, but it hadn't occurred to her they would take the stairs. She moved toward them. "Brett, can I talk to you a moment?"

Brett started at the sound of Ryan's voice. She knew they were on their way to meet with her, but she hadn't expected to be greeted in the hallway, and it took her off guard. She motioned Kenneth back through the door that led to the stairwell and whispered. "I'll be right back." She took long strides to where Ryan stood. "I thought we were meeting in the courtroom."

"We are, but I wanted to talk to you first. Alone." Ryan signaled for Brett to follow her into a corner. Ryan wasn't sure what she wanted to say, if anything. Mostly she wanted a moment alone with Brett before they entered their adversarial roles. She searched for words that might form a plausible excuse for this moment, but came up virtually empty. She pointed at the stairwell doors. "Was that your client?"

Brett nodded.

"He looks young."

"He is."

Ryan took a deep breath. She had to move this along or Jeff and his police escort were going to come looking for them. She didn't want to though. Brett looked stunning. Her honey brown hair was perfectly coiffed and her lightweight red wool suit was perfectly pressed, absent of any evidence of breakfast residue. She wondered how long this look would last before forces of wind and mishap gave Brett the mussy, but adorable, look Ryan had come to know. She wanted to tell Brett that as fantastic as she looked in this moment, she almost preferred the rumpled version, but she knew the comment would be totally inappropriate. Try as she might, she couldn't think of anything else to say.

Brett watched the shifting expressions on Ryan's face. She looked as though she was dying to say something, and her apparent inability to get the words out was making Brett nervous. Was she walking Kenneth into a hornet's nest? She decided there was only one way to find out. She placed her hand on Ryan's arm. "Ryan, is there something you want to tell me?"

Ryan's pulse raced. Her first instinct was to back away from Brett's touch, but the melting warmth of her hand caused Ryan's thoughts to puddle before they could solidify into articulate words.

Damn right there's something I want to tell you, but I never will. I want to eat breakfast with you and watch you spill coffee on your snow-white blouse. I want to mess up your hair myself. I want to put wrinkles in your suit.

Ryan willed her decidedly unprofessional thoughts away. She needed to surround herself with other people, and she needed to do it fast. Brett was still standing in front of her waiting for an answer, and Ryan clamped her jaw in fear of the improprieties that might tumble out. Suddenly she realized she did have something she could tell Brett without risking personal or professional compromise. "I wanted to give you the lay of the land before we go in. Jeff and I will be there, of course, along with Detectives Paulson and Harwell from Richardson PD. Judge Langston offered her jury room for the meeting." Ryan paused. "There's a chance Mr. Duncan might drop in."

"The Boss Man taking a personal interest in this case."

"Absolutely."

"A little unusual considering he's retiring. He must really want his protégé to succeed."

Ryan wasn't sure how to take Brett's observation, but she didn't have time to consider it for long before Jeff's voice interrupted her thoughts.

"Are we good to go?"

Brett started to answer, but Ryan held up a hand and responded. "We'll be right there." Jeff's eyes swept slowly over them, then darted around. Ryan stiffened. She knew he had seen Brett's hand, still on her arm, and she knew he was seeking out Brett's client. She waved him off and enunciated each word of her command. "We'll be right there." When he finally left them, she faced Brett. "You know I can't promise any particular outcome, but I do promise to hear him out before we make any decisions."

"And the decisions are yours to make?"

Ryan knew what she meant. Brett wanted to know who ultimately held sway over her client's fate. Ryan knew Leonard would want to have input, but he would defer to whatever she recommended as a way of showing his faith in his chosen successor.

"Yes. No matter what happens in there, this is my case and I call the shots." Translation—she may take the backseat on the debrief session, but when it was over, Ryan would be the one who doled out a plea offer. Ryan knew Brett would read between the lines.

Brett squeezed her arm. "All right then. Let's get started."

❖

Brett squared herself for the unknown challenges ahead, grateful to Ryan for the small heads up she'd received in the hallway. Any connection Brett felt with Ryan disappeared the moment she walked through the door of Judge Langston's jury room. Ryan was seated at the farthermost point of the table with Jeff at her side, and she barely glanced up from the papers she was examining to acknowledge their entrance. The two others, whom Brett assumed were the detectives assigned to the Dinelli murder, walked toward her. Brett didn't recognize the detectives, but one of them obviously already knew Kenneth.

"Well, hello. Kenneth, right? You remember me, don't you? I'm Detective Kim Paulson." Paulson moved right up against Kenneth. She shoved her hand out and Kenneth shook it tentatively. Brett found herself inching over as if to shield Kenneth from the detective's pushy approach. She appraised her from her own superior height. Paulson didn't have that woken up in the middle of the night, wear your breakfast on your sleeve look that many homicide detectives seemed to perpetuate. Rather, she looked as if she had stepped from the pages of a fashion catalog. Paulson was sharply dressed in a tailored pantsuit and designer boots. Brett guessed the man standing behind her was her partner, but the two couldn't have looked more different. The larger man definitely looked the part of the overworked veteran peace officer fresh from an all night scene.

Paulson turned her attention to Brett. "You must be Kenneth's attorney. He caught a case with me last year when I was with vice, but we worked it out without him needing to bother with an attorney." Despite her friendly smile, Paulson's tone gave Brett a hint of her disdain for defense attorneys. "I must say I didn't expect to see him here today."

Brett didn't know what to say. When she had asked Kenneth if he had a prior record, he made vague reference to a juvenile drug case from years ago, but he'd said nothing about an arrest within the past year and court records and a background check didn't reveal any arrests or charges. Apparently, whatever had happened, it had been resolved outside the system. She wondered if Kenneth had served as a confidential informant for Paulson in exchange for the charges being dropped. She could only hope that if things had gone well in that regard, Paulson might be willing to cut Kenneth some slack when it came to the current case.

The debrief started with Ryan making it clear, on the record, that she couldn't make any promises about the outcome, but that if Kenneth provided her with credible information that helped them close their case, she would give him some consideration. She both read and provided a copy of his constitutional rights and he agreed, in writing, to waive his rights and talk freely. Her words were delivered in crisp, sharp tones, and Brett could tell Kenneth was reasonably intimidated.

Brett told the assembled group that Kenneth would like to begin by reading from his well-worn paper, and Ryan had graciously agreed. The reading was rough, and even though the statement was short, Brett would've sworn it took Kenneth an hour to get the words out. Ryan, Jeff, and Detectives Paulson and Harwell then started tossing questions at him, and based on the level of detail, Brett saw no end in sight. She hoped Tony had gotten the text she had managed to type out under the table, asking him to clear her schedule because this session was obviously going to take a lot longer than she had originally thought.

"So why don't you describe your partner in crime, this 'John with no last name' guy you're so tight with?"

Detective Harwell fired the hard-edged questions, and Paulson swooped in every so often and tossed a softball Kenneth's way. Brett was mildly amused at the good cop, bad cop routine and wondered if they drew straws in advance to see who would play which role.

While Harwell wielded an accusatory tone, Paulson had a way of lining her questions with references to her prior relationship with Kenneth. "Remember when you helped me out before? I need you to think carefully and tell me everything you saw just like you did then." Brett started to think that perhaps the good cop thing wasn't an act. Kim Paulson seemed to have a soft spot for Kenneth, which took her up a notch in Brett's estimation.

"Like what about him?" Kenneth's question seemed genuinely curious, but Harwell's response was volatile.

"Like what the hell do you think?"

Brett caught a glimpse of Paulson squeezing Harwell's forearm under the table. The burly detective seemed to relax into the touch, and Brett flashed back to her brief contact with Ryan in the hall. The memory was distracting. She wondered what would happen if she touched Ryan outside of this place where their professional roles were so squarely defined. She spared a look at Ryan, hoping for some small connection, even if only a nod to confirm Kenneth was on track for some small measure of mercy, but Ryan's head was buried in her file, her hand busily scribbling notes. Brett had no idea what she could be writing. It seemed as if the detectives had asked the same ten questions over and over. How did Kenneth know John? What did he look like? Whose idea was it to go to the house? What did the woman in the house look like? Where did they pawn the stolen goods? Who set the fire? How?

Everything Brett had heard, both when she first met with Kenneth in her office and today, convinced her that this wasn't the traditional capital murder case. Someone who committed arson that resulted in someone's death could certainly be charged with capital murder, but in this situation the young men had set fire to Mary Dinelli's house to cover up the woman's death. She hoped Ryan was listening closely, but she couldn't tell. Detective Paulson was very attentive though, and Brett decided to focus her attention on bringing the detective around to her way of thinking. She listened to Kenneth's description and waited for an opportunity to cultivate Paulson's good will.

"Tall, skinny."

"Is he white like you or something else?"

"White like me."

"How old?"

Kenneth began to shift in his chair. "I dunno. Not old." He shot a look at Paulson, then Brett. Brett could tell he was wearing thin under the pressure. She decided to act.

She waved her BlackBerry. "I hate to disrupt the flow, but I need to get in touch with my office. It's important." She stood and made her way to the door, indicating Kenneth should follow. He looked at Paulson again, as if for approval and waited for her nod before he followed her out of the room. Brett was glad to see the bond develop between them. She showed him to a seat in the courtroom and told him not to talk to anyone until she got back. She stepped out into the hall and punched in the numbers to her office. Before she could finish, she felt a tap on her shoulder. She turned to face Kim Paulson's deep blue eyes.

"Can I talk to you for a minute?"

"Sure."

Paulson signaled for Brett to follow her. Brett followed the detective down the hallway that led to a separate entrance to the jury room. Harwell, Jeff, and Ryan were all waiting. Brett felt a sense of dread coming on. Harwell stood and waved her into a seat. He was the first to speak.

"We need to talk."

"I thought that's what we were doing. What's up?"

"I don't know what to make of your kid," he said.

Brett resisted the urge to point out Kenneth was not "her kid." She was torn between feeling protective and pissed. She resolved to figure that out once she knew who to focus her feelings on—Kenneth or the prosecution team. Whatever Harwell had to say wasn't likely to be good news. "No offense, detective, but I don't know what to make out of what you just said. Kenneth's answered all of your questions. He may not be the most articulate *kid*, but he seems to be genuinely interested in cooperating with all of you." She turned to Paulson, engaging her directly. "You know him. What do you think?"

Paulson seemed to warm to the direct attention. She moved closer to Brett and offered a reassuring smile. "He certainly has been forthcoming, and he hasn't tried to minimize his involvement. Here's the deal: he knows many of the facts, spot on. And, if you're any good at all, which Ms. Foster and Mr. Oates say you are, you know we've managed to keep a tight lid on this case. So Kenneth knowing critical facts, well, that makes him seem like a real credible witness."

"But." Brett knew one was coming and she wanted to deal with it head-on.

Harwell took over. "But he got a few things really wrong."

"It's been a while. Are you sure he isn't suffering from a bit of memory lapse?"

"John, aka Juan Rodriguez, is a Mexican, still wet from crossing." He paused at Brett's visible cringe, but not for long. "He's five seven, and weighs two hundred and thirty pounds. That sound like a tall, skinny white guy to you?"

Brett recognized the question was rhetorical and she was glad. She didn't really want to argue the point, especially while she was still trying to process the information volcano that had just erupted in her head. So they already have John in custody, or have at least questioned him. That fact certainly diminished the effect of any information Kenneth provided. But what was the relationship between John and Ross Edwards? Were Ryan and Jeff waiting to try John after they finished with Ross's case, or was John a key state's witness slated to testify at Edwards's trial? She sat silent, processing this development.

"There's more."

Brett looked up at Ryan who had just spoken for the first time since she admonished Kenneth about his constitutional rights. She followed Ryan's eyes, which were trained on the proximity between herself and Paulson, but she couldn't read her expression. Her eyes were distant, her brow furrowed.

"Let me guess, you can't tell me," Brett said.

"I can, but I won't. Your client has offered a strange mixture of fact and fiction. He knows plenty that wasn't in the papers, but some crucial areas are way off. Will he take a polygraph?"

"I'll talk to him about it."

"Can you do it right now?"

Brett was confused, not by the request itself, but by the urgency. She hadn't discussed a polygraph with Kenneth, but she knew it was a possibility. Lie detector tests weren't admissible as evidence of either guilt or innocence, but they were routinely used by prosecutors and defense attorneys to evaluate the veracity of witnesses. Brett often sent clients who could afford a private test to have one done where their guilt or innocence turned on a simple yes or no question, but when she did, she selected the examiner, and the results of the test were her confidential, privileged work product. What Ryan was suggesting was a police polygraph, which meant the results would be there for all of them to see.

"I have to have your word you won't bring perjury charges."

"How could I on the basis of a non-scientific test?" Ryan offered a hint of a smile.

"I have no doubt you would find a way. I would win that fight, but I don't want to engage. Give me your word, and I'll talk to him about it." Ryan nodded and Brett left to find her client.

She approached him as he emerged from the men's restroom, and she got right to the point. "They want you to take a polygraph. Do you know what that is?"

"Yes."

"Tell me."

"It's a lie detector test."

"How does it work?"

"I don't know. They hook you up to a machine and ask you questions and decide if you're lying or not. Who asked me to take one? That bitch prosecutor or the cop?"

Brett flinched at the epithet he used to describe Ryan, but held back a retort. To him, Ryan probably did appear cold and uncaring. She hadn't asked a single question and kept her head buried in a file folder during most of the interview. Brett's brief glimpses of another side of her didn't give her the authority to refute his assessment. She knew without asking that the cop Kenneth referred to was Paulson.

She dodged his question about who had requested the polygraph, responding instead to his description of what the exam would entail. "The test is much more involved than that. Before they hook you up to a machine, the examiner talks to you for an hour or so. He or she will ask you a ton of questions, some about what happened to Mary Dinelli, some about things that don't have anything to do with that. Then they hook you up to the machine and ask you more questions. Some of the questions will be softball questions, based on the casual conversation you had with the examiner. These are designed to determine how your body reacts when you're telling the truth. Next, the examiner will ask you some carefully crafted, very tightly worded questions about the events surrounding Mary Dinelli's death."

"The cop wants me to take it? The girl?"

"Yes." Brett resisted the urge to school him on the difference between a girl and a grown woman.

"Okay."

"Okay? Really? How do you plan to pass the polygraph when you don't know the answers to the questions?"

Kenneth flinched slightly, the only sign he had something to hide. Brett pushed on. "You obviously know some critical details about this case, but there are some key facts you've gotten wrong. Facts you should know if you were there."

Kenneth shrugged. "If she wants me to take a polygraph I will."

❖

When the break was over, Brett told the prosecution team they were ready to resume. She had sidestepped the issue of the polygraph, but it was obvious Paulson at least thought she planned to defer since Brett hadn't called a halt to the meeting altogether. She wanted to play this out a bit longer before she let them know for sure Kenneth would agree to the exam. She didn't have much confidence that he was making a good decision, but ultimately the decision was his to make. Her job was to run interference at this point. Before they had reentered the jury room, she had pulled Paulson aside and suggested she question Kenneth a bit more about the facts of the case.

Moments later, they were all seated back around the table, but the atmosphere had changed. The mood had morphed from idle anticipation to surging anxiety. Brett wasn't a stranger to the dynamics surrounding a breaking case, no trial attorney was. The rules of discovery in Dallas County were such that she often received critical pieces of the state's evidence in the middle of trial, which meant most of her strategy consisted of trying to anticipate the other side's tactics. She might be used to it, but she still experienced the same gut churning angst every single time. Today was no different.

Paulson took the lead. "Kenneth, we're setting up the polygraph now. We'll have to leave the courthouse and take you to the station. You're not under arrest. Do you understand?"

Kenneth nodded without looking at Brett. His developing bond with the detective was becoming more and more apparent. Brett stepped back and let Paulson fall into the role of confidant. Under her watchful eye, only good could come from the burgeoning relationship between her client and the person charged with investigating him. She would step back in when it was time for Kenneth to make the hard decisions, just as she had when it came to the discussion surrounding his decision to take the polygraph in the first place.

Paulson continued, apparently deciding to take Brett at her word before actually bothering with the trouble of the polygraph. "Kenneth, some of the things you've told us today have been very helpful, and we appreciate you coming forward with this information." She paused and stared him down with a combination of concern and authority.

"But here's the deal. Some of the things you have told us are dead wrong. We know John. He's already talked to us about what happened."

Kenneth didn't meet her eyes. His hands gripped the seat of his chair and he swung his feet back and forth under the table. Paulson leaned in, her voice almost a whisper. "You don't know John Rodriguez, do you?"

Kenneth didn't respond.

"You weren't at Mary Dinelli's house the night of the fire." It was a statement, followed by another. "Or any other night."

Brett recognized Kenneth's body language. She saw it often when she hung out with her young nieces and nephews who thankfully hadn't fully developed skills of deception calculated to disguise. Kenneth was clearly squirming at having been caught.

"Someone told you to come in here and confess, didn't they?" Paulson looked at Brett as she spoke. The expression on her face told Brett that Paulson knew her words would deliver a shock. Brett met her stare for a brief moment and then turned to Ryan. Her head was no longer in her notes. Ryan was riveted on this intense exchange, but she broke her concentration to meet Brett's eyes.

Ryan was certain Brett had no prior knowledge of her client's deception. No one could fake the shock she saw reflected in Brett's expression. Certainly, Brett must have had questions about her client's motivation for coming forward, but she wasn't part of the scheme herself. Ryan had no doubt the force behind Kenneth's admissions was Ross Edwards, even if the effort was well concealed to hide his involvement. She'd never met the man, but she had seen his videotaped statement to the police. That was no confession, but it was a revealing insight into the charming con who she had no doubt was responsible for snuffing out the vulnerable Mary Dinelli's life. The way he deflected questions about Dinelli's death, with a smug smile and hints about how the police might find the real killer, had driven Ryan crazy. Her whole team was thrumming with anticipation. If Ross was behind Kenneth's faulty confession, then they needed to act and they needed to act fast. With solid proof of his meddling, they could convince the judge to hold his bond insufficient and take him into custody.

The key now was getting Kenneth to reveal the full story behind what brought him in today. They needed to know every detail of how Kenneth became involved with Edwards and what, if anything, Kenneth really knew about Mary Dinelli's death. Ryan resisted the urge to jump into the interrogation. She grudgingly admitted Paulson had quickly formed a bond with the kid, but she wanted the revelations to come faster. Once they had Kenneth's full story, they still had to draft a motion to hold Edwards's bond insufficient and a search warrant for his home and get both documents served before he had a clue his plan was headed for disaster. She drew comfort from the fact that as long as they were in this room, Ross Edwards, wherever he was, thought his plan was working, but lingering in the back of her mind was a nagging question: why hadn't Ross given Kenneth more detail to back up his story? Ryan let the query eat away at her for a short while before, out of necessity, she finally wrote it off to a couple of possibilities. One, Ross wasn't a sly con, just a smarmy one. Two, Ross figured all he needed was a little reasonable doubt in the form of Kenneth Phillip's confession in order to throw a wrench in the state's case.

Ryan looked at Brett. Something was amiss. Her hair was no longer perfectly in place and she had a stain, probably coffee, on her sleeve, yet those details were more endearing than a source of concern. Finally, Ryan put her finger on it. The easy confidence that she had witnessed from Brett every time she had seen her during their brief acquaintance was gone. She appeared disconcerted. Ryan glanced at her watch. Five minutes wouldn't make or break their case. She signaled to Paulson to stop her questioning and called for a short recess. Jeff and the detectives left the room, but she lingered for a moment and pulled Brett aside.

"Take a minute. Talk to him." Ryan almost reached for her arm again. She wanted to convey more than her words only could accomplish. Understanding, compassion, comfort. She didn't dwell on the impetus behind those desires, as unusual as that was for her.

"I intend to." Brett was angry and she felt betrayed. Ryan could see it in her eyes.

"I want to nail Edwards and I'm willing to do what I have to in order to accomplish that." Ryan didn't want to parse the details, but she was letting Brett know as long as Kenneth told the truth, now and at Ross's trial, he would be safe from prosecution.

Brett fixed her with an intense gaze. "I understand."

Back in the room, Ryan tried to focus on Kenneth's words, but she could barely contain her excitement. Under Paulson's gentle direction, he revealed how he was arrested by a man, dressed in plainclothes, who said he was DEA agent Richard Emery. The man caught him selling dope and said he could make the case go away if

Kenneth would help out with a sting operation they were conducting. Kenneth thought Emery wanted him to assist with an undercover drug buy, but the agent had something different in mind.

"He said the feds were investigating the Dallas County District Attorney's office."

Jeff, who had hardly said a word during the entire meeting, snorted. "Really? What for?"

"Hell, I don't know. Illegal prosecutions or something like that."

"Or 'something like that'?"

Paulson shot Jeff a shut up look and resumed control of the interview. "What was your role supposed to be?"

"I was supposed to falsely confess to killing that woman."

"And then?"

"They would get you for trying to send me away without checking out real proof."

"Guess that didn't work out so well." This time it was Ryan who didn't hold back. "Seriously, kid, what were you thinking? You could have gone to prison for the rest of your life."

"He seemed for real. He showed me his badge. He told me he could nail me on a conspiracy charge. He said that I was facing ten years to life. I can't do federal time."

Ryan shook her head at his simplistic summary of the situation. She looked down the table at Brett, willing her to see the sympathy in her eyes. Brett still looked pissed, but her anger was tangled up with shock. She was probably used to her clients lying to her about their involvement in criminal activities. But their lies usually absolved rather than implicated them. Well, Brett might be off the hook soon. If Kenneth's story checked out, he wouldn't need a lawyer. At least not for this offense.

Ryan warmed to the thought of being on the same side as Brett. Maybe that dinner wasn't out of the question. She willed herself to focus. She had to nail this new evidence down before she could contemplate anything else.

"How did you get in touch with Ms. Logan?" The question allowed Ryan to stay focused on Brett.

"I dunno. The guy told me he set up a meeting with her. He said to take my mom and go."

Paulson took up the questioning again. "What did your mom have to say about all this?"

"She's thinks I'm kind of a loser anyway."

Ryan edged in. "That didn't really answer the question. Did she have any idea what you were really up to?"

"I wasn't up to anything." It was the first time Kenneth had exhibited any defensiveness during the long meeting. Brett shot Ryan a cautionary glance, but it was Paulson who interceded.

"We understand. We're not trying to accuse you of anything. We just need your help. Would you be willing to look at some pictures?"

Ryan held her breath. If Kenneth picked Ross Edwards out of a photo array as the guy who conned him into making a false confession, then she could immediately get a search warrant to rip Edwards's life completely apart. Not only would the case against him be rock solid, but she would have a choice of other charges to nail him on.

Kenneth nodded his assent at the same moment Brett's BlackBerry chose to ring loudly enough to wake the dead. Brett reached for the offending noisemaker. "Sorry, I thought I shut it off, but I must have turned the volume up instead during our last break." She glanced at the screen. "I need to take this. It's Kenneth's dad and he's called about six times since this morning." Brett stood and walked to a small hallway that led to the bathroom designated for juror use. Ryan was annoyed at the interruption, but apparently not as much as Paulson who glared daggers Brett's way. Kenneth on the other hand looked positively flummoxed.

Brett returned to the table after a brief moment. "I told him you were okay. That this was all a big mistake, and you would be coming home tonight. We got disconnected after that, so I don't know how much else he heard. I'll call him when we're done here." She looked at Ryan and Paulson with pointed interest. "Which shouldn't be too much longer, for today at least. Right?"

Ryan started to reply, but Kenneth interrupted her, turning to Brett. "Ms. Logan?"

"Yes?"

"My dad is dead."

CHAPTER FOURTEEN

She'd been saving the bottle for a special occasion. Brett read the label out loud despite the fact she was completely alone in her apartment. "Chateau Lafite Rothschild Paullic." *Who says special occasions have to be celebrations? Surely, finding out you've been duped into helping a client make a false confession was an occasion worthy of fine wine.* She poured a healthy glass and surveyed her apartment. It was a wreck and so was she. She had used her last bit of energy to toss her heels to the side of the tiny foyer. Her hose and suit jacket lay in a heap on top of them.

Brett shoved a stack of papers off her couch, ignoring Tony's voice in her head cautioning her not to get his carefully arranged work out of order. She couldn't care less about being organized, about working at all. All she wanted was to drink away any ability to think.

The expensive wine didn't work. Brett's mind swirled with the revelations of the day. She was used to hearing lies from her clients: I didn't do it; I didn't know what they were really up to; I didn't intend to…fill in the blank. A client confessing to a murder he hadn't even remotely been involved in was a once in a lifetime occurrence. *Thank god.* Brett swallowed another deep draught of the fancy wine as if it could wash away the bad taste left behind from the things she had said in support of her client's lie.

She recalled watching Kenneth pick Ross Edwards, without hesitation, out of a photo array, the last shades of her disbelief fading as his finger jabbed at the smiling face of the man who duped him into confessing and duped her into taking the case. Not only had Kenneth lied to her about having anything to do with the death of Mary Dinelli, but Ryan believed the man who had pressed Kenneth into duplicity had had direct communication with Brett, posing as Kenneth's father.

Kenneth's revelation that his father had died when he was a small child, led to a barrage of questions, all directed at Brett. Caught up in the moment, both detectives and prosecutors had honed in on every detail of every e-mail and phone call Brett had shared with the voice posing as Kenneth's father. They hadn't asked for access to her cell phone and e-mail accounts, but Brett figured the request would come soon.

As for Kenneth, he professed no knowledge of any contact between Edwards and Brett. He said he was told to take his mom and meet with Brett. He had been given a time, a place, and a story to tell. He did what he was told and expected his reward to come in the form of avoiding responsibility for a drug deal gone bad.

The prosecution team abandoned their pursuit of a polygraph, presumably because they were hearing what they wanted. Armed with probable cause to believe Ross Edwards was not only guilty of obstructing the investigation of Mary Dinelli's murder, but now most certainly guilty of the murder itself, they rushed to prepare a motion to hold Edwards's bond insufficient and, for the second time in the investigation of this case, an application for a search warrant for Edwards's apartment, phone records, and e-mail accounts. Brett's instincts told her it wouldn't be long before they came knocking at her door for follow-up. The prospect drove her to pour another glass of wine.

Ryan rarely participated in search and seizure operations, but she wouldn't have missed this one for anything. She wanted to look Edwards in the face and see if Ross was still smiling when they took him back into custody and uncovered his elaborate, albeit stupid, scheme. She wanted him to know she was on to him, could see through his charade, and wouldn't hesitate to send him to a gurney with a needle waiting.

What she hadn't expected and didn't want, was the crush of press waiting when she stepped out of Edwards's apartment. She was used to talking to the press about the status and outcomes of cases, but the contact usually came through a phone call, not the flash of camera bulbs and rolling video cameras in her face. *Leonard.* She knew he had to be behind this. She had called him on the way to Edwards's place to brief him on the situation, and she had done so because she believed he might be approached by the press for a statement. He had obviously decided to turn Edwards's arrest into a political gambit for his chosen candidate.

On the fly, Ryan made a brief statement commending Detectives Paulson and Harwell for developing evidence further supporting the grand jury's original indictment of Ross Edwards. She told the microphones thrust her way that she looked forward to sharing this new evidence with the jury they planned to empanel in a couple of weeks, and she was confident in a quick and sure guilty verdict. Then she turned to Jeff and told him to get her out of there. She had somewhere else she desperately wanted to be.

The steady buzzing of the doorbell streamed under Brett's subconscious and lapped away at her slumber. She waved her hand, still loosely holding an empty wine glass, in the air as if to ward off the invasion. It didn't work. Brett set the glass on her coffee table and stood shakily. Her skirt and blouse were wrinkled and she was certain her hair was completely smashed on the left side of her head. She checked her chin for dried drool, but that was as far as she was willing to go after the day she'd had. Whoever was so insistent about seeing her would have to make do with the rumpled version.

Brett squinted at the peephole before opening the door. She wasn't surprised by the identity of her evening visitor. She opened the door and invited Detective Paulson into her apartment.

"Come in. The place is a mess. Who am I kidding? I'm a mess. Is there some reason this couldn't wait till tomorrow?" Brett sat back on the couch. Detective Paulson stood before her, but Brett was too tired to care about her significant lack of manners. She didn't ask her to sit.

"Sorry to bother you, Ms. Logan."

"Call me Brett." Paulson nodded. "Where's your partner?"

"He's logging in evidence at the property room."

"I don't mean to be rude, but shouldn't you be helping him?" Paulson smiled. "May I sit?"

Brett waved at the chair opposite the couch. "Sure. Have a seat."

Paulson ignored the direction and sat on the couch beside Brett. "Are you okay? You look pretty beat."

"You sure know how to talk to women." Brett sized Paulson up. She hadn't flinched at the remark, and Brett idly wondered if Kim Paulson was family. She certainly was a looker, and she had a way of warming up to whoever was in her current focus. Unlike Ryan Foster, whose sharper edges were generally off-putting. *Generally.* During her last few encounters with Ryan, Brett witnessed a softer side. She had actually seemed to care about the impact of today's events on Brett. A thought occurred to her. "Did Ryan send you to check on me?"

"Ryan? Oh, you mean Ms. Foster?" Paulson shifted closer. "No, I haven't talked to her. I took it upon myself to check in on you. I get the impression young Kenneth really sprung a shocker on you today. Plus, I wanted to talk to you more about how Kenneth came to you in the first place. We should have those facts nailed down before we talk to Ross Edwards."

"I'm fine. Just tired. Do we really need to talk about this tonight? We've both had a long day."

"Mind if I have a glass of that wine?"

"Excuse me?"

"I'm happy to go off duty. You're right. It has been a long day and it's time to call it quits. So what better way to end the day than a glass of fine vino?" Paulson lifted the bottle, which Brett noticed held barely a full glass. "Nice vintage."

This woman is full of surprises. Brett decided Paulson was flirting with her and the thought made her uncomfortable though she couldn't put her finger on why. Kim Paulson was a beautiful woman, intense and compelling. But something about her was off. Ryan Foster was equally intense, but her presence had the vastly different effect of making Brett want to move closer. Sitting next to Paulson, Brett's instinct was to find a task to occupy her in some other room in the house. Silly, really. Especially since Paulson was here and Ryan Foster was not. Brett reflected. It had been way too long since she had enjoyed a glass of wine with a beautiful woman. Obviously, her barren personal life affected her perspective.

Brett shook her head. Why was she even thinking about Ryan anyway? Paulson was probably a perfectly great dating prospect, but Brett didn't trust her own instincts right now. She searched her mind for a polite way to refuse Paulson's hint for an invitation to stay. The formerly frustrating door buzzer saved the day.

Brett opened the door to the second surprise of the evening. "Ryan?"

Ryan looked over her own shoulder as if Brett's questioning tone indicated the presence of another person. "Yes, it's me." She flashed the quirky smile Brett had become fond of.

"Come in." Brett held the door open and followed Ryan's eyes as they honed in on the couch. She observed the crackle of conflict as Ryan and Paulson sized each other up, and felt strangely embarrassed that Ryan had found another woman on her couch.

Ryan strode across the room and shoved her hand at the last person she had expected to see sitting in Brett's apartment. Her anger was only slightly minimized by the discomfort Paulson obviously experienced at seeing Ryan. Or maybe she was just embarrassed to be holding an almost empty bottle of wine. Paulson set the bottle on the coffee table and took Ryan's offered hand. Ryan held it, squeezing hard enough and long enough to send a message.

It didn't work. Paulson remained seated. Ryan decided to be more direct. "I think Detective Harwell could use your help."

"He's fine."

"He's very capable, but I want the forensics on Edwards's computers started right away, and I want the phone record subpoenas on my desk later tonight. If you leave now, the two of you working together should be able to accomplish that." Her authoritative tone left no room for argument. The computers would need to be transported to their local IT expert, and Ryan had already told Harwell she didn't want to wait till morning to start the process. She could draft the subpoenas herself, but she wanted to talk to Brett alone, so ordering Paulson to take care of it would solve her immediate issues of both time and convenience.

Paulson stood and made her way to the door, ignoring Ryan. Ryan wasn't fooled. She wasn't Paulson's boss, but any cop in the county was smart enough to know Ryan had the ear of District Attorney Duncan. A call of reprimand from Duncan down the chain could inflict permanent damage. "Brett, thanks for your hospitality. I hope you get some rest and feel better soon."

Ryan's ears perked at the intimate tone. *Since when did Ms. Logan become Brett?* She waited till she was sure Paulson had made her way down the front walk before she focused on Brett. She looked like hell. Ryan guessed she needed more sleep than her lopsided hair indicated she had gotten. Did she share a bottle of wine with Paulson before or after her nap? Had they napped together? Ryan forced her face into an expression that didn't reflect the frustration she felt at finding Paulson cozied up on Brett's couch. Then she faced her.

Brett had dispensed with hostess formalities. She reclined on the sofa, a glass of wine in her hand. She spoke first. "I don't think I've had this many visitors since I moved in. To what do I owe the pleasure?"

"Frankly, I don't know why Paulson was here, but I came by to let you know a few things about the investigation."

"Oh, so you didn't come by to see how I was doing?"

Ryan shuffled. Brett's voice was lilting, but held a tinge of hurt. Ryan did care how Brett was holding up, but she was doing her best to maintain a level of professionalism. What she really wanted was to drain the last of the bottle of wine Paulson had been cradling, and take the place she had vacated on Brett's sofa. She was twitching with need. Tonight was the first night she had failed to keep an appointment she made with the service. She needed the relief, but on her way home to change into more appropriate clothes, her instincts told her to take a detour. A single phone call netted Brett's address.

Now, sitting in Brett's apartment, she wondered if she had made the right decision. Brett was clearly out of it, and who could blame her? They had both had a crazy day, though their experiences were vastly different. Where Brett felt betrayed, Ryan was vindicated. Where Brett looked foolish, Ryan looked wise. But the upshot was the blurring of lines between them. Brett, whether she realized it or not, was now a potential witness for the state, which placed her solidly in Ryan's camp. They were no longer adversaries. At least not for the moment. Ryan decided to take advantage.

"Have you eaten?"

"What?"

"You look beat. You'll feel better if you eat."

"I don't want to."

"Change into something comfortable. I'll wait."

Brett's tone changed from petulant to indignant. "Excuse me? I'm not accustomed to being ordered around in my own house, Ms. Foster."

Ryan smiled to soften the atmosphere. "Sorry. Look, I didn't mean to order you around. I just thought you could use something to eat and frankly, I could use the company. You'd be doing me a favor."

"I am starving." Brett gave Ryan a once over. "Are you wearing that?" Ryan shrugged and nodded. *That* was a tightly tailored charcoal gray wool suit, black silk shirt, and heels. Her suit looked fresh from the cleaners and her pantyhose were still intact, whereas Brett's lay in the heap across the room. Ryan's hair was still tidily tucked into a French braid and her mascara wasn't smeared with sleep. Brett could only imagine how she looked, and she had no desire to appear in public with Ms. Perfect. "Where did you plan on taking me?"

Ryan hadn't thought that far ahead. She fished her memory for the place Brett had suggested the night of the fundraiser. "How about Five Sixty?" Brett's only response was wild laughter.

"You've got to be kidding me?" Brett stood and smoothed out the wrinkles in her skirt. "I'd love to go to Five Sixty. When I look good. I'm way past that tonight. Take off your jacket."

"I beg your pardon?"

"You heard me. It's my turn to bark out some orders. You're way overdressed for where I want to go."

Ryan wasn't sure why, but she complied. "Okay, now what?"

"Your hair."

"My hair?"

"Braid be gone. Now." Brett couldn't help it; she reached over and fingered Ryan's perfectly coiffed hair. Ryan's slight flinch didn't go unnoticed. Brett quickly drew back. "I'm going to throw on some jeans. There's a brush on the bathroom counter. Help yourself. I'll be ready in five."

❖

"These are delicious. Don't make me eat them alone."

Ryan watched Brett's eager consumption of the largest cheeseburger she had ever seen. She'd heard of Snuffer's, Brett's restaurant choice, but this was her first time to experience the institution first hand. Despite Brett's insistence that she try one of the famous half-pound burgers, she ordered a salad in deference to her shape and the late hour. But Brett wasn't going to take no for an answer when it came to the appetizer she ordered. Ryan reached across the table and tentatively poked her fork at the mound of cheese pouring over the sides of the basket of French fries.

Brett held out her hand. "Give me your plate." Ryan handed Brett her plate and watched as she thrust her fork into the globby mess. She added jalapeños, bacon bits, and ranch dressing to the heaping plate and shoved it back to Ryan. No salad would offset the effect of this cholesterol nightmare. Her plan to ignore the full plate was thwarted by Brett's stare. Ryan took as small a bite as she could and placed it in her mouth. It was heaven. She reached for another bite, vowing to put in an extra few miles on the treadmill, even though she knew it was futile.

"Were you at Edwards's house when they did the search?"

"Yes."

"What did you find?"

Ryan hesitated. She and Brett were no longer on opposite sides, but she probably shouldn't be sharing information about an ongoing investigation with a potential witness. She reached for her beer—Brett had insisted it was a beer kind of a joint—and took a deep draught while she thought about her reply. *What the hell?* She was excited about what they had found. She probably should've been having this celebratory drink with Jeff, but she had been too focused on her other plans to think to ask him to join her for a drink after they had executed the search warrant, and besides, she didn't think fraternizing with one of her employees was a good idea. Of course those "other plans" had fallen by the wayside once Ryan thought about Brett. Ryan ignored the nagging internal voice that warned having a drink with Brett might be a mistake as well.

"We found enough to nail this case shut, and he'll be preparing his defense from a jail cell for the duration." She could tell by Brett's raised eyebrows that she wanted to know more. She wanted to tell her. She wanted to tell her that they had found draft after draft of the "script" Kenneth Phillips had read during the first moments of the debrief. They had found a fake DEA badge, and she was certain his phone records and e-mails would show direct communication with Brett and her office about representing Kenneth Phillips. "Let's just say we found definitive evidence he communicated with Kenneth about what Kenneth had to say to us today, and I expect we'll find more in the next few days from the evidence we seized."

"What are your plans for Kenneth?"

"I'll grant him immunity and he'll testify at Edwards's trial."

"He'll need an attorney to walk him through the immunity agreement."

"Uh, I thought you were his attorney."

"I think I might have a conflict now."

"Not if he has immunity."

"I assume you're talking about use immunity?" Brett referred to an agreement where the prosecution agreed not to use his testimony against him, which was more common than transactional immunity, which would mean he couldn't be prosecuted at all, no matter where the evidence against him came from. At Ryan's nod, she continued. "What if he gets on the stand and says something different?"

"We can deal with it then. I think he trusts you. The last thing we need is to have to involve another attorney at this stage."

"You mean the last thing Kenneth needs, don't you?"

"Sure, that's what I meant."

Brett wasn't entirely sure that was the case, but she decided to write Ryan's exuberance off to the excitement of experiencing such a huge break in her case. She decided to change the subject. "Did Kenneth get home okay?" Paulson had volunteered to drive him home since he'd taken a cab to the courthouse that morning.

"Sure. I'm sure Paulson got him settled in. Speaking of Paulson, how do you know her?"

"I met her for the first time this morning." Brett sensed more behind Ryan's question, but she decided to let Ryan get to it in her own time.

"She seemed kind of chummy at your place."

"Yes, she did."

"And you like that?"

Brett cocked her head. What was Ryan trying to get at? She had a sense, but wasn't sure whether or not to follow her instincts. Ryan's questions had all the signs of a curious, perhaps even jealous, admirer, but Brett held back on any such conclusions. She was definitely attracted to Ryan, but didn't harbor any hope the attraction was mutual. Word on the street was Ryan was an ice-cold celibate bitch. Brett was no longer buying the ice-cold bitch part, but celibate? Maybe. It didn't seem as if relationships of any kind were in Ryan's repertoire.

Fuck it. Brett decided she was done dancing around the question. "Are you asking me if I like Detective Paulson?"

Ryan flushed deep red and shoved a forkful of cheese fries in her mouth. Avoidance. Definitely a sign, but Brett was sick and tired of vague signs. She wanted definitive answers. "Are you asking me if I'm a lesbian?"

Ryan met her eyes straight on. She swallowed and cleared her throat. Arms folded, she leaned in, and sotto voice replied, "I know you're a lesbian."

Brett faked a shocked expression. Clutching her chest, she returned the whisper. "Oh my god! My secret's been exposed!"

Ryan's blush grew deeper. "Are you making fun of me?"

"Me? Making fun of you? Hey, it's my personal life that's at issue here."

"But it's not like you keep it a secret."

"No. I don't." Brett looked closely at Ryan, who seemed to blanch under the scrutiny. There was something more to this conversation. Some undercurrent she wasn't quite getting. She wanted to examine her instincts, but decided to wait. Right now, all she really wanted was to act on them. For the first time since they'd left the apartment, Brett took in Ryan's less than buttoned-up appearance. Her hair, still kinked from the tight braid that restrained it during the day, kicked around her face in stubborn waves. Brett wanted to touch the wayward tendrils, not to tame them, but to relish their happy freedom. She glanced up at Ryan's face and fixed her with a steady look that said she wasn't finished taking in the full picture. Ryan flushed again, and the look was positively captivating. The wave of red extended down her exposed neckline. Brett lost all interest in her meal, hungering only to touch the glowing skin at the base of Ryan's throat, sure it would be soft, hot, and firm. As captivated as she was, Brett was still conscious of where they were, who Ryan was. She didn't touch. Not with her hands anyway. "You are gorgeous. Do you know that?"

Brett wasn't sure what reaction she expected from Ryan. Shock, revulsion, a face slap maybe. No, Ryan's position as a candidate dictated there would be no public humiliation, even if initiated by the other party. Ryan remained calm, poised. "I think I should take you home." Her stoic reaction belied any possibility her response was a double entrendre. Brett merely nodded in response.

The drive was short and miserable. Ryan silently cursed the late hour. She could still show up at the party, but the likelihood anyone of choice would be waiting for a third tier late arrival was dim at best.

She had no desire to place herself in a position of rejecting whoever might be left, if anyone was. She was always careful to arrive in time to enjoy the variety of choices available at the exclusive events. A late arrival would be insult enough. If she showed up now, she couldn't add another insult by declining the hospitality of whatever man or woman might be waiting to service her needs. Such a slight to the host could result in a restriction of future privileges. Ryan didn't let her mind consider the possibility that not showing up at all might constitute an even greater slight.

She snuck a glance at the passenger seat. Brett hadn't said a word during the drive. Ryan had quickly become accustomed to her banter, despite the most recent uncomfortable subject, and she missed the smooth and easy tones of Brett's friendly voice. She didn't know what to say to spark the conversation back to life. *Thanks for the compliment. You're beautiful too. In fact, just the other day, I was running my hands all over this woman dressed in white leather wishing she were you. I fucked her senseless, and when she returned the favor, I pretended it was you, making love to me, as if I was the most important person on earth and touching me was salvation.*

Ryan shook her head as if she could splinter her thoughts with the action. She couldn't afford to let Brett detect what she was thinking. Her secrets were her only salvation, not Brett's touch, physical or emotional. She sensed the silence between them only fueled the intensity of their encounter at the restaurant, but she couldn't find words mundane enough to break the spell, so she didn't speak at all.

Brett's silence was another issue altogether. Ryan felt as if Brett could see through her, and what she saw was a poser. High-powered prosecutor reduced to silence by a single compliment from a beautiful woman. Wannabe politician unable to engage in small talk at the first sign of a controversial issue. Super Chief, supervisor of dozens, unable to manage her own emotions long enough to make it through dinner. Ryan desperately wanted Brett to be the one to break the silence, but she knew she wouldn't. Ryan didn't merit closer attention from the captivating woman beside her.

The drive was even shorter than she remembered. As she pulled into the parking lot, Brett's hand was on the door handle, her good-bye quick. "Thanks for dinner. Just let me out here."

Ryan ignored her and parked the car in one of the slots closest to the building that housed Brett's unit. Brett was already out of the car before she could make her way around to the passenger side. Brett seemed intent on making it to her apartment door in record time, and Ryan took long strides to catch up to her. Pulling up alongside, she lightly touched Brett's elbow with her hand. A protective, intimate gesture. The touch was met with a forceful shake of Brett's arm, clearly demonstrating Brett didn't welcome the closeness. Ryan waited to the side while Brett fished in her handbag for her elusive keys, ignoring Brett's annoyed glances in her direction. *She wants you to leave. She doesn't want you to stand here staring at her. She is clearly frustrated with you.*

Ryan didn't care. She wasn't ready to leave. She wanted to say something to Brett, but she didn't want to speak her truths out here on the doorstep, surrounded by the possibilities of observation. She waited out Brett's frustration and breathed a quiet sigh when Brett found her keys and inserted them in the lock. Brett pushed open the door and walked inside. When she turned and started to push the door back, Ryan was waiting there, standing in the threshold. Ryan moved closer and pushed the door shut behind her. She opened her mouth to speak, but the words pulled up short before they left her lips, like hesitant jumpers on the edge of a cliff. She could see the gorge below, the significance of the distance downward, the most certain devastation at the end of a floating free fall. She considered her options and took the only viable course. She pulled Brett into her arms and kissed her hard on the lips.

❖

The ride from the restaurant to Brett's apartment was interminably long, and all Brett wanted was for it to be over. *I should've known she'd be a homophobe. Damn Republican candidate for head of all things law and order in Dallas County.* Brett didn't mind that she'd outed herself to Ryan, but she wanted to smack herself for caring what Ryan thought. And for thinking, even for a split second, that Ryan might be able to take an intimate compliment or at least not ignore it completely. The woman had the social skills of a two-year-old. And the body of a model. *Whatever.*

Ryan obviously thought Brett couldn't make it to her own front door without assistance. Brett dug deep in her purse for her keys, studiously ignoring Ryan's presence at her elbow. As she crossed the threshold and Ryan followed her in, Brett's annoyance grew. She whirled around, ready to order Ryan out, but the look on Ryan's face stopped her in her tracks.

The stoic mask was gone, replaced by imploring eyes and an almost wistful expression. Ryan looked as if she were about to say something, and Brett's curiosity beat back her irritability. She waited through the silence, but the words never came. Ryan tugged her close and kissed her fiercely.

Brett stiffened, her instincts signaling the situation was off, wrong, crazy even, but as Ryan's lips let go their insistent pull, the breath of air that passed between them was painful in its separation. She crushed into Ryan's chest and demonstrated her own version of ferocity. She wouldn't have guessed Ryan's lips would be so smooth, so hungry, so strong, but they were perfectly matched with hers. Brett melted into the most intense, most delectable, most irresistible kiss she had ever experienced.

She wanted more. Ryan's hands were in her hair, sending shocking shivers throughout her body, and Brett reached up and guided Ryan's hand down her neck, down her sweater, lingering at her breast. Ryan took her lead, squeezing and pinching at her obvious arousal. Brett silently praised herself for choosing a skimpy lace bra that was only barely present.

She wanted even more. She reached for Ryan's other hand, but Ryan had her own ideas in mind. Ryan gently slid the palm of her free hand down Brett's side, letting teasing fingers play in the waistband of Brett's jeans. Her fingers reached down and skimmed the band of Brett's panties, before drawing back to trace long, slow trails along Brett's abdomen, over and over until Brett was sure she would go insane.

Ryan deftly unbuttoned Brett's fly and trailed her fingers deep down to lightly play against Brett's panties, skimming the fast-hardening folds of skin beneath. Without missing a beat, she pushed up Brett's sweater and shoved her bra to the side. Her mouth took the place of her hand at Brett's swollen, aching breast, and she used her now free hand to hold Brett secure as she began bolder moves below Brett's waist.

Ryan's touch was intense and sure, and Brett's body coursed toward climax. She arched her pelvis slightly out of reach to slow the pace. She had no doubt she wanted Ryan, but even as long as it had been since she'd experienced this incredible pleasure, she wanted to savor it, together, with Ryan. She tilted Ryan's chin up and gazed into her eyes. What she saw was abandon, fierce and wild. She wanted to bottle it, but she was scared if she disturbed the emotion it would disappear. She kissed Ryan's lips, their tongues meeting again in an explosion of desire. Brett wanted them both naked, free to explore, free to share mutual pleasure. She wanted more than a quickie in the foyer. Brett murmured against Ryan's lips, "I want you. In my bed. Come with me. Please?"

Ryan could barely make out the words through her haze of desire. Brett wanted her. Excellent news since her mouth, fingers, and the rest of her body craved contact with Brett beyond the bounds of any hunger she'd ever experienced. She wanted Ryan to come with her. Again, excellent. Based on the pulsing rhythm of their touch, they would come together in an explosion. The specifics of Brett's invitation finally broke the surface of Ryan's scattered thoughts. *In her bed?*

Ryan's thoughts raced ahead. She would be naked, in Brett's bed, for hours perhaps. She had shared a bed with other women, but she knew doing so with Brett would be different than with an anonymous stranger at a prearranged party. Brett might want to talk about something meaningful. The women Ryan paid for talked to her only if she wished, and their conversations had no significance other than to put forth the pretense their interchange was more than a business transaction. Would daylight catch her still here, redressing in her suit from the day before? Treading the walk of shame back to her car, up the sidewalk in her quiet suburban neighborhood? Striding through the courthouse halls, wondering who was gossiping about her tryst with a prominent defense attorney?

Ryan knew the only answer was no, even though it meant denying herself the fulfillment she had glimpsed before but was doomed to never experience again. Anonymous sex was far safer than gliding around the edges of something deeper, something real. Decision made, she gently drew her hands away from their intimate contact with Brett's taut and willing body. She glanced away from Brett's pleading eyes, unwilling and unable to endure the unbridled desire that would pull her back toward their mutual passion.

Brett didn't resist when Ryan pulled away. Ryan may be a skilled poker player in the courtroom, but this evening she had telegraphed all her emotions with signals sure and true. Brett knew Ryan's desire to join her in bed was as strong as the force that cautioned against the idea. She also knew which force would win. She released Ryan, with her eyes and with her hands. She could make Ryan's decision easy or hard, and she knew if she made it hard, it would be even harder on herself.

Brett's bed had been lonely for a long time. By her own choice. She was tired of getting involved with women who expected her to change who she was for them. *Work less, socialize more. Don't become so immersed in the lives of the less fortunate. Don't isolate your work from me.* The pleas ostensibly requested self-improvement, but Brett had always resisted, sensing compliance would make the other woman happy at the expense of losing a piece of herself. She'd dabbled in such sacrifices and found she always lost her sense of self in the process.

Ryan clearly would have been okay with a quick sex session, still clothed, in Brett's foyer. Brett wasn't. Naked, in the bed, all night or nothing. One last look at Ryan's frightened expression gave her the answer. *Or nothing.*

CHAPTER FIFTEEN

Y ou've looked better." Tony handed Brett the triple shot cappuccino she had demanded the moment she walked through the door.

She hadn't slept at all the night before. Thinking about her heavy schedule the next morning hadn't mixed well with memories of Ryan's searing kisses and hasty rejection. She finally dressed and drove to the office, surprising Tony at her uncustomary very early arrival. She wasn't in the mood to talk, just drink. Since she had to be in court in an hour, she would have to satisfy herself with caffeine for a drug.

Tony wasn't getting the hint. "Here's your mail. I put the most important piece on top."

"Is it a big fat check?"

"Hardly. It's a big fat orange invitation." Tony grinned and held the burnt orange envelope just out of Brett's reach.

"Kind of late, isn't it?" Brett didn't need to open the fancy envelope to know the contents, but she reached for it anyway. Every year her father organized a weekend full of events to celebrate the Texas versus OU football game, aka Red River Shootout, where his University of Texas Longhorns took on the Oklahoma Sooners at the Cotton Bowl. The game was this weekend. As if the game itself weren't a big enough affair, the Cotton Bowl was situated smack in the middle of the state fairgrounds and the largest state fair in the country was already in full swing. Brett's father traditionally hired a limousine to cart their entire family to the game. Attendance was mandatory.

"I've been hiding it."

Tony's expression held no remorse. He knew she had mixed feelings about this event. She could rave about her alma mater with the best of them, but a whole day with her siblings and family units was a bit much. As much as she loved them all, the time together would be a constant reminder she wasn't living up to the Logan family standards: marriage and kids. For the first time she could ever remember, she actually cared she wasn't living up to those standards. At least the marriage part.

Her last girlfriend, Stephanie, had moved out of their apartment while Brett was immersed in trial. Stephanie left a small note on the coffee table to commemorate their time together. *Hope you win in trial because you're not winning anywhere else.* In the following weeks, Brett relished her newfound independence. She didn't do anything different, but she didn't have anyone hounding her about what she was doing. The silence was indeed golden, for a while anyway. She wasn't sure when the balance tipped, but at some point the freedom no longer outweighed the comfort of being loved. Watching her family interact made her crave the substance of commitment, though obviously not enough to do anything about it since her habits hadn't changed since Stephanie exited her life.

Brett would go to the game. Surrounded by her mom, dad, and brothers, she would play the role she had become accustomed to as the not quite perfect kid in the perfect family.

❖

"You look like shit."

Ryan wondered when Jeff had decided they were enough of a team that he no longer had to defer to her authority. Telling your boss she looked like shit was most certainly insubordination, but she knew he was right. She hadn't slept, instead she spent the night questioning each decision she had made. She shouldn't have had dinner with Brett. She shouldn't have kissed her. She shouldn't have held her, placed her hands down her pants, suckled her breast into her hot and ready mouth. The list of things she shouldn't have done poked and prodded at her throughout the night. She shouldn't blame Jeff for pointing out the effect of her punishing regrets. Besides, after the events of yesterday, he probably assumed they had experienced the ultimate prosecutorial bonding experience: a major break in the case.

Ross Edwards's fate was sealed. Any spark of reasonable doubt that might have existed had been snuffed out with Kenneth's revelations and the telltale evidence found at Edwards's residence the night before. Ryan briefly wondered how a person could be so cunning, yet so stupid at the same time. Edwards's plan to have Kenneth confess was half-baked. He hadn't given Kenneth all the information he needed to seal his own fate—if he'd told Kenneth the fatal injury had come from a gunshot wound rather than a fireplace tool, they might have bought the kid's story.

Ryan shrugged. Though the subject intrigued her, she had long ago resigned herself to the realization that the internal workings of the criminal mind would often elude her. In this case, it was probably something as simple as Edwards had figured Kenneth would serve his purpose merely by providing reasonable doubt. His lawyer would be entitled to know if someone else had come forth confessing to the crime, even if the prosecution team didn't plan to offer that testimony at trial. The defense attorney could then offer the evidence about that confession and try to convince the jury that the mere fact of another confession, however lame, should shed some doubt on Edwards's guilt. After all, why would someone confess to doing something, especially something as heinous as murder, if they hadn't actually committed the crime?

Ryan winced at the thought of a defense attorney using one of the most common arguments of prosecutors. Usually, it was the other way around, with defense making arguments about false confessions. *My client may have said he did it, whatever it was, but he didn't mean it. He was coerced or threatened.* When the prosecutors got their turn, they invariably countered with the simplistic, but believable notion—innocent people don't confess to bad acts. Ryan had made that argument plenty of times in the past. She wondered how many times she'd been wrong.

She was full of feeling wrong today. Time to focus on what was right with this case since it was the only thing she had going for her right now. On her way home from Brett's, Leonard had called, cheering through the phone line. He was ecstatic about the break in the case. *Seal this case up, and you'll be the next DA. No doubt.* This case. This election. These things were her future, and Ryan knew her future was where her focus should be.

"I need to talk to you two."

The voice was Brett's. Ryan was instantly stripped of her resolve, and her focus blurred from the facts of the case to her memories of Brett, pliant and willing, in her arms. She wanted to pull Brett aside, talk to her, size up her reaction to last night, but she didn't trust herself to limit the bounds of such an encounter. Right now, all she could focus on was her desire to kiss Brett's lips, feel her smooth skin, and take what Brett had been so willing to offer. She made a snap decision to act as if nothing had happened between them.

"We need to talk to you too. Jeff's going to want to meet with you and Kenneth about your testimony since he'll take you both on direct." She ignored Jeff's shocked look at her uncharacteristic selflessness. She knew he assumed she would hog the star witnesses for herself. She hated to admit it, but if last night hadn't happened, she probably would have.

Brett didn't respond directly. She had her own concerns. "I understand you may want me as a witness, but Kenneth's going to need a new attorney. I wanted to give you a heads up. I'm headed to talk to Judge Langston about it now." Brett hadn't slept the night before either, but she'd put the time to good use. After considering all the angles, she had come to the conclusion she needed to withdraw from representing Kenneth.

"What?" Jeff and Ryan spoke at the same time.

Ryan shot Jeff a look that said she would respond. She took a deep breath. "Ms. Logan, if you're concerned about a conflict, we're willing to extend full use immunity to Kenneth. Of course that is dependent on his waiver of attorney-client privilege."

"Ms. Logan?" Brett let a smile slip into the corners of her mouth. Was Ryan really trying to act like nothing had happened between them? If nothing else, the shared experience of revelations during Kenneth's debrief should have swept away such formalities between them. The woman was unbelievable, but Brett was willing to play along. To a certain extent. "I think you should call me Brett."

Ryan tried to ignore Brett's pointed look, but the hint of a smile was contagious. "Sorry. *Brett.*"

"Thanks. Full use immunity is great, but it doesn't cover him if he lies to you. He needs to have another attorney advise him about what can happen if he doesn't hold up his end of the bargain." Brett paused, as if considering her next move. "I'm headed to chambers now if you want to come with."

Ryan stood. "Great idea." She motioned for Jeff to stay behind. She didn't need his help for the maneuver she had planned, plus she was gambling she might catch a moment alone with Brett. She needed to set things straight between them.

❖

"Ms. Logan, Ms. Foster, good to see you both."

Brett hadn't expected to run into the judge in the hallway, and she didn't want to have this discussion out in the open. "Good morning, Judge. We were actually on our way to see you. May we have a few minutes?"

"Certainly. I have to take care of something in Judge Hall's court. I'll be back on the bench in about five minutes."

"We'd like to talk to you in chambers if you don't mind."

Judge Langston glanced at Ryan who affirmed Brett's request with a nod. "Very well. Go on back. I'll be there as soon as I can."

Brett led the way and seconds later, she and Ryan were seated on the loveseat directly across from Judge Langston's desk. Ryan was acting like Brett had a dreaded disease, and she sat with her legs tucked off to the side, as far away from Brett as possible. Brett stared at Ryan. Ryan stared back. Ryan spoke first.

"I'm sorry about last night."

"Me too, but I suspect we have different motivations for our apologies."

Ryan was confused. She wanted to know more, but she was wary of going down a path from which there would be no easy return. Curiosity won. "And you're apologizing because..."

"Because I wanted something you are clearly not ready or willing to give." There, thought Brett, I said it and I'm glad I did. Ryan just sat there, apparently flummoxed. She opened her mouth several times as if to say something, but no words came out. Brett watched the process, determined not to bail Ryan out.

"Brett, I—"

"Sorry, ladies, I hope I didn't keep you waiting too long." Judge Langston sailed into the room and sat behind the desk. Brett followed her eyes to the crystal framed clock on her desk, nine thirty. Thank goodness they weren't going to be captive for teatime.

Ryan moved to the edge of her seat and started speaking first. "Thanks for seeing us, Judge. We have a situation—" Ryan felt a light touch near her knee and caught Brett's hand making the subtle motion. She caught the hint. She reluctantly ceded the conversation to Brett. "Brett, I mean, Ms. Logan, can explain."

Brett nodded in Ryan's direction, but focused her attention on the judge as she explained the situation with Kenneth. "Judge, you remember the conversation we had the other day, about the person you appointed me to represent? Pre-indictment confession to a capital murder?"

"Yes."

"Some things have come up on that case. I need to go ahead and divulge this person's identity and ask you to appoint new counsel."

Judge Langston turned to Ryan. "Is this information in relation to the search warrant I signed for you last night?" At Ryan's nod, she turned back to face Brett. "I know the basics, but fill me in on the points relevant to your request to be removed from the case."

As Brett outlined the circumstances of the debrief session with her client, Judge Langston listened intently, and then summed up what she had heard.

"The young man wanted to confess, but not because he did the murder, but to get out of trouble on another case?"

"That's correct, Judge."

Judge Langston directed her next question to Ryan. "And you have evidence to support that the defendant in the Dinelli case, Ross Edwards, arranged this faux confession?"

"Yes, Your Honor. Strong evidence," Ryan replied.

"And you believe that he's telling the truth? Not about the murder confession, but about being persuaded to tell a lie?"

"We obtained credible evidence in response to the search warrant we executed yesterday."

"Do you intend to list Ms. Logan as a witness in your case?"

Ryan hesitated, for several reasons. One, she found it strange to be talking about Brett as if she weren't in the room. Second, it felt decidedly weird to be talking about Brett at all when their proximity conjured up sexy images of her hands in Brett's pants. Ryan's breathing became shallow, and she willed herself to concentrate on the judge's question.

"Based on what we found last night..." Ryan paused and flicked a glance in Brett's direction. "Pardon me, Ms. Logan, we haven't had a chance to share this information with you yet, but we were able to obtain copies of cell phone records for a phone registered to Edwards. It appears that he called you on your cell and at your office several times over the past week, and based on the length of the calls, he either left lengthy messages on your voice mail or actually talked to you or someone in your office." Turning back to the judge, Ryan answered the question she'd been asked. "Yes, we intend to list Ms. Logan on the witness list. I don't have a good idea at this point if we will need to actually call her as a witness. We will introduce phone records and, perhaps, with the testimony of Kenneth Phillips, we will not need her testimony."

Brett knew the final decision to call her as a witness at trial was a decision that would be made on the fly, during the trial itself, and totally dependent on how the rest of the testimony was shaping up. The judge wasn't asking Ryan for a firm commitment, only an assessment of the likelihood. Ryan had given Brett her opening.

"Judge, I don't think I should assume dual roles at this trial. If Ms. Foster wants me on the witness list, my client needs new counsel." Brett knew it wasn't as simple as that, but she wanted it to be. Her hope was that either the judge would agree and appoint someone new to advise Kenneth, or Ryan would agree not to call her as a witness. She could tell by the expressions on the faces of both of the other women that they were engaged in complex thought. Not a good sign.

Ryan spoke first. "Judge, I'm prepared to offer full use immunity to Mr. Phillips if he will agree to waive attorney-client privilege and testify truthfully at trial. I think that alleviates any concern about a potential conflict."

Brett didn't wait for the judge's reply. "It doesn't, Judge. Who is going to review the waiver and immunity offer with Mr. Phillips? I'm supposed to advise my client how to proceed and be willing to testify that he was complicit in a scheme to obstruct justice at the same time? And what if he gets on the stand and tells a decidedly different story than the one he told the prosecutor? There won't be any immunity then. What if he wants to seek counsel prior to answering questions from either the state or the defense? If I'm a witness, I won't be in the courtroom while he's testifying."

Brett took a long, deep breath while she waited for her onslaught of words to wash over the judge and Ryan. She wondered how much she harped on the issues just to get off the case. While she should have been relieved the case wasn't turning out to be the capital murder nightmare she'd initially envisioned, the situation was still fraught with its own complex circumstances, even without factoring in the strong pull of attraction between her and Ryan. She knew when the waves receded, all of her professional concerns could be allayed, but she wasn't sure the personal ones could withstand the light of day. Ryan had practically run from her house after their encounter, and Brett could imagine a dozen reasons why she did. In fact, it surprised her Ryan was arguing in favor of her remaining on the case. Maybe it was a means to erect a barrier between them.

Brett couldn't deny she had her own motivations to be off the case. She felt betrayed. Kenneth Phillips had started out a sad, lost soul, but he was really just a punk kid, willing to do whatever it took to avoid taking responsibility for his crimes. She knew many of her clients were no different, but she was finally forced to face in stark relief the reality she usually managed to gloss over. When it came down to it, Brett could only hope the mere appearance of impropriety would relieve her of any further responsibilities to young Kenneth Phillips.

Judge Langston had different ideas.

"I think we can handle these issues with a minimum of fuss. It is my opinion we will just make things more complicated by introducing new counsel." She addressed Brett. "If defense counsel waives the rule just for your testimony, you can be present in the courtroom when Kenneth testifies. If they won't, then perhaps Ms. Foster will adjust her strategy so you can testify first. If you don't feel your new position as witness comports with your ability to properly advise your client about his rights as to waiver and immunity, then I would be happy to assess his understanding and advise him myself."

That's a lot of ifs, Judge. Brett didn't bother speaking the words, since Judge Langston had clearly made up her mind. She saw the judge sneak a look at her watch, and she looked at Ryan who she could tell was thinking the same thing. It was getting dangerously close to teatime and they both had better things to do. Brett resigned herself to continued involvement with Kenneth Phillips, the Edwards case, and with Ryan Foster.

❖

Ryan spent the rest of the day working on the case. She enjoyed the fast pace just before a trial. The new developments only made things more exciting. Kenneth Phillips, his revelations, and the evidence the detectives had discovered at Edwards's home meant hours of additional preparation, but Ryan welcomed the challenge of reworking their strategy. And having a smoking gun was nice too. She and Jeff still had the issue of no direct evidence—no one had seen Ross Edwards pull the trigger that snuffed Mary Dinelli's life, but she knew Ross Edwards had been involved with Mary Dinelli before she died, he had hired a punk ex-con John Rodriguez to torch Dinelli's home, he had been seen with the woman who posed as Dinelli as she cashed Dinelli's veteran's benefits. Now, she had solid proof Edwards had scammed someone else into confessing in his stead. The circle of circumstantial evidence was drawing close to a single center point: Ross Edwards arranged the murder of Mary Dinelli, then defiled her memory by stealing every last dime she had and having her home burned to the ground.

"Is Jeff around?"

Brett's voice reminded Ryan she couldn't do the job on her own. As they left Judge Langston's chambers earlier that morning, Jeff had nabbed Ryan to ask her several questions about pretrial matters. Brett, who was still by her side, had told Jeff she would stop by later to schedule her witness prep with him. Ryan was grateful Jeff was taking the lead with regard to Brett. She didn't think she could handle proximity with Brett, especially with the undiscussed encounter that hung between them. The courage she'd summoned to talk about it had vanished when Judge Langston interrupted them in her chambers. She hadn't planned on Brett stopping by when Jeff was out meeting with their forensics expert.

"Uh, hi. Jeff's running lead on witness prep, but he's not here right now."

"Interesting. Are you really letting Jeff handle all the witness prep? Even important ones like Kenneth?" Brett purposely asked a provocative question to get Ryan's attention since she didn't think Ryan was listening to her. She seemed focused on some object over Brett's shoulder. Brett followed her gaze. *Shit.* Was that sawdust all over her suit? She remembered there had been some construction on the tenth floor. She reached up to wipe it off and caught the hint of a grin on Ryan's face. "What are you laughing about?"

Ryan looked embarrassed. "I wasn't laughing." She wasn't, at least not out loud. "Okay, okay. I was merely wondering how you afford your dry cleaning bill." She couldn't hide the grin any longer. Brett laughed out loud and Ryan joined in.

"I make so much money doing these court-appointed cases, I can afford to wear a new suit every day," Brett joked. "Seriously,

I'm sure I've sent all my dry cleaner's children to college. I can't seem to get from my apartment to the car without wearing evidence of my every activity." Brett let her voice drop to a soft, smooth tone. "Leave it to you to notice."

Ryan blushed. Deep. She could feel the surge of warmth all the way to her toes. What was it about Brett that made her feel so off her game, or even made her feel at all? More than she wanted to know the answer, she wanted to relive the rush she felt kissing Brett the night before. That would never happen. She would make sure.

"Jeff should be back any minute. We'd like to meet with Kenneth tomorrow. If you can't wait for Jeff now, I'll have him call you to schedule a time. I imagine we'll take a few hours. We could meet with you after."

Brett thought about the long list of activities her father would have planned for the day before the big game. Cocktails with Texas alums, dinner with university bigwigs, more cocktails. The festivities would start early and run long. She ignored Ryan's suggestion that she talk to Jeff about scheduling. "We can do the meeting with Kenneth in the morning, but I'll have to take off after." Brett reached into her bag for her BlackBerry to check her schedule and brushed against the edge of the envelope Tony had handed her that morning. "Next week's packed for me as well." She made a snap decision. "I'll meet you Saturday. In fact, I'll pick you up. Ten a.m. See you then." Game day at the State Fair would provide many more opportunities to have a more personal conversation than the courthouse halls would allow.

Ryan opened her mouth, but the words weren't faster than Brett's exit. There were a million reasons she couldn't, shouldn't meet with Brett on Saturday. She was supposed to visit her aunt. She didn't want Brett at her house, hell, how did Brett even know where she lived? She didn't want to be alone with Brett.

Ryan knew the last reason fell more into the "shouldn't" than the "couldn't" category. She resolved to tell Brett her plan was unworkable. She would see her tomorrow when they met with Kenneth, and she would make other arrangements when others were present to prevent personal conversation. *Yeah, right, because conversation is what you're really worried about.*

CHAPTER SIXTEEN

Y ou're early today."
Ryan was very early, and she knew she'd pay for it.
Aunt Eunice may have a crippled body, but her mind was razor
sharp.

She had shown up for their meeting with Kenneth the day
before fully prepared to tell Brett she couldn't meet with her today.
Brett foiled her plans by announcing to Jeff and the detectives that
she wouldn't be able to stay after Kenneth's meeting, but she was
meeting with Ryan on Saturday instead. Remembering the rush she
felt the other night convinced Ryan to trade a tongue-lashing from
her aunt for time alone with Brett.

"Yes, I have an important meeting today. I'm sorry I had to
adjust my schedule."

Aunt Eunice frowned. "You don't need to act all uppity. I
know it's the weekend. If you want to socialize, by all means do
so, but don't pretend you're working. If visiting me has become an
imposition, then don't do it anymore."

Ryan knew it was no use to argue the point. Her aunt knew
the facts. Ryan had graduated from law school. Ryan worked at the
district attorney's office. But Eunice had never bothered to delve
deeper to associate Ryan's education and position with anything
other than the mere fact her niece had a degree and a job. Ryan
didn't bother talking to her about accomplishments at the office or
the possibility she might be the next elected official in charge of

enforcing the law in one of the largest counties in the nation. She knew none of that would mean anything to her aunt. She secretly feared Eunice would think she was exaggerating. One lesson her aunt had emphasized was humility.

Instead, Ryan discussed mundane matters. What was happening at the nursing home, and other unimportant, innocuous daily news. Despite her attempts to keep the conversation low-key, her aunt invariably veered onto a tangent about the liberal doings of the African-American president. Ryan tried to tune her out, but the constant harping finally broke through. She would never talk back, but she could leave. The clock on Aunt Eunice's nightstand signaled she had only been in the room for forty-five minutes. Ryan didn't care. Her aunt was already angry about the change to their schedule. It wasn't as if Ryan would suffer some additional consequences by cutting the visit short.

As she started out the door of the facility, she heard a voice call her name. She turned to see an employee of the nursing home heading her way.

"I just wanted to check in and see if you have any questions or concerns about your aunt."

Ryan was puzzled by the question. Her aunt just was. She didn't spend much time thinking about her well-being beyond the weekly visits she was required to make in order to keep guilt at bay. She supposed she should feel guilty for not being more involved in Eunice's daily care, but she didn't care about doing anything other than fulfilling the visitation duty Eunice expected. Anything more, even if well-meaning, would probably be dismissed by her as an intrusion.

Ryan realized the woman was still waiting for a response to her question. "Everything seems fine." Her eyes flicked to the woman's name tag, Lori Logan, and she remembered Brett said that her sister-in-law worked at the facility. Was this her?

As if she could hear her thoughts, Lori stuck out her hand and said, "I think you know my sister-in-law, Brett Logan. I'm Lori Logan, the director of nursing. I see you here all the time, but I don't think we've ever been formally introduced."

"Nice to meet you." Ryan wanted to make some clever remark, signifying some insider tidbit about how well she knew Brett, especially recently, but nothing came. She felt a rush of warmth and wondered if Lori could see her blush. She needed to make her exit before she made a fool of herself. "It was nice to meet you," she repeated. "I have to get to a meeting."

"Sure. No problem. Glad to hear things are going well with your aunt." Lori waved as Ryan exited the doors. "Don't let the meeting run too long. We'll be waiting."

Ryan was already out of the building as Lori's final message drifted out to her. She didn't understand the remark but didn't bother running back to clarify. Lori was probably referencing her next visit, which in Ryan's opinion, would come much too soon.

❖

Getting Ryan Foster to give up her address had been a battle. Brett finally had to point out that if Ryan owned a house, it would only take a few clicks on a keyboard to locate it. She knew Ryan had to be smart enough to know that, but for some reason she still guarded her privacy as if she housed state secrets.

Brett pulled up in front of a modest ranch style home. The yard was neatly kept, the trees trimmed. No signs of age on the shutters or trim. The tan brick exterior was bland. Brett idly wondered why she had expected to garner some clue about the complicated internal workings of Ryan from the exterior appearance of her house. If that was the case, she was out of luck. Brett parked her car and walked up the drive. As she raised her hand to ring the bell, the front door opened causing her to gasp.

"You scared the living daylights out of me!"

Ryan looked appropriately apologetic. "I'm sorry. I saw you pull up." She walked out onto the porch and locked the door behind her. "Ready to go?"

"You didn't have to stand at the door waiting. I'm a few minutes early."

"Not a problem. I've been ready."

Brett had hoped to get a glimpse at the inner sanctum, but it was apparent that wasn't going to happen. She looked at Ryan hoping perhaps her attire would be inappropriate for the day's activities and she could suggest they go back inside to look for something suitable. She took in Ryan's outfit and was pleasantly surprised. Ryan's hair was in the familiar French braid, but otherwise she was stylishly casual, wearing a neatly pressed oxford shirt, crisp jeans, and leather loafers. "You look great."

Ryan glanced down. "Um, thanks."

Small talk during the drive was strained. Neither one seemed to want to fill the space between them with trivial conversation, nor did they seem willing to talk about the professional and personal intimacy they had shared. Luckily, the drive from Ryan's place to Brett's parents was short.

As they pulled into the drive, Ryan spoke. "Who lives here?"

Brett grinned. "Potential voters." She opened her car door and waved for Ryan to follow. "Come on in and meet my parents."

The word "parents" nearly sent Ryan into a tailspin. She struggled to mask her anxiety with her courtroom game face. She tamped her stress level down with logic. Brett's father was Gerald Logan, friend of Leonard, and a senior partner in a powerful Dallas law firm. He was a staunch Republican, definitely poised to support Ryan's campaign. She was headed into friendly territory. Still, of all the scenarios she'd envisioned for this day, the last place she expected Brett to take her was her parents' home. She certainly would have dressed more formally if she'd known where she was headed.

"Ryan Foster! What a terrific surprise." Gerald Logan stood in the front entryway and his voice boomed toward them.

Ryan forced a hand forward. "Good afternoon, Mr. Logan. It's a pleasure to finally meet you."

"It's Gerald, please." He rocked back on his heels and shot a glance at Brett. "Brett, I thought Ms. Foster was a Harvard girl?"

"That's what her bio says, but today she shall be an honorary Longhorn."

"I should hope so. The limo leaves in ten minutes, and you better be on board. The kids are staking out seats and your brothers and the gals are out by the pool finishing brunch. There might be a scrap or two left if you hurry."

Brett nodded and signaled for Ryan to follow her. She did. She didn't have the wherewithal to do anything else since she was completely perplexed by his questions about college and references to a limo that they were supposed to be leaving in shortly. What had she gotten herself into?

"Come on. I'll explain." Brett's eyes were twinkling with mischief. Once they made it into the spacious house, she pulled Ryan into an unoccupied room. "I'm sure you know it's Texas/OU weekend?"

"Yes." Ryan tried to cipher Brett's point.

"We're headed to the Cotton Bowl."

Ryan shook her head. "Oh, no. I'm not."

"Yes. Yes, you are."

"We're supposed to be meeting to discuss your testimony. After I meet with you, I plan to tackle hours' worth of work I have to do on this case." She did have hours' worth of work to do, but she had half-hoped her time with Brett might turn into something more. Of course, now that Brett was trying to get her to spend the entire day with her, she felt herself backing off.

Brett wasn't having it. "I'm a litigator. Do you really think I need much preparation to anticipate your questions and give the answers in the way you want? I swear we'll have time to go through the highlights, but I can't miss this game. It's a family tradition. Besides, I thought you might enjoy spending a few hours with a potentially huge campaign donor." Brett tried not to wince at the partial lie. She didn't care if they had time to review her testimony, and she cared even less about her father and brothers giving Ryan's campaign a single dime. She did want to spend time with Ryan, though, and she had plans to get her to herself at some point during the day to talk about the burst of passion they had shared in Brett's foyer.

Her father's booming voice sounded through the hall. "Brett, we're loading up." Brett tugged at Ryan's arm. "Come on. It'll be fun. When's the last time you had a Fletcher's Corny Dog?"

"Uh…"

"Oh my." Brett put the back of her hand up to Ryan's forehead. "At least tell me you've heard of this delicacy?"

Ryan let out a pent up breath. "Absolutely. I don't live in a cave."

"Brett!"

Brett recognized the urgency in her father's voice. "Come on, non-cave dweller. Let's go."

The Hummer limousine was obscene. As they climbed in, Brett calculated she could fit a half dozen of her little Priuses into the beast of a vehicle and still have room for a few passengers. Her nieces and nephews were running around the perimeter of the lighted dance floor. Leave it to Dad to rent the biggest and the best. Brett was embarrassed at the excess and wondered what Ryan thought about her and her family. *Too late now.* They were headed to the State Fair grounds, and neither one of them had a means of escape.

❖

Ryan took one look at the long line. "I don't mean to be rude, but can't we just get something to eat inside the stadium with everyone else?"

"In a word? No." Brett wedged her way into the small opening as the line inched forward. "They don't serve corny dogs or beer at the game."

"That's crazy. The stadium's located on the fair grounds."

"It is crazy. At least the corny dog part. No beer is an NCAA rule."

"I don't need a beer anyway. I'm working." Work was not the reason Ryan didn't want a beer. Her lack of restraint the last time she drank one with Brett was the true deterrent.

"You're not working yet. I refuse to answer any questions until both of us have a beer and a corny dog."

Ryan sighed. She resigned herself to Brett's wishes. *I can always pour the beer out when she's not looking.* "Fine." She looked at the line again. "I don't mean to keep grilling you, but I don't see anyone walking away from this booth with either beer or corny dogs."

Brett tried not to roll her eyes. How could she be so attracted to someone who had no clue about the real world? She forced any sign of condescension from her voice, but she knew some trace of incredulity remained. "We're in line to buy tickets. Then we get in another line for munchies. Seriously, Ryan, have you never been to the State Fair?" The expression on Ryan's face made her instantly regret her remark.

Brett's question stung. Painful memories stabbed like sharp stakes into the soft spots of Ryan's psyche. Spots Ryan thought were long scabbed over.

Every year, Texas schoolchildren slogged their way through the first six weeks of the fall semester buoyed by the prospect of their first break. Fair Day. They each received a free admission ticket and a day off to attend, but the getting there part was up to them. Ryan remembered the day each year the tickets had been handed out. She always took the ticket even though she knew she would never get to use it. Her parents would never take her, and they wouldn't let her go unchaperoned. Julia had encouraged her to sneak away, but even the enticement of Julia's company wasn't enough for Ryan to risk her parents' wrath. She knew better than to ask her aunt. Chaperone or not, her aunt thought the State Fair was a cesspool of sin and excess, and Ryan's attendance was completely out of the question.

She knew her home life was different than most, but she always did her best to fit in. Once the fair hit town, Ryan read the newspaper religiously for details about the various scheduled activities so she could swap stories with her classmates the morning after Fair Day. Until she met Julia. Julia with her open, easy ways. Julia with her brutal honesty. Julia who would have scoffed at her own parents if they said she couldn't go to the fair, who would have snuck out her bedroom window for a trip to the midway.

No, she couldn't lie to Julia, but she wouldn't cross her parents for her either, at least not by openly defying them. They'd never said she couldn't sleep with Julia, never said she couldn't caress her during a seemingly innocent sleepover, never said she couldn't worship the ground she walked on. Looking back, Ryan had to admit she had walked a crooked line between obedience and defiance. Julia's love was the one thing her parents hadn't realized they needed to guard against, but her love had never been enough to compel Ryan to choose sides.

"Hey, are you okay?"

Ryan looked into eyes full of concern and the visions of Julia from her memory faded into the very real face of Brett whose brow was furrowed and whose stare was penetrating. Ryan saw something other than concern in the emerald green gaze, something familiar.

"Yeah, I'm okay." And strangely enough, she was. Ryan felt the sting of her childhood memories recede. She wasn't a child anymore, subject to the whim of her volatile parents and her stern aunt. Brett wasn't Julia, daring her to be something she wasn't. She was just a colleague, sharing the day with her. Ryan could have a beer, watch the game, eat a corny dog, and no harm would come of any of it. She looked into Brett's eyes and appreciated the frank feeling she saw reflected there even though she didn't entirely understand her reaction. "Let's go get that beer."

At halftime, the interrogation began. "So tell us about your campaign. I assume you'll make an official announcement soon? Any ideas about changes to the office?"

Brett punched her dad in the arm. "One question at a time, nosy. I didn't bring Ryan here to be interrogated."

Brian piped in. "Why did you bring her, sis?" He leaned toward Ryan. "No offense. But seriously, I know Brett came to your last fundraiser, but I'm pretty sure she only came because I promised to buy her dinner after. You two seem like a mismatched pair. Not that we're not happy to see the wayward Logan keeping more respectable company."

During the course of the game, Ryan had become accustomed to the good-natured banter of the Logan family. It had not occurred to her they might wonder why she was present at this traditional family event. They hadn't asked, and Brett hadn't offered any explanation. The Logan family couldn't have made her feel more welcome.

Yet, Brian's comments were laced with innuendo. *Did Brett's family know Brett was gay?* Ryan chided herself. Of course they did. If Ryan could find out with a few clicks of her mouse, then this seemingly close-knit family would know the sexual orientation of one of their own. She searched their expressions, words, and behavior for signs of rejection, but she couldn't detect a trace of judgment. Ryan had never known unconditional love, but she could feel its presence now. Directed at Brett, anyway. As for her, well, that was a different story. If this obviously conservative Logan clan could somehow read her thoughts and discern her cravings for their daughter, their sister, she knew they would turn her out as the pariah she was. As it was, the fact they were questioning her basis for any kind of relationship with Brett was a cause for alarm.

Brett felt the tension in Ryan's body even before she saw the panicked look in her eyes. The angst jumped off her skin in hard waves, and Brett feared it would propel Ryan to leap out of her seat and tear out of the stadium. She resisted her impulse to touch Ryan, to ground her into the moment, sensing even the slightest touch from her would send Ryan over the edge. Instead, she fixed Ryan with her eyes, forcing all the comfort, all the soothing she could muster into a steady gaze. Without breaking eye contact, she answered Brian.

"Ryan and I have a particularly messy case together. We couldn't get plea negotiations wrapped up last week. We had a meeting scheduled for today, but I didn't want to miss the game, so I offered her my extra seat. I figured we could talk about the case in between plays." Brett felt Ryan relax, slightly.

Brian nodded enthusiastically. "Nothing like putting the opposition in close proximity with potential donors to further your own ends." He patted Brett on the back. "Sis, I didn't know you had it in you."

Brett resisted the urge to punch him. *Great.* Now her family thought she was trying to bribe a prosecutor. She instinctively knew Ryan would prefer them think that than that she was Brett's date. What she didn't know was why she was so focused on protecting Ryan. *Because she needs protecting.* Ryan's apprehension about this entire outing had been palpable. Brett didn't understand the source, but she wanted to root it out and banish it, freeing Ryan from the tension that gripped her so tightly. If a little lie and innuendo of her own could accomplish comfort for Ryan, she would happily comply.

❖

Texas won. That simple fact was all Ryan registered from the experience. As over ninety thousand fans flooded out of the Cotton Bowl, she found herself plastered against Brett, the only physical contact they had had during the rest of the game. Before the conversation at halftime, Brett had interacted with her easily, punctuating her words with light touches to Ryan's shoulder, hand, leg, all innocent gestures that an affectionate person might use while sharing conversation with a close relative, friend, or spouse. Their interactions took on a sharper edge after Brian's comments. Brett still sat next to Ryan, but Ryan could feel the invisible barrier between them as Brett took extra care not to be in Ryan's personal space. No more shoulder bumps, no more thigh squeezes, no more hand-grabs, no matter how exciting the play on the field. They sat through the rest of the game like strangers. As much as Ryan hated the claustrophobia of the exiting crowd, she welcomed the chance to feel Brett against her, welcomed the comfort of her closeness.

The Logan clan gathered in their predetermined spot outside the stadium. The crowd around them was even bigger now, filled with regular fairgoers in addition to the football fans. Ryan could see that Gerald Logan was addressing their group, but the music from the band playing nearby made it difficult to hear his words. She glanced around for Brett who had moved a couple feet away from her side and was whispering in her sister-in-law Lori's ear. Ryan stared at them until she finally caught Brett's glance, and mouthed, "What's he saying?" Brett held up a finger, signaling she would fill her in shortly. After a few moments, the Logan crowd splintered into small groups all headed in different directions. The kids toward the midway, strings of tickets grasped in their eager hands. The adults toward the exhibit buildings. Only Brett and Ryan remained.

"The limo doesn't leave for three hours. I told Lori we would catch a cab back to the house."

"We're leaving?" Ryan was genuinely surprised.

"Isn't that what you want?" Brett's tone was even, but Ryan caught the flicker of hurt in her eyes.

I don't know what I want. I want to be close to you. Alone. Ryan knew if she and Brett left now, distance would be more likely. Brett had obviously wanted to share this experience with her. The game, her family, the spectacle of the fair. During the first half of the game, she'd listened as Brett described for the kids all the offbeat foods she was going to eat, most of them fried, including Twinkies, butter, bacon, cheesecake, even peanut butter, jelly, and banana sandwiches. Ryan's usual tendency to be disgusted by such a display of excess was stifled by the pure childlike joy she witnessed on Brett's face as she regaled the attractions of the fair. She found herself wanting to experience all the fair had to offer with Brett as a guide. *I guess I do know what I want after all.* She risked honesty.

"I don't want to leave."

"You don't?"

"I don't." Ryan realized she needed to be more clear. "I want to spend the day with you. Here. At the fair." She stifled the fleet of butterflies in her belly. She had tons of work to do, but she knew that wasn't the source of her anxiety. She was both excited and scared about being alone with Brett.

Brett's face sported a wide grin. "Excellent." She pulled a folded up piece of paper from her back pocket. "I'm giving you one last chance to back out."

"I'm not backing out."

Brett waved the paper under Ryan's nose. "We'll still need a cab later, because three hours is not enough time to make it through my list."

Ryan grabbed the list from Brett's grasp and glanced at the numerous items. "What's a Crazy Mouse? Pig Races? *Fried butter?*" She gave Brett a stern look. "You know that's wrong, don't you?" Ryan laughed at the responding pout. "Come on, show me the fair."

CHAPTER SEVENTEEN

I can't believe you're making me exercise at the State Fair."
Brett quit pedaling and crossed her arms. What she really
couldn't believe was that she was sitting in a swan-shaped pedal boat
in the middle of the Leonhardt Lagoon. Brett couldn't remember the
last time she'd spent an entire day at play. After the game, she'd
checked in with her answering service, then she turned off the
ringer on her BlackBerry and stowed it in her purse. Ryan had been
an engaging companion. She'd indulged every one of Brett's fair
favorites with good humor. Brett was having so much fun she forgot
all about her muted connection to the outside world. Amazing, since
she usually checked her phone at least every fifteen minutes even
when she was on a date.

"We've done everything on your list. Now it's my turn." Ryan's
strong legs provided power enough for both of them, and she was
having the time of her life steering them around the smallish body
of water. Ryan was thankful for the relief from consuming fried food
and welcomed the opportunity to work off the pounds of fattening
food she'd put away during the day. "Lean back and relax. I've got
this."

Brett did as instructed, watching Ryan all the while. She looked
happy. Brett realized she'd never seen Ryan look happy before.
Intense, focused, driven, but never happy. Maybe Ryan reserved
pleasure for personal time. Whatever the case, Brett was glad Ryan
had chosen to share some of that personal time with her.

"What do you do for fun?" Ryan seemed startled at the question, and Brett immediately wished she'd just let the moment be. "Never mind. It's none of my business. We just had so much fun today, I almost forgot the real reason we're supposed to be spending time together. We can talk about the case whenever you want. If you want to leave—"

Ryan interrupted her rambling. "Nothing."

"What?"

"I don't do anything for fun."

Brett would have said the same about Ryan as a joke, but she never thought it was true. "Seriously?"

"Seriously."

"What do you do in your free time?" Maybe Ryan's idea of fun was just slightly different from hers.

"Work out. Visit my aunt. Read case law. Pretty pathetic, don't you think?"

"A little." Brett ducked to avoid the teasing punch Ryan threw her way. "How about dating?" She saw Ryan's open expression start to shut tight.

"What about it?"

Brett evaluated her options. Veer away from the subject and recapture the casual intimacy they had shared all day, or dive in and hope neither one of them drowned. She decided she wanted the information enough to take the risk. She took a deep breath. "Just curious." She saw Ryan relax slightly and decided to take a more circuitous path. "I have a hard time finding time to date or anyone willing to date a workaholic. You?"

"I don't date."

"So we have something in common."

"Ever."

"Excuse me?"

"It's not just that I don't date. It's that I never have." Ryan couldn't believe she'd shared this fact, especially with someone like Brett. Attorneys were born to interrogate, but it wasn't as if Brett were exerting a lot of pressure. Her guard must be down. *Too late now.* What she wasn't prepared for was the silence that followed her revelation. She waited, but Brett said nothing. Ryan saw a mixture of pity and sadness reflected in her eyes. She wanted neither. "I'm ready to head back." She leaned forward, pumping her thighs and driving her feet hard against the pedals. Ryan looked away from Brett to hide the blur of tears in her eyes. She didn't see Brett's hand move onto her thigh, but she felt the pressure of her touch. "Don't."

Brett held her tighter. "I won't do anything you don't want me to."

"I don't know what I want." A necessary lie.

As if she could read her mind, Brett pressed. "I think you do. I think we want the same thing."

"It doesn't matter. It can't happen."

"I don't believe you've never dated. I think you have. I think someone hurt you."

Ryan now knew why Brett was such a good attorney. She could read minds and people couldn't resist her. "Yes."

"You don't have to tell me, but if you want to I'm a good listener." Brett paused. "And I care. I really do."

"Why?"

"Because I find myself hopelessly attracted to you." Brett looked down at her hand on Ryan's thigh and smiled. "And not just to your fantastic body."

"You shouldn't."

"Can't help it. Tell me you don't feel something for me and I'll leave you alone."

Ryan knew if she denied the attraction, Brett would know she was a liar. The scene in Brett's foyer foreclosed any conclusion to the contrary. "You know how I feel."

"I know you're physically attracted to me. I can only hope you're attracted to me for other reasons as well."

Ryan nodded.

"Well, that's something." Brett cocked her head. "Let me guess, you don't like the way it makes you feel."

Ryan shook her head. "It's not that simple."

"Okay."

"I have a campaign to think about. You're a witness in a case." Ryan knew the excuses were lame. She braced herself for a retort.

"I could say you're a chicken, at least when it comes to the campaign. You'd rather be an elected Republican than have a relationship?" Brett knew she was jumping to conclusions. Ryan had barely confessed an attraction, let alone a desire for a relationship, but her own desires compelled her to push the boundaries.

"As for me being a witness, well, that should be over within a couple of weeks." Brett knew something deeper lurked beneath the surface of Ryan's reluctance, but she wasn't entirely sure she wanted to be the one to unearth the issue. Ryan saved her the trouble.

"I've only felt this way about one other person in my whole life."

"Bad breakup?"

"The worst. We were in high school."

"Ah. High school romances are the worst. And the best. They definitely leave a lasting impression." All Brett's internal alarms were ringing. *She hasn't been with anyone since high school?* Brett tried not to dwell on the more significant truth behind Ryan's revelation, but she couldn't help but wonder if Ryan would ever recover if she hadn't after all these years. She decided to ask more questions in lieu of mulling over the meaning. She'd start with the basics. "Girl?"

"Her name was Julia." Ryan choked out a laugh devoid of humor. "I'm sure it still is."

"What was she like?"

"A free spirit. Beautiful. Independent. Beautiful. Brilliant." Ryan leaned back and closed her eyes. "Did I mention she was beautiful?"

Brett smiled. "I get the picture. So what happened?"

"I was too chicken."

"Sorry. I didn't mean to call you chicken before. I realize everyone has their own comfort level about revealing personal information."

"But you think I hide things to further my career?"

Brett had no intention of letting this conversation dissolve into a discussion of political correctness. She was interested in Ryan's personal intentions, not her professional ones. "The girl, Ryan. Tell what happened with the girl."

"She loved me. I loved her. But our love didn't come without conditions. For either of us. She wanted me to be more like her. I was too uptight, too frightened about what other people would think, too scared of what my parents might do if they found out about us. She pushed me to do things outside of my comfort zone. I pushed her to be more discreet.

"I wasn't kidding about never dating. I never went anywhere with Julia in public, not on a date anyway. Ironically, if I had, I might have avoided my worst nightmare." Brett was quiet. This time Ryan recognized it for what it was. Space. She needed it. She'd never talked about Julia with anyone. The last time she'd spoken her name out loud had been the last time in her life she'd lost control.

That day her parents came home a day early from an emergency out of town trip and found her and Julia on Ryan's bed, half-dressed and tangled in each other's arms. The Fosters had reluctantly agreed to let Ryan stay at Julia's house that weekend since they hadn't had time to make other arrangements. Ryan convinced Julia this was a perfect chance for them to be together, and they didn't need to be in public to show their love. They snuck into Ryan's house where they would explore their love in private. Their privacy was short-lived, and their intimacy was marred by Ryan's parents' condemnation of what they called vile and reprehensible behavior. They sent Julia home. Ryan, they packed into the car and drove to live with her aunt. Ryan had wailed the whole way, anguished cries of desperation laced with pleas of understanding. All her efforts were ignored. She never saw Julia again. Never spoke her name.

She vowed she would never lose control of her emotions again.

Ryan had managed to keep that vow until she met Brett. From the day she'd watched her in court, to their passionate embrace at Brett's apartment, to this day, spent sneaking glances and light touches, Ryan's control had been slowly, steadily slipping away.

Brett watched the emotions play out on Ryan's face. Feelings too coarse to process, even after all these years. She didn't have any personal frame of reference. She'd always been confident about being out. Her parents weren't necessarily happy about it, but they spent too much time encouraging their children to be independent to really put up a fuss. Frankly, her father was more concerned about her chosen field of practice than who she slept with. She was always encouraged to bring a date along to family affairs, but Brett hadn't brought many into the Logan circle. Either she didn't care enough to go through the introductions, or she didn't want to add another voice to the chorus telling her she should have a job with more regular hours and less angst. Since most of her former girlfriends had this litany down, she found it easier to keep them at a distance when it came to her family.

She almost envied Ryan her heart-wrenching memories. At least Ryan had the capacity to care about something other than the cases she worked on. Brett often wondered if her ability to muster feelings about people other than her clients was stifled by the energy she threw into her work. But her feelings about Ryan weren't stifled. As much as Ryan had the tendency to infuriate her, she cared what she thought, how she felt, what she needed. Right now, she could tell Ryan needed understanding, compassion, space. Brett was going to give her all three.

"Look, I'm sorry I brought up such a difficult subject." Ryan started to protest, but Brett held up a hand. "Don't get me wrong. I want to know more." She stared into Ryan's eyes and ran her hand slightly higher on her leg. "And I want more. But I can wait." She moved her hand back to her own lap. "Let's get through this trial, and we'll pick up where we left off. Okay?"

Ryan wanted to say waiting wouldn't solve anything. The campaign would still be an insurmountable obstacle, but Brett had already heard that excuse. Even if she didn't win the nomination, her career couldn't withstand an affair with a prominent defense attorney, let alone a woman. She wanted to reaffirm her vow to never risk losing control again, but she was no longer confident she could keep the promise of her past.

CHAPTER EIGHTEEN

Monday, after lunch, Brett poked her head in Jeff Oates's office in the DA workroom. He wasn't there, but Detective Paulson was sitting at his desk, sorting through the files spread out in front of her. She looked up and smiled at Brett. "Come on in."

"That's okay, I was looking for Jeff."

"I know. He's expecting you." She waved Brett toward an open chair.

Brett continued standing. "Any idea when he'll be back?" For some reason she couldn't quite explain, Brett didn't want to be trapped in the tiny room with Kim Paulson. She was there to see Jeff for her witness prep. She still thought it was unlikely she'd even be needed as a witness, but she understood that Jeff and Ryan would want to prepare for any contingency.

After Saturday, she and Ryan had agreed all Brett's contact with the DA's office about the Edwards case would go through Jeff. Brett had spent several hours the day before conducting research on the potential ethical issues of appearing as a witness for the state in light of her attraction to Ryan. Ryan had done the same. It was a gray area. They weren't in a relationship. Even if they were, it wasn't necessarily unethical for her to be a witness as long as they disclosed the existence of the relationship. As things stood, Brett determined there was nothing for them to disclose, but for the sake of propriety, she agreed with Ryan that all her interaction with the prosecution should be through Jeff. She imagined Jeff was ecstatic to learn two key witnesses for the state had reverted back to his control.

"I'm sure he'll be back soon. I think he just went downstairs to grab a sandwich," Paulson said. "How was your weekend?"

Brett resigned herself to taking a seat. "It was good. Thanks."

"Do you go to the game every year?"

"Pardon me?"

"I think it's great your whole family goes to the game together."

Brett's thoughts spun. She wasn't processing fast enough to respond. How did Paulson know she'd been at the game? Okay, maybe Paulson had seen her there, but how did she know that the people with her were family? Had she seen her with Ryan? Maybe Ryan told her? Brett recalled the undercurrent of hostility she'd detected between them at her apartment. No, there was no way Ryan would have mentioned her attendance at the game with Brett to anyone, let alone Paulson. She decided to do some detecting of her own.

"Are you a Texas or OU fan?"

"I'm Switzerland." Paulson laughed at her own joke. Brett didn't, but Paulson didn't seem to care that Brett didn't find her amusing. "I graduated from Texas Tech. Go Raiders."

Brett tried again. "I guess you saw me at the fair Saturday."

"We decided it would be a good idea to keep an eye on you. For your own protection."

"We?"

"Mike and I."

"Is that so? I thought you had Ross Edwards safely behind bars?"

"Yes, but his female accomplice has never been apprehended. Until she is, you might be in danger for exposing this part of their scheme."

Brett seriously doubted Ross Edwards's girlfriend was anywhere near the action. She'd probably taken off the minute he got caught and was looking for her next partner-in-crime. She focused instead on the fact Paulson had been tailing her. "When did you start following me around?"

"You make it sound so clandestine."

"It is. I can't have law enforcement tailing me. I have client confidences to protect. A fact you are well aware of. My clients won't feel comfortable coming in to see me if cops are parked outside my door."

"See many clients on the weekend?"

"Matter of fact I do."

"Hi, ladies." They looked up as Jeff entered the room. Paulson got up from her place behind his desk and grabbed another chair from the outside office. When she returned to Jeff's closet-like office with the extra seat, Brett started to feel claustrophobic.

"Jeff, can we do this somewhere else?" Brett pointed at the boxes lying nearby. "You don't want your witness tripping over evidence and ruining her favorite suit, do you?"

He gave her a sheepish grin. "Sorry. I guess it is a little crowded in here. Tell you what, it's a nonjury week." He referred to certain prescheduled times during the year when no jury trials were scheduled in order to allow the court to take care of administrative matters. "The jury room should be free. I'll ask the bailiff."

Brett stood. She didn't want to be stuck in the room alone with Paulson again. "No, you eat your sandwich. I'll check on the room. Be right back."

Brett exited the workroom and nearly ran into Jake Simmons in the entryway to the courtroom. "Hi Jake, how're you doing?"

"I'm fine, considering."

Brett could tell by his tone that fine was a relative term. "What's up?"

"Seems like lately everything you want me to look into has me going up against a brick wall."

"Is that so?"

"I don't like brick walls."

Brett knew him well enough to know he wasn't frustrated with her, but rather with his own inability to gather information. She waited.

"That girl, Ann Rawlings?"

Brett nodded for him to continue.

"She's in a lot of trouble. I don't mean legal trouble."

"Care to share?"

"Yes." He inclined his head toward the DA workroom doors. "But not right here. Actually, I think it would be best if we went to see her together."

"I don't know if I can break away to get to the jail this afternoon." Brett had an idea. "Gloria owes me a favor. Maybe I can get her to bring Ann over this afternoon. The judge is at a conference so nothing's going on. We should have the holdover all to ourselves."

"I'll be nearby. Just give me a shout and I'll stop back over whenever you're ready." Jake left without another word. Brett was beyond curious about what had him so concerned, but she knew if it was something time sensitive he would have told her. He was a man of few words and probably just figured it would be easier to reveal whatever he had learned to both Brett and Ann together rather than repeat the story twice. She shook her head and went to check on the jury room.

❖

Ryan looked at her watch. Again. Brett was meeting with Jeff, and she desperately wanted to be there. Not because of the case.

These feelings were so out of character, but Ryan was starting to slow down long enough to try them on and see if she could make them fit comfortably. She hadn't reached comfort yet, but rather a heady mix of angst and craving.

She looked at the papers on her desk and willed herself to focus. Despite their agreement to wait till after the trial to engage in anything personal, Ryan had called Brett the day before, mere hours after they had parted on Saturday night. Ostensibly, it had been a professional call. They discussed the ethical issues about Brett being called as a state's witness by a prosecutor who wanted to get in her pants. The situation gave Brett more pause than it did Ryan, and Ryan tried to see Brett's point of view.

"If I were a defense attorney, I'd want to know the prosecutor had shared an intimate lip lock with a state's witness."

"I suppose I can see that, but there are a lot of things Edwards's attorney would like to know that I'm not legally or ethically required to tell him."

"It doesn't feel right."

Ryan felt her defenses click into place. *"Are you saying you plan to tell him?"*

"No. Frankly, it's your duty to disclose if there's anything that needs to be disclosed."

"I can tell you right now, I'm not telling him anything."

Brett's voice was a balm to her rising anger. *"Hey, sweetheart, don't be angry. I just want to talk it through to make sure we're doing the right thing."*

Ryan was silent while she absorbed Brett words. Sweetheart? It was the kind of casual endearment she had heard Brett use with others, but directed at her it felt more than casual. It felt loving. She sighed. Perhaps this little exercise was necessary after all. *"Okay, let's talk it through."*

"Thanks. Now for starters, under what circumstances would you feel you needed to disclose a relationship between a prosecutor and a witness?"

Ryan thought for a moment. *"Definitely if they were married. Maybe even living together."*

"The DA's office has rules about whether a prosecutor can work on a case with a defense attorney if they are related or are in a relationship, right?"

"Right, but when they aren't in a legally defined relationship, the rules are kind of gray. Basically, if the relationship is such that your obligations to your partner might outweigh your duty to prosecute the case, then you shouldn't work on the case."

"I've looked at this and I think that's the rule that applies to this situation as well."

"Then we have nothing to disclose."

Brett sighed. *"I suppose you're right. I certainly don't feel obligated to say something that isn't true out of some obligation to you."*

No, you shouldn't feel obligated to me at all. Ryan had left the obvious unspoken. No, Brett had no obligations toward her at all. And, although they had decided to wait until the trial was over to explore any possibilities for something personal, she didn't hold out any hope the removal of their self-imposed barrier would have any effect on whether they could have a chance at more.

❖

Brett sat close to Jeff and as far away from Paulson as she could get. They had reviewed everything she knew, which wasn't much, several times, but Paulson kept interjecting questions and asking Brett to repeat what she knew.

"The first communication I received was by e-mail." Brett handed over a piece of paper. "Here's a copy. As you can see, there's no signature."

"How many times did he e-mail you?"

Brett chose her words carefully. "Whoever it was e-mailed me four times."

"We're going to need to work on how you phrase your answers," Jeff said, "'Whoever it was'?"

"Ah, that's the point I've been trying to get across. I think you're going to have trouble getting my testimony in at all, at least with regard to these e-mails and phone calls."

"How do you figure?"

"What I have to say isn't relevant. I don't know who was sending me e-mails or who was calling me. And the content of those e-mails and phone calls is hearsay."

"Not necessarily," Jeff responded.

"How do you plan to prove what was said was said by Ross Edwards?"

Paulson interjected. "Why does he have to? Seems pretty clear from the phone and e-mail records he was communicating with you."

"You can't offer a statement that was made out of court into evidence at trial. There are some exceptions to that rule, and one of them is that the statement was made by the defendant, but the state has the burden of proving the statements were made by Edwards. If you have the very e-mail he sent me from his computer, you might get there with the e-mails, but the phone calls were where most of the details were conveyed. If I were the defense attorney, I'd be objecting all over the place that you can't prove that my unknown caller was Ross Edwards."

"Then I guess we're lucky Luke is trying this case, not you," Jeff said.

"If he asks to talk to me, I'm going to sit down with him. Tell him everything I know."

"I'd expect you to. I don't want to interfere with his ability to review the evidence. Once we tell him what it is." He grinned. "I would appreciate it if you wouldn't feel compelled to give him legal advice."

"Ross Edwards isn't my client. Despite what you may think, I don't feel like I need to defend the world. Just the people who come to me for help. Ross Edwards is not one of those people. I'll tell the truth. Nothing more, nothing less."

"Perfect." Jeff picked up his list of questions. "I'm confident Judge Langston will give us a fair hearing on the hearsay issue. We'll establish that based on the timing and circumstances of the phone calls you received in combination with Edwards's phone records, your testimony is probative and relevant. You don't need to worry about how we plan to get the evidence admitted. Just tell the truth and we'll take it from there."

Jeff sounded extremely confident, but Brett had a sinking feeling nothing about this case was going to be as easy as he thought.

CHAPTER NINETEEN

The first thing Brett noticed was Ann Rawlings wasn't doing well. Her carefully manicured nails were chipped and her hair was limp and dull. Brett wondered if her psyche was in worse shape as well and whether her condition might render her more willing to talk about her case.

"Ann, this is Jake Simmons. He's an investigator who works for me. I asked him to join us here today."

"I don't understand."

Brett was hopeful. At least she said something. "I reviewed the police report and I have some questions."

Ann sighed. "I can't tell you much."

"Can't or won't?" Jake asked.

Ann's jaw was set and she averted her eyes. Brett took her turn at getting her to cooperate. "We're here to help you. Jake works for me, so anything you tell either him or me is protected by attorney-client privilege." *Your secret's safe with me.*

"You don't understand."

"We might understand better than you think."

Jake had pulled Brett aside before they entered the holdover to meet with Ann. He laid out the basic facts. The location where Ann had been arrested was a luxury townhome, now vacant, but still furnished. The upscale North Dallas location of the townhome was an unusual location for a prostitution arrest. Even more unusual was a vice sting conducted in the wealthy neighborhood. The ownership of the building was a tightly woven and well layered secret, but after calling in some favors, Jake had managed to trace at least a partial interest back to the top law enforcement official in Dallas, Leonard Duncan.

Brett didn't have a clue what to do with that piece of information. Her only inclination was to dig deeper, but her instincts told her to do so could be perilous. She decided to start with her client and find out what she could, but she knew whatever she found, the implications ranged far beyond this particular case. The notes from the police report rang alarm bells in her head. *Wild sex party.* If her beginning suspicions were true, that the DA was somehow involved with this case, Brett wondered why that particular statement had made it into the final report.

She started with a direct approach. "Ann, I need to know who you were working for."

"I don't know."

Brett noted her demeanor and decided she was telling the truth, in some respect, at least. "But you have some ideas?"

Ann nodded.

"Can you tell how your, um, arrangement came to be?"

Silence.

Jake assumed a fatherly role. He hunched down and placed his hand on Ann's knee. "You seem like a real sweet young lady. I don't know how you got in this mess, but I'm here to tell you what I know. This lady," he jerked a thumb in Brett's direction, "She's the best there is. If anyone can help you out of the mess you're in, she can." He paused and gazed into Ann's eyes, neither one of them blinking. "You wanna know how I know?" He didn't wait for her to answer. "My daughter, my only daughter, she got herself into serious trouble. I raised her to know right from wrong. She had everything she could possibly want or need, but she fell in with a bad crowd. Next thing you know, she was wearing a jumpsuit like you're wearing, sitting in a federal prison, looking at the possibility of spending the rest of her life behind bars." He glanced at Brett again, then back to Ann. "Ms. Logan saved her life. If you give her a chance, she can save yours."

Brett watched the interaction between them. While she wouldn't have made such grand promises on her own, she wondered if Jake's words would open the vault of information Ann had locked down tight.

"It was supposed to be a modeling job."

Brett held back a sigh at the clichéd non sequitur. She nodded for Ann to continue.

"They provided us with clothes. They took pictures of us. At first, it seemed like a great opportunity."

Brett wanted to know who the "they" was, but she also wanted to keep Ann talking so she started with more subtle questions. "Did it appear that anyone lived in the townhome, or was it just a studio?"

"I don't think anyone lived there. The first time I was there, the photographer had a professional setup. He took what he said were going to be our portfolio shots."

"And later?"

"Later things changed. The photos they took were spontaneous, action shots."

Brett took the hint. "You were working then?"

"I went there because it was a good paying modeling job." Ann's voice rose slightly as she showed emotion about her situation for the first time since Brett had met her. Brett already had a pretty good idea about how it had all gone down, but she still wanted to hear, in Ann's own words, how she'd been persuaded to sell her body.

"I'm not here to judge you."

Ann's guarded expression told Brett she wasn't convinced.

"I need to know everything if I'm going to help you."

"They brought people in to meet us. Important, rich, pretty people. These people were supposed to be well connected in the fashion and film industries. We were supposed to make them feel welcome, let them get to know us. 'Network for future opportunities' is what they said."

"And?"

"We networked. They asked for hospitality. We gave them all the hospitality they could handle. Several of us were allowed to stay at the townhouse and we were expected to entertain whenever they brought guests over." Ann's tone was bitter, and Brett didn't need to ask for clarification. She could only imagine the sexual favors these naïve model wannabes had to perform to further their careers. As Ann described the encounters, Brett's anger grew. All the "models" were dressed in white to signal to the party guests their availability, if not willingness, to provide private entertainment. Ann recognized a few of the guests from local publications and she soon realized that the invitations included many local dignitaries and even a state senator.

Parties were also held in various other locations around the area, always in private homes. Ann never saw money change hands, but she and the others were paid well for their services. Payments laced with many strings. Silence, loyalty, servitude.

"Why did you stay?" The moment the words left her lips, Brett wished she hadn't asked the question since Ann probably didn't have a logical answer. Ann surprised her.

"I didn't have a choice." Her words were strong and clear, and for the first time, Ann faced Brett and stared directly into her eyes. Brett read every signal, including powerful desire to survive. Ann Rawlings had stayed because she feared for her life. Certainly that was the reason she hadn't hired her own lawyer or confided in Brett the first time they met.

"Tell me about this other girl." Brett glanced at her notes. "Heather. Tell me how you met her."

"I barely knew her. She came to the house the day before I was arrested. She was just another model. I had no idea she was only sixteen, but I don't know what I would have done if I had known. Probably nothing. She was just like me. Looking for work. We had plenty to share."

"What happened the night you were arrested?"

"One of the guests from a previous party came by the house earlier in the day. I don't know his name. We didn't use names with guests. He said he wanted to arrange a more intimate gathering. He pointed out Heather and asked me to arrange for her, myself, and one other girl to be available for a few select guests that evening. He offered triple what we usually made and paid half up front. Compared to our usual arrangements, lots of guests, okay money, this seemed like a perfect situation."

Brett decided to venture her first probing question. "Who usually arranged the parties?"

"We call him Al, but I doubt that's his real name. He's the one who I met when I responded to the ad for a model. He introduced me to several other people, men and women, but I don't remember their names. Then, when I started attending the parties, I learned to stop using names altogether. I can barely remember the names of the others who lived at the townhome. It was easier to adjust to the rules if we obeyed them even when we didn't have to."

Brett nudged her back into the story. "So you were present for this more intimate party. What happened?"

"Most of the others were at another location for the evening. Three guests showed up at the house with the one who had paid us the money. He said one of them was only there to watch. Heather, Ginger, and I were just beginning to pair off with them when the cops busted in and arrested us."

"What about the guests?"

"I don't know. The cops took us to jail in a van, but only us three."

"Do you know any of the guests at the private party?"

"Except for the one who made the arrangements, I had never seen them before."

"Men or women?"

"Both."

"Would you recognize them if you saw them again?"

"Absolutely."

Brett signaled to Jake who had been watching the exchange between them in silence. She had asked him to find a photo of Leonard Duncan to show Ann. She was dying to know if one of the mystery guests had been the powerful man himself. She forced herself to wait for the answer as Jake pulled a brochure from his suit pocket and handed it to Ann. "Take a look at the picture on the back cover. Do you recognize that man?" Jake asked.

Ann held the brochure in both hands as she studied the photo. From where she was sitting, Brett could see the front cover and registered irony when she realized the document Ann was holding was a brochure detailing the accomplishments of Ryan Foster. Leonard's enthusiastic endorsement must be located, along with his photo, on the back cover.

Ann finally spoke. "Yes. He was there that night. He was going to a room with Heather when the cops broke in." She glanced back at the brochure. "He's the DA?"

Brett nodded. She could tell Ann knew how that truth complicated matters. Brett made a mental note to ask Jake to check for arrests of johns at the same location that night. She knew he wouldn't find any. It was likely the "guests" were safely whisked away while the expendable models/prostitutes took the fall.

Jake's discovery that Leonard was a part owner in the house, along with the fact he had attended at least one sex party there was mind-blowing. Brett didn't have a clue how the pieces of the puzzle fit together, but at least she had pieces to work with instead of a blank slate. She needed some time to process, on her own, without her client's worries clouding her ability to think.

"Ann, thanks for opening up. I'm going to check on some things and I'll be in touch. Jake probably has a few more questions for you. Tell him everything." Brett stood to exit the holdover and she held out a hand. Ann seemed to mistake Brett's offer of a handshake for a request to return the brochure and shoved the paper toward Brett, flipping it over in the process. Brett noted Ryan's gorgeous campaign photo centered on the cover and wondered if Ryan had a clue about her mentor's involvement in a prostitution ring. *Doubtful.*

"Who is that? Does she work for the DA?"

Brett looked up. Ann was pointing at Ryan's photo. She opened her mouth to answer, but a twisting pain gripped her belly. Ann's expression was a mixture of recognition, fear, and resignation. Brett stalled the inevitable with a question. "Do you know her?"

"I've seen her."

"At the townhouse?" Brett asked hesitantly. She knew once she started down this line of questioning, she would have to go all the way.

"No."

Brett sighed with relief, but before she could ask a follow-up question, Ann added, "Not at the townhouse, but at the other parties. She's a VIP guest."

Chapter Twenty

Ryan had abandoned the office hours before. She knew Brett was still at the courthouse. She'd seen her Prius still parked in the garage early in the afternoon. She didn't know if Brett was still meeting with Jeff and the detectives, but since her desire to find out was so strong, she decided to distance herself to lessen the temptation to interrupt. She spent an hour at the gym and then headed home to work without distractions.

The workout helped drain some of her pent up energy, but her focus was fractured and had been ever since Saturday. Since Julia, Ryan hadn't shared any truly personal information about herself with another human being. For years, she stuffed her feelings, longings, and regrets deep inside. Sharing even a little bit with Brett had created an unstoppable force. She tried to squeeze the cap back on, but the prospect of a true connection with another person caused her emotions to expand. She could no longer fit her emotions back into a sense of order. Ryan made resolutions in order to buy back her ability to focus. *When this case is over, I will...* She wasn't ready to fill in the blank, but she knew that whatever action she took when this case was over, it would involve Brett. She had to wait just a bit longer to explore the intense attraction. She would need the added time anyway to figure out how to work around the obstacles.

For now, she sat at her dining room table, files spread across the table. Kenneth and Brett would be Jeff's witnesses, but she would put on the expert testimony designed to tie Edwards to the scheme to divert attention from his guilt. She spent several hours culling through the appropriate phone and e-mail records and drafting a chart to illustrate the connections to the jury. For most lawyers, the work would be tedious and boring, but Ryan recognized the beauty of having evidence in black and white, displayed on a big screen, for the jury to review over and over again. Charts admitted into evidence would go back to the jury room and would be more powerful persuaders during deliberations than the faded memories of witness testimony.

She became so engrossed in her work the loud chime of the doorbell startled her. She lived in a neighborly area but didn't cultivate the kind of relationships that welcomed uninvited guests to her door. Solicitors were rare. She was tempted not to answer, but she had gathered the mail about thirty minutes before. If the person at the door was a neighbor who had seen her and knew she was home, she didn't want to risk offending him or her. The cursed campaign meant she had to consider such things.

The last person she expected to see when she cracked her door was Brett Logan. She recovered quickly from her surprise and smiled broadly. "Hi. I was just thinking about you. Did you finish with Jeff?" Ryan was so glad to see Brett she forgot to care how much she hated unexpected guests, or guests at all. "Come in."

"I don't think so."

Ryan stepped back and looked into Brett's eyes, registering anger mixed with something else. *Loathing?* Ryan was confused.

Brett had left the holdover and gone directly to Jeff's office looking for Ryan. When he said she was working from home, Brett left the courthouse, got into her car, and drove directly to Ryan's house. Now that she was here, standing on Ryan's porch, she didn't have a clue what to say or why she had bothered to make the trip. She didn't want to enter, but she didn't want to throttle Ryan on her doorstep, which is what she was likely to do if she stood there much longer with anger surging inside her. Ryan stood in front of her, seemingly oblivious to her mental machinations. She was dressed more casually than Brett had ever seen her, in denim cut-offs and a Harvard hoodie. Brett wouldn't have thought Ryan would have owned anything so casual. She was barefoot. Her hair was loose and slightly wild. She wore only a touch of makeup. Brett didn't recognize this woman. *How ironic.*

"On second thought, I will come in."

Ryan didn't say a word. She pulled the door back to allow Brett entrance, glancing up and down the street before shutting it tight. When she turned around Brett was fuming.

"Who do you think you are?"

"Excuse me?"

"It's a simple question. Either you're a person who obeys the law and prosecutes those who don't, or you are a hypocrite." Brett could tell Ryan had no idea what she was talking about. She didn't care. She may not have agreed with Ryan's black and white view of the world, but at least she could respect her for having convictions and standing by them. Now that she knew Ryan was a preferred customer in an exclusive prostitution enterprise, her respect was shattered along with all the intimate feelings she had for her. If Ryan's sexual escapades weren't enough, Brett now knew Ryan was duplicitous as well. Ryan's words reverberated. *"I'll run this through the grand jury myself. It's time we stopped prostitution at the source."*

"Brett, I don't understand what you're—" Ryan's words were cut short by the hard press of Brett's lips against hers. Brett's tongue fought for entrance and claimed Ryan with firm, forceful strokes. Brett's car keys hit the floor with a sharp crack, and suddenly her hands were all over Ryan's body, roughly tearing at her clothes. Within seconds, Ryan felt her shorts drop to the ground and Brett's fingers dug at her naked flesh. She groaned instinctively at the insistent touch, even as she sensed Brett's true goal had nothing to do with pleasure. She longed to surrender to the ecstasy, but she couldn't until she was certain Brett was motivated by something other than the desire to control. Arching away, Ryan reached for Brett's chin and slid her hand along her cheekbone. She looked at Brett's forehead, creased with anger, and shuddered. "Look at me."

Brett's eyes opened and gazed at her, questioning.

"Why are you doing this? You clearly don't want to."

"Interesting how that works, isn't it?" Brett's voice dripped sarcasm.

"What?" Ryan knew she was missing signals, but she couldn't wrap her head around Brett's actions.

"Next time you're having sex with someone, think about whether they chose to be with you or whether they just don't feel like they have any other choice."

Ryan's mind spun. One minute Brett was passionate, the next she was full of disdain. Ryan didn't know what Brett expected, but she desperately wanted to. "Brett, I don't understand what you're trying to say. If we could just sit down and talk."

Brett bent for her car keys and strode to the door. "You want to talk? No thanks. I heard your last sad story and bought every line. That won't happen again. When you're ready to talk about Ann Rawlings let me know. Until then, stay the hell away from me."

❖

Brett picked up the demitasse Tony placed on her desk and drained it. "More?"

"If you drink any more of that black tar, you'll never get to sleep tonight." Tony cocked his head and squinted at her. "I think working on cases that don't pay well is sucking the life out of you."

"I recall asking for coffee, not advice," Brett snapped.

"Get your own coffee. I stopped being your lackey long ago. If you want a servant, look elsewhere." Tony turned and started toward Brett's office door.

Brett knew she'd crossed the line. They often had good-natured spats, but she'd been a bitch all afternoon. She wasn't surprised Tony was tired of putting up with her.

"Wait! Please."

He stopped.

"I'm sorry."

"And?"

"And?"

"I'm waiting for some explanation for why you're acting like such an ass. I'd just as soon you hadn't come back to the office at all today if whatever happened at the courthouse has you so out of sorts."

"I have a problem. Actually, I have a series of related problems, and I don't have a clue what to do."

"Personal or professional?"

"Both."

"Ah. Seems complicated. Do you want to talk?"

"Yes. And no." Brett laid her head on her desk. She wanted to talk, but she needed time to process before she would even know where to start. "I think I need to get a better handle on the situation before I can even articulate the issue. Does that make sense?"

"Sure it does." Tony walked back to her desk and picked up the demitasse. "Maybe some espresso will help. If it doesn't, know I'm always here for you."

"I know, T. Thanks." Brett watched him leave the room. She wanted to leave. Get in her car and drive far away from all the work sitting on her desk. Far away from this case. Far away from Ryan Foster.

She didn't know what to do. The ethical issue she and Ryan had discussed the day before seemed inconsequential compared to the dilemma she faced over what to do about Ann Rawlings's case. She knew she needed to take some action, but she was paralyzed. The truth was she just couldn't wrap her mind around the image of Ryan as a patron at a sex party. Ryan, of all people. Straitlaced Ryan Foster. Who was she kidding? Straitlaced Ryan Foster who growled like a tigress when kissed while her body responded with raging fervor and passion.

Maybe she could imagine that Ryan Foster. Maybe the duality was part of the attraction that made Ryan Foster the woman Brett couldn't stop thinking about, who made her heart race, who she would have to learn to forget.

❖

Ryan waited till nine o'clock to enter the building. She had been itching to get into the courthouse since the moment Brett left her house, but she needed privacy. Monday night during a nonjury week would provide her with the freedom to find what she needed.

She spread Ann Rawlings's file on her desk. She didn't see any of Cindy's notes and wondered if Cindy had even reviewed the file since Ryan had flagged it.

Ryan took her time reading the police report. The address was vaguely familiar, but she couldn't quite place it. She typed the street address into Google and within seconds, a map appeared. She could recite the likely geographic areas for a prostitution arrest in Dallas, but this wasn't one of them. No, this location was more likely to serve as a site for a well-heeled campaign fundraiser.

I don't get it. Ryan scanned the narrative on the police report. Rawlings was arrested following a 911 call reporting a "wild sex party." Ryan reread the words and her gut started to churn. She looked at the address. She never wrote down any of the addresses. Ever. She memorized them as they were read to her. She took deep, calming breaths. She had an excellent memory. She did not remember this address. There was no connection.

Her eyes kept roving back to the phrase "wild sex party." She wouldn't characterize the events she attended with those words. Not exactly. The parties she attended were not wild. They were calm, distinguished affairs. No drugs were allowed and alcohol intake was moderate, a strictly enforced rule. Sex took place behind closed doors, not in a sprawling mass of bodies draped all over the living room furniture, and all activities were between consenting adults.

"Next time you're having sex with someone, think about whether they chose to be with you or whether they just don't feel like they have any other choice."

Ryan flashed back to Brett's words. Ann Rawlings was charged with compelling prostitution. She had a minor working for her. Ryan shook her head. She sensed Brett's words were a clue as to why she was angry, but she just didn't get it.

She reviewed the file again. The location of the arrest bothered her especially since many of the private parties she attended took place in that very area. She didn't know the logistics, but she knew the parties were insulated from police action. She'd seen enough local officials present to conclude arrangements had been made to deter enforcement on the off chance someone reported unusual traffic at a particular residence.

Ryan checked her memory. There had been a party that night, also in North Dallas. Ryan decided police dispatch must know the exact location of the parties in order to prevent sending cars to one of the gatherings. Apparently, "wild sex party" wasn't enough of a clue to dissuade them from further investigation. Either the address of the Rawlings arrest wasn't on the not respond list, or an exception to the no-enforcement rule had been made that evening.

Ryan realized how little she knew about the exact arrangements for the parties. Every month for the past year, she made a credit card payment to a professional cleaning service ostensibly for work they performed at her house. Ryan cleaned her own house, but her payments bought her full access to all the parties she wished to attend. Access was simple. She called a prearranged phone number, stated her customer number, and received the code word and location for the evening's events. She wasn't naïve enough to think she was completely insulated from detection, but she knew the secrecy of the parties was successful because of the mutual discretion of all involved. Any attendees who exposed fellow partygoers risked exposure themselves. Based on what Ryan had seen, none of the individuals she'd seen at the parties could afford such a risk.

Yet, she hadn't considered the discretion of the men and women who were present at the parties to please the guests. She assumed they were paid well for their services, based on the high cost of her cleaning bill, but she hadn't given any thought at all about how they came to be employed and who employed them. Ryan looked at the jail photo of Ann Rawlings. Despite the grainy texture and circumstances under which the picture was taken, Rawlings's ravishing beauty was apparent. Ryan felt a prick of recognition. She was certain she had never had sex with her, but she was fairly certain she had seen her before, and she was fairly certain she knew where.

❖

Whoever was ringing the doorbell wasn't going to give up. Brett had finally left the office since she wasn't accomplishing anything of substance. Peace and quiet was what she needed to process the day's events. Dinner was a cardboard flavored Lean Cuisine and a glass of wine. She was about ready to turn in when her late night, insistent visitor arrived. Brett was tempted to yell, "Don't want any," but she reasoned the sound of her voice would signal her presence just as surely as if she opened the door. *So much for peace and quiet.*

Ryan Foster was the last person she expected to see.

"I thought I told you I didn't want to see you."

"Actually, you said something along the lines of stay the hell away from me until I'm ready to talk about Ann Rawlings." Ryan shuffled in place as if unsure what else to say. "I'm ready."

Brett couldn't quite read the expression on Ryan's face. Resignation? Fear? Her instincts screamed at her to tell Ryan to leave. She ignored them. Brett held the door open and Ryan walked through. They stood facing each other in the foyer. Brett flashed back to the last time they had stood there and the desire she felt in those moments. Things had changed drastically in a few days, but her craving wouldn't abate. Her hunger wasn't limited to wanting to feel Ryan's body against hers. She wanted to recapture the bits of tenderness they had shared. She didn't hold out any hope, but she could at least hear what Ryan had to say. She led the way to the living room, sank into the couch, and waved to the seat across from her. "Have a seat."

Ryan sat stiffly on the edge of her seat. She wasn't sure where to start, in part because she had as many questions as answers.

"You said you were here to talk about Ann Rawlings," Brett said.

"I don't know where to start."

"I'm not in the mood to cut you any slack."

"I understand." Ryan lied. She suspected the source of Brett's anger, but until Brett actually spoke the words, she wouldn't be sure. All Ryan knew for certain was that she didn't want to have to be the one to say it out loud.

"Do you?" Brett pressed the point. "I'm not so sure about that and I'm not sure I care. You said you were here to talk about Ann Rawlings, so talk."

"I have some questions."

"I doubt I can answer." In response to Ryan's questioning look, Brett said, "Attorney-client privilege."

Ryan tossed out an overture. "She's not a common prostitute. I don't think she was a pimp either."

"I know."

"Who is her employer?"

"Seems like you should be the one to answer that." Brett waited for Ryan's reaction. She wasn't convinced she really wanted to know exactly what Ryan knew.

Ryan ignored the jab. "Do you know or not?"

"Don't push me, Ryan. I'm not going to share anything my client has told me with you or anyone else."

"Can you at least tell me if she knows the name of her employer?"

Brett considered the request. The ownership of the townhome was information Jake had provided, not Ann. Surely she could tell Ryan that much.

"I don't know. Not exactly."

"You have an idea, though. Right?"

Brett decided to dispense with subtleties. "Ann Rawlings was arrested in a townhouse in North Dallas. Leonard Duncan is one of the owners of the property." Brett cursed inwardly. She should have known once she started she wouldn't be able to stop. She studied Ryan's face for a sign she knew what was coming next. "He was there the night she was arrested."

"No." Ryan shook her head. "That's not possible."

"Don't pretend you didn't know." Brett watched Ryan carefully. Her face was pale, her eyes wide. She was genuinely shocked by the news of Leonard's involvement. Or she was a consummate actress.

"I don't believe it." Ryan spoke the words, but they were more about survival than truth. A nagging doubt crept into her conscious. *Leonard? Really?*

"Save it. I know you knew. Why else would you walk the case through grand jury yourself?" As the words left her lips, Brett wondered why Ryan hadn't pulled the file off the docket rather than just flag it. She should have known someone else could have accessed the information Brett was able to obtain. Doubt crept along the surface of her awareness. *Maybe it wasn't an act. Maybe Ryan didn't know.*

"Brett, you have to believe me. I had no idea Leonard was involved. It's not in the report. I flagged that file because you challenged me, and I didn't want to back down. You were so insistent that day that I was out of touch. I wanted to show you I knew a thing or two about handling run-of-the-mill cases. I never even gave this case a second thought until earlier today. Frankly, I forgot about it."

Everything about Ryan's demeanor told Brett she was telling the truth. She looked Brett directly in the eyes; she leaned forward. Her arms were open. Brett believed her, but it didn't change anything. One major issue still stood between them.

"What about the sex parties?"

Like a flower when the sun goes down, Ryan shrank and withered, telling Brett everything she needed to know.

"I think you should go."

"Please, Brett, let me explain."

"Don't."

"Please," Ryan begged her. She didn't have a choice. Disgust was clearly etched on Brett's face. She couldn't walk out with Brett thinking she was a slut or, worse, a common criminal.

As if she could read her mind, Brett said, "Seriously, Ryan. You shouldn't tell me anything else. In fact, you shouldn't talk to anyone else about this unless it's your lawyer."

"I don't need a lawyer."

"Dear, that's what they all say right before they give a confession sure to land them in the slammer. If you haven't learned anything from our short time together, I would've hoped you learned the benefit of waiting until your attorney is present before baring your soul." Brett delivered her lecture with a smile she didn't feel. She stood and waved at the door. "It's late, Ryan. Go home."

Ryan remained seated. She took a deep breath and prepared to come clean. "About a year ago, Braden Marcus brought me a file. It was a municipal case, petty code violation. A nosy neighbor had called the city to report unusual activity at a house in East Dallas. The over-zealous code inspector decided the landlord must have been running an illegal multi-family rental based on the number of non-related adults living on the premises. Braden told me to get rid of the case. To handle it personally."

Brett nodded. Braden Marcus was Duncan's first assistant, the second most powerful person at the courthouse, and Ryan's direct supervisor. Ryan would naturally do what he asked.

"I got the message loud and clear. The charge was only a class C misdemeanor, but the property owner was someone who would draw headlines for even a minor infraction. I talked to the code inspector and he insisted the citation was justified. I went to the house myself. It was a huge place just off Swiss Avenue. I don't know how many people were there, but I met five. Five of the most gorgeous men and women I've ever seen in my life." *Before you.* "One of the women did most of the talking. She said they were models, on a shoot. I believed her. Every one of them was model-perfect. She assured me they would be more circumspect about their comings and goings. She said the shoot would be over soon and they would be moving to a new location. I sensed something was off, but I wanted to believe them."

"You wanted to impress Braden."

"Yes, but there was something more than that." Ryan took a deep breath. "I wanted to impress the woman. She was tall, dark, exotic. When she spoke to me, she stood close, practically rubbing against me. Her voice purred. She was the first woman since Julia that I had let physically close enough to arouse me. I'm sure it sounds silly to you, like I was thinking with all the wrong parts, but in that moment I didn't care about the consequences. I only wanted to melt into her embrace. She ignited a long dead fire within me, and in that moment, I would have done anything she wanted."

As much as she dreaded the climax of Ryan's story, now that she was well on the path, Brett wanted to know where she was headed. "What happened next?"

"I mustered the tiny bit of self control I had and left. I called the code inspector and told him I had handled the situation. I told him there would be no more problems with that particular residence. He was impressed I had given the matter my personal attention, so he backed off. One less time he would have to come to court."

"Who owned the house?"

Ryan ignored the question. "The next day, Braden brought me an invitation to a campaign party for Senator Story. He asked me to represent Leonard at the function. Senator Story had sponsored many of the bills Leonard wanted pushed through the legislative session, and I was supposed to be on hand to demonstrate our mutual support."

Brett decided Ryan was determined to tell the tale her way. She resigned herself to nodding at appropriate moments.

"The senator pulled me aside. Thanked me for handling a potentially volatile situation regarding his property in such a discreet manner. Said that someone else wanted to thank me as well and would I be so kind as to accompany him to a VIP party later that evening. He said 'she' would surely appreciate my presence.

"Have you ever been so desperate for something you would risk anything to have it? Or better yet, ignore the risk? The me that I show to the world is a person who takes risks for the sake of her cases but not in her personal life. Her personal wants and desires take a backseat to duty. Can you imagine how lonely, how tiring that can be?"

"Yes." Brett didn't have to imagine. She knew. She'd forsaken many personal pleasures for her profession, thinking the sacrifice was fulfilling enough. Reflecting, she realized too much sacrifice had created a vacuum, and large pieces of her life were sucked into the void. Brett knew Ryan's pain, and even though she wouldn't have chosen the same cure, she empathized. "Tell me what happened."

"I went to the party. She was there. She devoted herself to me and my pleasure. What I wanted, what I needed was the only thing that mattered to her. We were together for hours. Passionate, mindless hours. We didn't talk. I never even knew her name. Yet at that moment in time, it was the most fulfilling experience of my life.

"I was hooked. When I received a phone call inviting me to another party, I was thrilled. I eagerly gave my credit card number, not caring about the cost or the consequences. I never saw her again, but I have been with countless other women. Each of them made me feel like the center of the universe. My pleasure was their primary concern. What I needed. What I wanted. I thought I had everything I could ever want."

"I suppose it was a perfect situation for you." Brett didn't try to hide the bitterness she felt.

"I thought so." *But then I met you.* Ryan wanted to say the words, but she knew Brett wouldn't hear them on the heels of Ryan's confession. *I'm falling in love with you.* The declaration wouldn't mix well with the fresh tale of Ryan's indiscretions. She would have to wait and hope she had another chance.

Brett wasn't in the mood to hear any more. "You should leave."

"Is that what you really want?"

"What I want isn't the issue." It was, but Brett didn't trust her desire. For the first time in her life, she had fallen for someone whose career made her uniquely qualified to understand her passionate devotion to her own career. She'd been foolish to mistake Ryan's awkward personal interactions for naïveté.

"I don't understand. You represent some of the most reprehensible scum on earth. How can you forgive them their indiscretions, but not mine?"

Brett shook her head. "I've never fallen for one of my clients."

CHAPTER TWENTY-ONE

Ryan hardly slept. Brett's words echoed throughout the night. She replayed the scene over and over. In various alternate versions, she took Brett into her arms and professed her feelings. Brett was receptive rather than repulsed. *In my dreams.*

She finally gave up on rest. At seven a.m., she was seated at her desk, dreading her next move. She debated whether to confront Leonard directly or take a more circuitous approach through Braden first. Once she initiated the discussion, she had no doubt she would lose her position, if not her career. She resolved she would make her last stand with the boss himself. She spent the next hour poring over the files on her desk, tying up loose ends. At eight o'clock, she picked up the phone and dialed Leonard's secretary.

"Hi, Doris, is he in? I need about ten minutes this morning. Thanks. Be right there."

Ryan stood and straightened her suit. She had no idea what her future held, but she was certain of what she would lose if she didn't come clean.

Leonard was seated on the couch in his office, drinking coffee from an enormous mug. He half stood as Ryan entered, then motioned for her to join him on the sofa. She sat in the chair opposite.

"Good morning, Ryan. What can I do for you this morning?"

Ryan glanced out at Doris sitting at her desk outside Leonard's office. Leonard nodded his okay for her to shut the door. "You look so solemn. Gunning for a raise?"

"Hardly. We need to talk."

"So talk."

"Do you know a woman named Ann Rawlings?"

"Doesn't ring a bell. Should I know her?"

"How about Heather Daniels?"

"Not familiar. What's up?"

Ryan placed a copy of the police report from Rawlings's file on the coffee table between them. "How about the address of this arrest? I think you might recognize it."

Leonard barely glanced at the papers. His face assumed a stoic mask, and he stared intently into Ryan's eyes. "What's this about?"

Ryan took a deep breath. "This woman was arrested for compelling prostitution at a house you own. Why don't you tell me what *that's* about?"

Leonard's laughter boomed against the tension but didn't release it. Ryan waited for the punch line.

"I own a lot of property, Ryan." His tone held the tiniest trace of condescension.

"There's more. Do I have to say it?"

All traces of amusement were gone from Leonard's expression. He reclined against the sofa, arms folded across his chest, regarding Ryan like a lion assessing his prey. "No. You needn't say anything else on this subject. In fact, I suggest you tread carefully."

Ryan ignored the threat and pressed on. "I can't keep this from the attorney handling the case." She knew she was offering her own threat, empty though it was since Brett already knew enough about Leonard's involvement to cause serious damage to the case against Ann Rawlings, not to mention Leonard's effectiveness as DA. She held out hope he would have some plausible explanation for the events surrounding Rawlings's arrest.

"There shouldn't have been an arrest that night—of anyone. But I haven't run this office for this many years without making some enemies. One of them tried to take me down." He pointed at the report. "This woman, she was collateral damage."

"I have to tell her attorney. It's *Brady*." Ryan referred to the precedent setting case that required the prosecution to share exculpatory information with the defense. The legal requirement was a moot point since Brett already had at least a hint about Leonard's involvement, but a growing sense of foreboding kept Ryan from sharing that fact with Leonard. She wanted to gauge his reaction to her thinly veiled threat to disclose his association with the Rawlings case. His response would be the touchstone for her own future.

"It's not any such thing. We have the ability to use our own discretion in determining what's *Brady* and what's not. I trust that upon further review you will do what's right."

She expected his deflection, but she was still disappointed. Ryan knew "what's right" in Leonard's mind consisted of doing whatever it took to keep information about his involvement from the public. She conceded she had stretched the boundaries of legal ethics in the past, but never to save her own hide. *You made yourself look good though.* Ryan's thoughts were interrupted by Leonard's sudden switch in topic.

"By the way, I hear you've been spending a lot of your free time networking at private parties. I'm proud of you. I think the contacts you make at such functions will serve you well in your campaign."

Ryan's stomach turned to stone. She'd been prepared to face the consequences of confronting Leonard about his own behavior, but she hadn't considered how he would use her own her actions to force her compliance. *Stupid.*

"I appreciate your, shall we say, cordial relationships with other women. Diverse support will serve you well in the election." Leonard's words oozed indirect threat. He wasn't done. "I trust you to do whatever needs to be done on this case. And, as for the Edwards case, I expect you to score a big win. It will benefit the entire office and be the perfect kick-off to your official campaign."

In the next few seconds, Ryan considered her lifelong goals: success, acceptance, love. The menace reflected in her mentor's eyes spoke a clear message. She had worked hard to achieve nothing. She resolved to change her focus. Ryan took a sweeping look at Leonard's plush office, the vast mahogany desk, the wall of accolades, the shelves lined with photos featuring Leonard, his hands clasped with those of the governor, senators, even a president. He had all the trappings of success. The kind of success she now knew she would never have.

❖

Brett slammed her hand against the clock again. She had no idea what time it was or how many times she'd hit the snooze to put off the start of the day. She wanted to pull the covers back over her head and forget the trouble she was sure still waited on the other side of her slumber. Brett stared at the ceiling and calculated. Was it really only Tuesday? Three days ago, she'd been floating along in a cheesy, yet romantic swan boat with Ryan at her side. Ryan, with her muscular thighs. Ryan, with her doting indulgence for Brett's obsession with all the harrowing rides and artery-clogging foods the fair had to offer. Ryan, with all her baggage.

Having baggage wasn't the issue. Brett knew most anyone she met her age or older would carry around traces of the paths they had taken before. She knew she was far from perfect. She was a workaholic who kept friends and lovers waiting while she focused her attention on the needs of strangers. She'd spent her life trying to prove her brand of success was every bit as worthy as the moneyed achievement of her father and brothers.

Ryan was caked with the dirt from the trails she'd chosen. Ann Rawlings sold her body because people like Ryan were willing to pay for it. One woman sat in a jail cell while the other was poised to ascend to the top tier of prosecution. Brett didn't group Ryan into the truly evil category she'd assigned to Leonard Duncan. She could see the genuine vulnerabilities despite Ryan's actions, but Brett wasn't sure time and circumstance would ever wash away enough to let the real Ryan shine through. She wished it would, while simultaneously wishing she didn't care.

Time to stop thinking and start acting. Brett threw back the covers and swung her legs out of the bed. She had to see Judge Langston for the second time in as many weeks to ask the judge to let her withdraw from a case.

❖

Ryan pressed the print button on her office computer. When the single sheet slid out of the printer, she grabbed it up and penned her signature before she had a chance to reconsider. She folded the signed document into thirds and placed it in her briefcase for safekeeping until she had formulated the rest of her plan.

She decided to take a walk. If she'd stayed in her office, she would have been subject to the constant ringing of the phone and probable visits from Leonard to discuss her once bright future. Ryan knew only two things were certain about her future: she wasn't going to be working for the DA's office much longer, and she had to redeem herself in Brett's eyes. She needed a plan. A plan to save the pieces of her soul she hadn't yet sold.

Ryan's first stop was the intake division. She strode over to Joyce Grandon's desk.

"Good morning, Joyce."

"Morning, Ms. Foster. What can I do for you?"

Ryan handed over a small piece of paper. "I'd like you to pull this case for me."

Joyce stood and Ryan waved her back into her seat. "Sorry, I meant pull it off the docket. I've done some checking and we don't have what we need to present an indictment. I'll notify the filing agency. Will you put the file in my office when you have a moment?" Joyce merely nodded, though Ryan was certain she had to be curious about the request. Ryan trusted her to be discreet. "I'd appreciate it if you deliver the file yourself."

"I will."

Ryan turned to leave, but thought of something else. "Joyce?"

"Yes?"

Ryan didn't respond at first, embarrassed to admit she didn't know the answer to the question she was about to pose. "What happens to an inmate if a case is never presented? I mean, how will the sheriff's office know to release them?"

"There's a procedure in place." Joyce paused. "Would you like me to take care of it?"

"Yes, thank you. We won't be presenting this case. Ever. If Cindy has any questions, have her see me." Ryan had no idea what she would tell the prosecutor in charge of presenting the case to the grand jury, but she figured by the time Cindy Laramie got around to asking, she might not even be here anymore.

Ryan left the eleventh floor and wandered the halls to consider her next step. The moment she saw Luke Tyson in the hall outside Judge Langston's courtroom, the next piece of the plan fell into place.

"Hello, Ryan. Are you doing the pretrial yourself?" Luke referred to the pretrial hearing on the Edwards's case set later that morning. Jury selection was scheduled to start on Friday, a tradition in a capital cases. The first day, jurors would show up and receive the lengthy written questionnaires used in death penalty cases, and early requests for dismissal would be entertained by the judge. The pretrial hearing scheduled for this morning was designed to resolve any remaining legal issues prior to jury selection. Both sides had filed fully briefed motions and were prepared to argue their respective sides to Judge Langston. Ryan's intention was to let Jeff handle the heavy lifting, but she suddenly had a very different idea.

"Luke, I think your client should plead."

He laughed. "Little late now, don't you think? Besides, you folks have never offered a deal."

Ryan took a deep breath. What she was about to do went against all her well-honed prosecutorial instincts, but her resolve was strong. She was going to make headlines, but not the kind likely to get her elected to public office. She gestured down the hall. "Let's find a quiet place and see what we can work out."

❖

Brett pushed through the courtroom doors. Judge Langston was on the bench and a hearing was underway. She shouldn't have been surprised to see Ryan. She knew she would run into her again soon enough, but she wasn't prepared for the jumble of emotions just being in the same room with Ryan evoked. Torn, she finally slid into a seat at the rear of the courtroom. She watched and waited.

"Counsel, Mr. Tyson informs me you have reached an agreement," said Judge Langston.

Jeff started to stand, but Ryan placed a hand on his shoulder, urging him to remain seated. She stood instead. "That's correct, Judge. Fully executed plea papers are in the file."

Jeff turned toward Ryan and Brett got a clear shot of his shock at Ryan's pronouncement. *Ryan's pleading this case?* Brett couldn't imagine Duncan would go along with a plea offer. He'd spent lots of political capital building up the Edwards case as a true example of why the citizens of Texas were justified in delivering the death penalty.

As Judge Langston read through the plea papers in the court jacket, Brett heard Jeff muttering in Ryan's ear, loud enough for her to hear his displeasure about the news. Ryan sat facing forward, to all appearances ignoring the arguments of her associate.

"Everything looks to be in order. Will the defendant please stand?" Ross Edwards stood in response to the judge's request, and Brett watched the almost mechanical plea proceeding. Pursuant to the agreement, Edwards was sentenced to forty years in prison. He would be eligible for parole in half that time. From what Brett could tell, he was likely to be in his seventies the first time the parole board considered his release. Definitely a win for the state, but Brett wondered what cost Ryan had paid to avert a trial and why.

When the hearing ended, Judge Langston exited the door behind the bench, and Ryan watched the bailiffs lead Ross back to the jail where he would await transfer to a division of the Texas Department of Corrections. Satisfied with the resolution of the case, she methodically loaded her file into her briefcase. Jeff finally realized Ryan wasn't going to respond to his scathing commentary, and he stalked off. Ryan imagined he would find many sympathetic listeners among their colleagues. Not much was worse to a veteran prosecutor than having your boss completely undermine all your hard work by pleading away a winnable case. She wanted to explain her reasoning to him, but too many details were linked to secrets she wasn't ready to reveal.

As Ryan walked toward the exit of the courtroom, she saw Brett seated in the back row. *How long has she been sitting there?*

Ryan wondered what Brett thought about the plea. *Is she here to see me?* She met Brett's stare and hurried toward her. A familiar reporter from the *Dallas Morning News* inserted himself into her path.

"Surprising development on the Edwards case, Ryan. Care to comment?"

She glanced around his shoulder, willing Brett to wait. "Not so surprising, Ralph. We had solid evidence against Ross Edwards. This morning, I had a conference with Edwards and Mr. Tyson, and I laid out the strong and compelling evidence in favor of a guilty verdict. He made the only logical choice. I expect he will spend most of the rest of his life in the penitentiary, and I hope he thinks about Mary Dinelli every moment of every day."

"If the evidence was so strong, why offer a plea?"

"Our job is to uphold the law and protect the citizens of Dallas County. Edwards's conviction and lengthy prison term means we did our job." Ryan shot a glance at Brett before she finished. "I personally contacted the victim's family before we extended this offer. Sure, we could have made even bigger headlines with a month-long trial seeking the death penalty, but today we accomplished justice, swiftly and efficiently. It's not always about…"

Brett didn't try to hide the fact she was listening to Ryan's conversation with the reporter. This cool, collected Ryan was vastly different from the haggard, pleading woman who'd shown up on her doorstep the evening before. Which Ryan had she fallen for? Which Ryan threatened to break her heart? Brett knew the answers weren't simple. The real question was, did she have the fortitude to find the truth?

She could tell the interview was winding down. Time to decide if she should stick around or duck out before Ryan got any closer. A tap on her shoulder made the decision for her.

"Brett, did you say you needed to see the judge? She's got about five minutes now if you want to head back to chambers."

Brett turned to face Judge Langston's coordinator. She had mentioned to Gloria she needed to talk to the judge about the Rawlings case. She looked back at Ryan then followed Gloria to the judge's chambers. Gloria chattered the entire way there. "I ran that case number. It's not on the computer anymore. I called upstairs and they said it was pulled off the docket. The defendant's being released."

Brett was surprised by Gloria's efficiency. Maybe she had the case number wrong. "You sure it was the Rawlings case?"

"Yes. Joyce, upstairs, said the case is over. You can go ahead and submit a pay sheet—"

"Thanks, Gloria," Brett cut her off. "Will you let the judge know I don't need to talk to her? I have something I need to take care of." Brett didn't wait for a response before she took off down the hall hoping to get some answers.

CHAPTER TWENTY-TWO

R yan wasn't in the courtroom. Brett's next choice was the
DA workroom. She swung open the door, but her entry
was blocked when Detective Paulson barreled past her. She wore
a fierce scowl and ignored Brett's greeting. Brett stared at her back
for a moment before entering the room. Jeff Oates was sitting in the
main area with Detective Harwell. Neither looked any happier than
Paulson. Brett couldn't really blame them.

Jeff spoke first. "Guess you heard your witness skills are no
longer necessary."

"I heard something about that. What gives?"

He shook his head. "*Ms. Foster* pled the case. First I learned
of a deal was seconds before it happened." The growl of his tone
signaled he was furious. "Any other details, you'll need to see her."

No wonder Jeff was pissed. He had worked hard to make
sure Edwards received the ultimate punishment. From a defense
attorney's perspective, the forty years Edwards got was a hefty
chunk of time, but Brett knew Jeff's view was skewed.

Brett had a million questions, but she decided further discussion
was only going to intensify his anger. She searched for a good excuse
for her appearance in the workroom. "Would you like me to call
Kenneth and let him know you won't need him?"

"You can. We were supposed to meet with him again tomorrow.
I can just tell him when he shows up."

She felt her sympathy for him fade as she realized he hadn't notified her he planned to meet with her client again. *Typical prosecutor.* Once he'd started thinking of Kenneth as his witness instead of her client, he totally disregarded professional boundaries. *Ryan wouldn't have crossed that line.* Brett pushed the thought away. She wasn't sure she was ready to examine what Ryan would or wouldn't do.

She started to remind Jeff to contact her if he wanted further contact with her client, but realized the point was moot. "I'll call Kenneth myself."

❖

Ryan changed into her favorite sweats. She'd left the office with every intention of heading to the gym for a sweaty bout with a boxing bag, but her car drove home as if it had a mind of its own. Once there, she didn't have the energy to do anything but sprawl on the couch. Her guilt about her lazy behavior dissipated when she realized where she was and what she did or didn't do wouldn't matter to anyone soon.

She glanced at the typed, folded resignation letter sitting on her coffee table. *You can tear it up. Go back tomorrow as if nothing happened. You can still have everything you worked for, everything you ever wanted.* Not so long ago, temptation would have ruled her actions. Surely, Leonard could fix everything, make it so her indiscretions would benefit rather than detract from her ability to do her job and ascend to his.

Ryan shook her head. She knew better. And now there was Brett. Doubtless, she felt betrayed by the revelation regarding Ryan's sexual indiscretions, not to mention the legal conflicts she now had to unravel. Her letter of resignation was a small step toward repairing some of the damage. Ryan decided to rest a bit before taking the next, bigger steps.

❖

Kenneth's cell number was disconnected, so Brett called Tony to get his address. As she recalled, the address his mother had written on the intake sheet during their first meeting was just a few miles from her office. She plugged the address into her GPS and left the courthouse garage.

The old Oak Lawn neighborhood was on the sketchy side. New homeowners found great deals on older houses with lots of future potential in this area bordered by decaying apartment buildings and aging strip malls offering a wide selection of liquor stores and pawnshops. Unfortunately, the recent tank in the housing market meant many put off restoration, and the result was a jumbled mix of vacant, dilapidated structures next to cozy, updated homes. Kenneth's home was the latter.

Brett parked her Prius and walked up the drive alongside a gas-guzzling SUV. She knocked on the door, but no one answered. After waiting several minutes, she decided to leave a note. As she dug through her purse looking for a pen and paper, she heard voices coming from the back of the house. Brett abandoned her search for writing materials and walked along the flagstone path leading to the backyard. What she saw there made her pull up short.

Mrs. Phillips was standing in the center of the yard yelling at a woman who was standing in front of her. She emphasized each word by poking a finger into the chest of the other woman, and when she finally stepped out of the way of the finger jabbing, Brett had a clear view of Detective Kim Paulson.

Curiosity held Brett in place. She listened to the exchange.

"You promised me he would get the death penalty."

"I said I would do everything I could, and I did." Paulson waved her hands in the air. "I can't help it if that bitch prosecutor sold out a perfect case."

"What did he tell them to get that deal?"

Paulson didn't answer, and Phillips's tone grew more anxious. "He gave me up, didn't he? I thought you were perfectly placed to make this work. 'I'll handle everything' you said. 'Don't worry.' He told them where to find me." Her voice was blaring now. "They could be on their way now."

"Don't be ridiculous. I'm in charge of this case. If they had information about you, I would be the first to know. They don't even know your name."

"Like you knew Ross was going to get a deal in the first place? You said they would never make an offer on this case. You said they were going to take it all the way. I know him. If he was offered the chance to avoid the death penalty, he would give up his own mother. If they put me on trial now, I don't have any leverage. They'll give me the needle for sure."

Brett was riveted by the scene. She didn't completely understand what was going on, but she sensed Mrs. Phillips was Ross Edwards's missing partner in crime. What Paulson was doing here was a complete mystery. Brett wanted to stay and see what else she could find out, but the anger brewing between these two women was likely to create a dangerous situation. She started to back away quietly, when a piercing sound rang from her purse.

Brett cursed under her breath. Her BlackBerry. She rummaged through the contents of her bag as she dashed away. She finally found the infuriating device and switched it off as she ran down the drive. Brett thanked the universe she hadn't locked her car. She jerked open the door, threw her bag on the floorboard, and slid into her seat. She jammed the keys into the ignition, started the car, and threw it into gear. Glancing at the street ahead, she saw no other cars, but she found herself looking directly into the angry eyes of Kim Paulson.

Paulson slammed her open hands against the driver's side glass, yelling for Brett to roll down the window. Brett responded by gunning the engine and rocketing down the street as fast as her little energy efficient ride would go. She blew two stop signs in a row, turning first right, then left, her route the product of pure adrenaline. Her glance flicked quickly back and forth between the rearview mirror and the path ahead as she fought for enough composure to figure out her next step. She jabbed at her BlackBerry and cursed its slowness. Finally, it powered back up, and she pressed nine-one-one. Before the first ring, she heard the screech of tires, and her rearview mirror filled with the image of a large SUV. As the vehicle bore down, Brett clicked off the call and jammed her accelerator to the floor.

❖

Ryan sat next to Brett on the swan boat. The setting sun cast light shadows across the still water like flickering candlelight. They were holding hands. No barriers existed between them now. No politics, no litigation. No longer adversaries, they were free to be lovers. Ryan could only hope Brett would still want her.

"I'm sorry for everything."

Brett squeezed her hand. "Shh, it's over now."

"I quit the office, the campaign. I have no future." Ryan paused, still surprisingly cautious about exposing the extent of her vulnerabilities. "I could be suspended, disbarred even."

Brett pulled her close and murmured softly in her ear. "Darling, you still have a future, even if it's not what you once thought it would be. We'll get through whatever we need to. Together." She lightly kissed Ryan's cheek and nuzzled her neck. "I love you."

Ryan didn't try to stop the tears. She no longer cared about preserving her tough veneer. All she wanted, all she had ever wanted, was this combination of tender closeness and all-consuming passion she had found with Brett. Everything else would follow. "I love you too."

❖

Until now, Brett had no idea her Prius could handle hairpin turns at high speeds. She wished she hadn't acquired that nugget of information through experience, but Paulson's SUV was bearing down fast, and she knew if she didn't keep accelerating, her little car would be crushed in its path. On pure instinct, she'd sped wildly through the neighborhood, making erratic, last second turns in hopes she could shake Paulson. She was still ahead, but she'd hit two curbs in her attempt to avoid her pursuer. Brett glanced at her white knuckles, and murmured a simple "thanks" to the universe for sparse midday traffic.

Brett's brief distraction was costly. Paulson pulled alongside and steered the front of her powerful ride into Brett's left rear bumper. Brett gripped the wheel tighter as she struggled to control her careening vehicle. She could hear the roar of the SUV as Paulson accelerated again. Brett had no idea how long she could keep up this pace. She needed help and she needed it soon. She glanced left and right. Not a soul in sight. A mixed blessing, considering Paulson would probably mow down anyone who got in her way. *Just think what she'll do if she catches you.* Brett punched the gas and launched her car to the right. As she sped down the sleepy residential streets, she focused. She had to get to a more populated area. Paulson wouldn't chase her like a maniac down a busy, commercial street. Would she?

Brett glanced back. Paulson was gaining, but her last crazy turn had bought Brett some time. She reached for her phone.

"Tony, it's Brett. I'm in a hurry, so just listen. I'm being followed by Detective Paulson." Brett wished she had shared with him, or anyone for that matter, the major ick factor Paulson had been putting off from day one. If she had, she might be spared having to explain now, under such extreme circumstances. "I know this is going to sound crazy, but she's bad news and she's trying to run me down. The cops aren't going to buy it, so I need you to reach Ryan Foster." After she disconnected from 911 earlier, Brett realized she had to find help from someone who wasn't going to give Paulson the benefit of the doubt because she was a fellow officer. She recalled Ryan's subtlety displayed dislike of Paulson. Besides, Ryan owed her. "If she's not in the office, see if you can get her cell. Try Gloria in Judge Langston's office. She'll have Ryan's number. Just tell her it's an emergency."

"And when I reach her?"

"Tell her I'm in trouble and patch her through."

❖

The ringing phone nudged her awake. Ryan yearned to remain in Brett's embrace, but the persistent tone edged out the dream, and

Brett's touch fell away. She pulled her cell toward her, planning to turn it off without answering. The only calls she ever received were from the office, and they could wait. She didn't recognize the number, but the caller ID spelled out the name Logan Law Firm. Ryan flipped open the phone. "Brett?"

"No, it's Tony, her office manager. She's in trouble. I'm connecting you now."

Ryan didn't have time to process the curt message before Brett's voice came through the line, firing off facts.

"Ryan, Paulson is involved with Ross Edwards's accomplice. I found out, and she's chasing me down right now." Brett struggled to keep her fear from overwhelming her cry for help. "She already clipped my car once. I just turned from Maple onto Inwood. I need help."

Ryan heard the desperation in Brett's voice. She remembered back to the Internet research she'd done after first meeting Brett. "Your office is on Oak Lawn Avenue?"

"Yes, Oak Lawn and Fairmount."

Ryan's first instinct was to jump in her own car and drive as fast as she could toward Brett. As much as she wanted to run to the rescue herself, she knew she could do more for Brett by staying where she was and sending help.

"Turn around and drive to your office. Stay on main streets. Use Harry Hines Boulevard to get back to Oak Lawn. I'll stay on the line with you, but I need to make a call on my home phone. I'm right here and help is on the way."

Brett listened through the line as Ryan dialed a number and waited through the rings. She heard her announce to someone on the other line that she was calling on behalf of DA Leonard Duncan and needed cars dispatched to Brett's office and along the route she told Brett to take. She cautioned whoever she was speaking with that Brett's pursuer was a Richardson cop, but that she was wanted and likely to be armed. She described Brett's vehicle, then switched back to Brett to get a description of Paulson's vehicle and the plate number. Finally, Ryan disconnected the other call and came back on the line with her.

"Brett? Can you hear me?"

"Yes, I'm here."

"She still behind you?"

"Yes. She's a few cars back, but gaining."

Ryan grabbed her wallet and keys, jammed her feet into a pair of running shoes, and ran toward her garage. "Listen to me closely. Lots of help is on the way. You're going to be okay."

"Uh huh."

Ryan wanted to reach through the phone, gather Brett into her arms, and whisper comfort. She did the next best thing, forcing her voice to remain calm and sure. "Brett, I won't let anything happen to you. I promise." Ryan peeled out of her driveway and sped toward Brett's office. She would continue to offer the encouragement Brett needed, but she longed to speak words of her dream instead. She debated holding back, hanging on to the hope she would have the opportunity to speak her feelings when the current crisis passed. *What if I never get the chance? Say it now.* "Brett, I—"

The screech of tires interrupted her declaration. She heard a loud crash, followed by a slam. Then silence. Ryan shouted Brett's name into the phone over and over, but no one answered. She jammed the accelerator to the floor and tore through town, desperate to make good on her promise.

Chapter Twenty-three

M a'am, can you hear me? Ma'am?"
Brett heard the voice, but it sounded very far away. She wanted to go back to sleep, but the voice was persistent. "Don't worry. We're going to get you out of here." Brett waved her hand toward the sound of the voice. Something about the voice wasn't right, but the reason why eluded her. She wished whoever was talking would be quiet, let her go back to sleep. She'd been dreaming. If she could remember the last part of her dream, maybe she could jump back in and find out the ending.

Ryan. She'd been talking to Ryan, and then nothing. A crash, and then Ryan's voice was gone, replaced by the determined male voice urging her not to worry. Brett's eyes flew open. She was lying back in the front seat of her car, with a deflated airbag on her lap. She wiggled her fingers and toes. Everything worked. She pushed the airbag away and reached for the door handle. The door wouldn't budge. She looked at the passenger side of the car. Her little Prius was hugging the side of another car. She was going to need help to get out.

Brett didn't have to wait long before the voice returned. It belonged to a handsome man wearing a firefighter's uniform. He was holding a strange looking tool with a claw on one end and a pick and wedge on the other.

"Good, you're awake."

"I am."

"Talk to me about how you're feeling."

"My forehead's burning, and I feel a little shaky, but otherwise okay."

"You have some skin burn from the airbag. We'll take care of it as soon as we get this door open. Hang tight and we'll get you out of there in a couple minutes." He signaled another uniformed man over, and together they worked on the door. Brett leaned her head back and tried to remember the events leading up to the crash. Ryan. She'd been talking to Ryan on the phone. The memory of the conversation flooded back. Paulson was chasing her, and Ryan was talking her to safety. Brett looked down at the console, but she didn't see her phone. She looked out the window, twisting her head back and forth. No sign of Paulson's SUV. She could see the Scottish Rite Hospital on her right, which meant she was on Oak Lawn Avenue, yards away from her office. Suddenly, she was desperate to get out of the car, get to her office, and get hold of Ryan, who had to be worried sick. Seconds after she had the thought, the firemen jerked the door open. Brett lurched out of her seat.

"Wait a minute, ma'am. Take it easy." Fireman number one gently pushed her back toward her seat, but Brett resisted. She wanted out. Now.

"Please, ma'am. We need to check you out."

Brett pushed past him. "I'm fine." She was, for the most part. She leaned against her car and surveyed the damage. Her car, on the other hand, was not fine and would need to be towed. She looked all around, but Paulson was nowhere in sight. Two Dallas police officers were walking toward her. She wanted to leave, but knew she couldn't without giving them her version of what happened, or at least what she thought had happened. She figured Paulson must have struck her car and pushed her into another vehicle, then fled the scene when she realized police and emergency personnel were on route. As the officers came closer, Brett tried to formulate a story that didn't involve explaining why Paulson had been chasing her in the first place. The real version wasn't something she wanted to get into with a couple patrol cops on the side of the road.

"Ma'am, are you Brett Logan?" An officer with sergeant stripes on his shoulder spoke first.

Brett resisted the urge to snap at him. She was tired of all being called ma'am. *Wait a minute; how did he know my name?* Was this one of the cops Ryan had called? She started to answer him, then another thought struck her. Maybe this guy was one of Paulson's pals. Brett began to slowly back away and bumped into someone standing behind her. She started at the contact, but before she could move away, strong arms encircled hers, and a familiar voice whispered, "It's me."

Brett turned to face the speaker. "Ryan, thank god it's you." Brett's previous anger dissolved into gratitude, solace, and anticipation.

Ryan looked deep into Brett's eyes, eyes reflecting relief, excitement even. She hadn't expected to be on the receiving end of either of those expressions from Brett ever again. She didn't want to break the connection, but they were standing on the side of road with other people all around. She leaned close. "Hold that thought."

Ryan knew the officers weren't likely to defer to a mere declaration of her authority, dressed as she was, so she flashed her badge. "Sergeant Jimenez, thanks for your quick response. I know your men want to get a statement from Ms. Logan about the accident, but she's a material witness in a very important case. I need her first. She'll give you a statement when we're done. I'll give you a call when she's ready." Ryan grasped Brett's arm. "Ms. Logan, are you ready to come with me?" She hoped her confidence wasn't misplaced.

Brett mustered a trace of a smile. "Absolutely, Ms. Foster."

❖

Ryan drove Brett directly to her apartment. While Brett called Tony to report in and have him cancel her afternoon appointments, Ryan called Jeff Oates and braced herself for his resistance.

"Jeff, it's Ryan. I'm at Brett Logan's apartment." She read off the address. "We have a break in the Edwards case." She listened to his rant about how the Edwards case was over thanks to her. "Hey, Jeff, focus. Remember Edwards's accomplice? Brett knows who she is. We'll need to draft some warrants, fast. Get over here quick, and bring an investigator from the office. Someone you trust. And most importantly, don't tell Harwell or Paulson. I mean it. I'll explain when you get here."

Brett changed into loose fitting sweats, and Ryan fussed over her until Jeff arrived. She asked a lot of questions about what Brett had witnessed at Kenneth's house. A quick search on the Internet revealed the house was owned by none other than Ross Edwards himself. Brett's theory, that the woman who claimed to be Kenneth's mother was actually Ross Edward's missing partner in crime, seemed more and more likely. Paulson's involvement was inexplicable, but Ryan hoped a search of the house would reveal answers.

A few hours later, Jeff and an investigator from the DA's office left Brett's apartment with enough information to get a search warrant for the house Brett had visited earlier that day, as well as an arrest warrant for Paulson. Ryan had instructed them to use the charge of failure to stop and render aid to draft the warrant for Paulson's arrest, based on the fact she'd left the scene after crashing into Brett's vehicle. They could amend it to include charges relating to her involvement in the Edwards case once they had more information to go on.

"Don't you want to go with them?" Brett asked.

Ryan shook her head. "No. This isn't my case anymore." Before Brett could ask more questions, she posed one of her own. "Are you sure you don't need to go to the hospital?"

"I'm sure. I'm worn out and I'm sure I'll be sore tomorrow, but nothing some more Advil and a good night's sleep won't cure."

Ryan decided Brett's words were a hint. "Well, if you don't need anything else, I'll head out. I'll arrange for a unit to watch your place until we have Paulson in custody."

Brett reached out to grasp Ryan's hand. With the simple touch, her suspicions and doubts ebbed away. Ryan's mistakes made her human. She hadn't acted out of a desire to be devious, but a desire to be loved. Ryan's words echoed: *"You represent some of the most reprehensible scum on earth. How can you forgive them their indiscretions, but not mine?"* Brett knew her initial response was lame. Her desire for Ryan should equate to compassion, not rejection. She turned Ryan's hand in hers and placed her lips against

Ryan's palm. She kissed her gently at first, then traced her long, prominent lifeline with her tongue, pressing hard. She sucked the skin between Ryan's fingers, enjoying the arousal reflected in Ryan's shallow breaths. Each time she touched Ryan, she wanted more. She lifted her head and pointed toward her bedroom. "I'd like you to take me to bed."

Ryan didn't hesitate. She helped Brett up from the couch and followed her to the bedroom. She was surprised to find a stark room, very much like her own bedroom. It looked as if Brett had purchased the entire model on the showroom floor and added no personal touches to the tableau. She eased Brett down on the pillows and sat gingerly on the edge of the bed.

"Come closer." Brett tugged at the strings of her hoodie. Ryan hesitated. This day had delivered clarity about so many things, her love for Brett the most prominent. She had made love only once before, though she'd had sex countless times. It was essential to mark the difference with a declaration, but she was frightened. Her earlier interrupted profession of feeling had been fueled by the adrenaline at the thought of losing Brett. The adrenaline was gone now, replaced by arousal. She still felt the same, but the fear of rejection was no longer masked by the fear of a lost opportunity. *Say it. Say it now.*

"Brett, I love you."

Brett tugged the strings, pulling Ryan closer. She gazed deeply into her eyes and knew Ryan had just bared her soul. She admired her bravery and rewarded it with a declaration of her own, which she knew, without a doubt, was true.

"I love you too, Ryan. I always will."

Brett sealed her vow by kissing Ryan's lips, hard and fast. She wanted Ryan to be sure of her feelings, her commitment. She would not let the events of the last few weeks thwart the passion she'd felt from the moment of their first connection. She would battle anything, anyone who threatened her chance at a relationship with Ryan.

Brett was surprised by the strength of her desire. She was used to fighting for others, not herself. No other lover had inspired such ferocious fidelity to personal rather than professional pursuits. But this day, when her life had hung in the balance and with it, the risk of a chance to reconcile with Ryan, her priorities found a new order. For the first time, she knew true love was worth fighting for. The more she considered what she could have lost, the more intense was her desire to claim her place in Ryan's heart.

Ryan sensed a shift. Brett's touch was fiercely possessive, and Ryan willingly submitted. Her mouth fell open against Brett's probing tongue, and she surrendered to her commanding strokes. Ryan's breaths were jagged, and she could no longer hold herself upright. She broke the kiss just long enough to slide her body along Brett's length, taking enormous pleasure from the easy way they fit together. *She loves me.* Ryan cherished the words and the feeling flowing from them. Brett turned into her embrace, and Ryan returned her kiss with slow, gentle strokes.

Brett tugged on the strings she still held and pulled the hoodie over her head. Ryan sucked in her breath when Brett touched her naked breasts. She'd bared her chest innumerable times before, for a seemingly endless parade of dispassionate encounters, such that the act had become rote, a well-known step on a well-worn path toward physical release. Only once in her life had the act of removing her clothes been a prelude to making love. Until now. The memory of her fumbling teenage frenzy hardly resembled the fiery passion she felt this day.

Brett took one of Ryan's nipples into her mouth, and rolled it across her tongue. With one hand she teased Ryan's other nipple to a fine point, while using her other hand to slide her hand into Ryan's loose shorts. Her fingers traced Ryan's throbbing lips before dipping into her dripping wet, silken folds. Ryan arched her back as she rose to meet the triangle of touch. She urged Brett to touch her harder, deeper.

Her previous encounters had always been about her own paid-for pleasure, but even when she played the role of submissive, Ryan always firmly grasped the reins of control. The familiar grip slipped as every sense point in her throbbing body ached for Brett's touch. With every stroke, Ryan was certain Brett's desire to please her was strong, and she knew a complete exposure of her own vulnerabilities was the most worthy gift she could give in return. For love, for Brett, she relinquished all command.

CHAPTER TWENTY-FOUR

Ryan reluctantly padded her way across Brett's apartment searching for her phone before its persistent rings could wake Brett.

"Foster here."

"Ryan, it's Jeff. Boy, do I have news for you. Where are you? Can you come downtown?" Ryan glanced back toward the bedroom where Brett lay sleeping. Her old self would have jumped at the opportunity to be in the thick of an investigation. She was a different person now. She wanted nothing more than to crawl back under the covers, curl up next to Brett's naked body, and revel in the warmth after the hours of lovemaking they had just shared. She noted it was just after midnight, and she remembered she had a letter of resignation with today's date on it, ready to be delivered. She wanted whatever information Jeff had, but as for the exhilaration of the quest? She would leave it for him to enjoy on his own.

"I can't come in. Can you give me a rundown now? Do you have Paulson?"

"Not yet, but we have the next best thing." Jeff paused, and Ryan knew he did it for effect. "We have her sister."

She listened as he detailed the events that had occurred since he left Brett's apartment. They had searched the house Kenneth Phillips had listed as his. The occupants were gone, but Jeff and his team found scads of evidence left behind: wigs, fake IDs, lots of high tech equipment capable of rerouting phone calls, even a voice-changing device. Jeff's excitement caused his words to tumble over one another. "Brett may not have even talked to Ross Edwards at all. One of them may have been calling her instead."

"Slow down. Who do you mean?"

"Sorry, I forgot to tell you we caught Kenneth's mother. I mean the woman who claimed to be Kenneth's mother, anyway. We found an online trail that led us to an airline booking. We picked her up at DFW. She spilled her guts when we told her she could get the same deal Ross got if she talked." He stopped suddenly, and his tone changed from excited to meek. "I hope you don't mind. I just thought since you offered Edwards forty years, you—"

Ryan cut him off. "Don't worry about it. You did the right thing. So who is she?"

"You're not going to believe this. Her name is Marian Paulson. And get this, she's Kim Paulson's sister."

Ryan sank into the nearest chair and listened to the rest of Jeff's recap. Hiring Kenneth to make a false confession had indeed been Ross Edwards's idea. Marian agreed to handle the details. Their goal was to cast reasonable doubt onto the case against Ross, but Marian saw an additional opportunity. If she could set Ross up in the process, she could ensure he would get the death penalty and she would walk free. All she had to do was convince Ross she had done everything she could to enact his plan and then blame Kenneth's poor acting abilities for the scheme falling apart. She had amassed enough evidence to prove Ross was involved in the setup from the beginning. She was sure he would never rat her out if it meant risking his own hide. Plus, he really did love her, and she trusted his feelings to keep him quiet. Her ace in the hole was her sister, Kim Paulson, the cop. Kim, out of a strong sense of family loyalty and a large chunk of money, had agreed to help her sister. She'd maneuvered herself onto the case and located a former confidential informant, Kenneth, to play the role of false confessor.

Ryan listened while Jeff wrapped up the rest of the tale. Bottom line, Paulson was still on the loose. She told Jeff to make sure every effort was exerted to find her, and then Ryan clicked off the line.

Brett was awake when she returned to bed. Looking sleepy, yet stunning.

"Hey, baby, who was on the phone?"

"Jeff. They picked up Kenneth's mom." Ryan slipped back under the covers and relayed the highlights.

"Wow, what a night. Do you need to go?"

Ryan tensed. Did Brett want her to leave? "Go?"

"Things are hopping. I figured you would want to take the lead."

Ryan relaxed and pulled Brett into her arms. "I think I'll stay right here." She smiled. "Maybe you'll let me take the lead now and then."

"Absolutely."

"I want to be here with you more than anything I have ever wanted."

Brett felt the weight of unspoken words. "I feel a 'but' coming."

"But even if I wanted to join them downtown, I can't. I'm resigning the office, effective today. I've already written a letter I plan to deliver today."

Brett nodded. She sensed Ryan had more to say and her silence was meant to give Ryan the space to get the words out.

"Obviously, I'm not going to run for office. I'm still considering what to do about Leonard, whether to report him and to whom. If I start talking, I could be opening myself up to suspension, disbarment, maybe even criminal charges. I probably need to consult with a lawyer. I want to do the right thing, tell the truth and nothing but. I'll understand if you don't want to go down this road with me."

Brett recognized Ryan's declaration as especially painful for someone who had spent her whole life living up to the expectations of others. Brett wanted Ryan to know, with absolute certainty, her only expectation had been fulfilled. She wanted Ryan to expose herself, not with the whole world, but with Brett, her lover. In return, she would embrace Ryan's vulnerabilities and love her completely. In that moment, she realized she wasn't much different from Ryan. She defined her success by the work she did, not the relationships she cultivated. Her love for Ryan shifted her focus, and she could see a clear path to balance. Now it was up to her to stand by Ryan while she found a balance of her own. Brett hugged her close and spoke her own truth, soft and sure. "Darling, I'm here for you. Always. We'll get through whatever we need to. Together."

Ryan snuggled into Brett's embrace and closed her eyes. "I dreamed this once."

"Good dream?"

"Great dream."

Brett kissed her forehead. "Let's make your dream come true."

About the Author

Carsen works by day (and sometimes night) as a criminal defense attorney in Dallas, Texas. Though her day job is often stranger than fiction, she can't seem to get enough and spends much of her free time plotting stories. Her goal as an author is to spin tales with plot lines as interesting as the true, but often unbelievable, stories she encounters in her law practice. Her first stab at fiction, *truelesbianlove.com*, was a pure romance, released as one of the debut novels in Bold Strokes' Aeros e-book line. Carsen received a 2010 Lavender Certificate from the Alice B. Readers for her second novel, *It Should be a Crime*, which draws heavily on her experience in the courtroom. *It Should be a Crime* was selected as a 2010 Lambda Literary Award finalist. She is hard at work on novel number five, *The Best Defense*, scheduled for release in July 2011.

Carsen is married (Canadian-style) and she and her spouse live near White Rock Lake in Dallas where they enjoy cycling and walking the trails with their four-legged children.

Books Available From Bold Strokes Books

Breaker's Passion by Julie Cannon. Leaving a trail of broken hearts scattered across the Hawaiian Islands, surf instructor Colby Taylor is running full speed away from her selfish actions years earlier until she collides with Elizabeth Collins, a stuffy, judgmental college professor who changes everything. (978-1-60282-196-5)

Justifiable Risk by V.K. Powell. Work is the only thing that interests homicide detective Greer Ellis until internationally renowned journalist Eva Saldana comes to town looking for answers in her brother's death—then attraction threatens to override duty. (978-1-60282-197-2)

Nothing But the Truth by Carsen Taite. Sparks fly when two top-notch attorneys battle each other in the high-risk arena of the courtroom, but when a strange turn of events turns one of them from advocate to witness, prosecutor Ryan Foster and defense attorney Brett Logan join forces in their search for the truth. (978-1-60282-198-9)

Maye's Request by Clifford Henderson. When Brianna Bell promises her ailing mother she'll heal the rift between her "other two" parents, she discovers how little she knows about those closest to her and the impact family has on the fabric of our lives. (978-1-60282-199-6)

Chasing Love by Ronica Black. Adrian Edwards is looking for love—at girl bars, shady chat rooms, and women's sporting events—but love remains elusive until she looks closer to home. (978-1-60282-192-7)

Rum Spring by Yolanda Wallace. Rebecca Lapp is a devout follower of her Amish faith and a firm believer in the Ordnung, the set of rules that govern her life in the tiny Pennsylvania town she calls home. When she falls in love with a young "English" woman, however, the rules go out the window. (978-1-60282-193-4)

Indelible by Jove Belle. A single mother committed to shielding her son from the parade of transient relationships she endured as a child tries to resist the allure of a tattoo artist who already has a sometimes girlfriend. (978-1-60282-194-1)

The Straight Shooter by Paul Faraday. With the help of his good pals Beso Tangelo and Jorge Ramirez, Nate Dainty tackles the Case of the Missing Porn Star, none other than his latest heartthrob—Myles Long! (978-1-60282-195-8)

Head Trip by D.L. Line. Shelby Hutchinson, a young computer professional, can't wait to take a virtual trip. She soon learns that chasing spies through Cold War Europe might be a great adventure, but nothing is ever as easy as it seems—especially love. (978-1-60282-187-3)

Desire by Starlight by Radclyffe. The only thing that might possibly save romance author Jenna Hardy from dying of boredom during a summer of forced R&R is a dalliance with Gardner Davis, the local vet—even if Gard is as unimpressed with Jenna's charms as she appears to be with Jenna's fame. (978-1-60282-188-0)

River Walker by Cate Culpepper. Grady Wrenn, a cultural anthropologist, and Elena Montalvo, a spiritual healer, must find a way to end the River Walker's murderous vendetta—and overcome a maze of cultural barriers to find each other. (978-1-60282-189-7)

Blood Sacraments, edited by Todd Gregory. In these tales of the gay vampire, some of today's top erotic writers explore the duality of blood lust coupled with passion and sensuality. (978-1-60282-190-3)

Mesmerized by David-Matthew Barnes. Through her close friendship with Brodie and Lance, Serena Albright learns about the many forms of love and finds comfort for the grief and guilt she feels over the brutal death of her older brother, the victim of a hate crime. (978-1-60282-191-0)

Whatever Gods May Be by Sophia Kell Hagin. Army sniper Jamie Gwynmorgan expects to fight hard for her country and her future. What she never expects is to find love. (978-1-60282-183-5)

nevermore by Nell Stark and Trinity Tam. In this sequel to everafter, Vampire Valentine Darrow and Were Alexa Newland confront a mysterious disease that ravages the shifter population of New York City. (978-1-60282-184-2)

Playing the Player by Lea Santos. Grace Obregon is beautiful, vulnerable, and exactly the kind of woman Madeira Pacias usually avoids, but when Madeira rescues Grace from a traffic accident, escape is impossible. (978-1-60282-185-9)

Midnight Whispers: The Blake Danzig Chronicles by Curtis Christopher Comer. Paranormal investigator Blake Danzig, star of the syndicated show Haunted California and owner of Danzig Paranormal Investigations, has been able to see and talk to the dead since he was a small boy, but when he gets too close to a psychotic spirit, all hell breaks loose. (978-1-60282-186-6)

The Long Way Home by Rachel Spangler. They say you can't go home again, but Raine St. James doesn't know why anyone would want to. When she is forced to accept a job in the town she's been publicly bashing for the last decade, she has to face down old hurts and the woman she left behind. (978-1-60282-178-1)

Water Mark by J.M. Redmann. PI Micky Knight's professional and personal lives are torn asunder by Katrina and its aftermath. She needs to solve a murder and recapture the woman she lost—

while struggling to simply survive in a world gone mad. (978-1-60282-179-8)

Picture Imperfect by Lea Santos. Young love doesn't always stand the test of time, but Deanne is determined to get her marriage to childhood sweetheart Paloma back on the road to happily ever after, by way of Memory Lane—and Lover's Lane. (978-1-60282-180-4)

The Perfect Family by Kathryn Shay. A mother and her gay son stand hand in hand as the storms of change engulf their perfect family and the life they knew. (978-1-60282-181-1)

Raven Mask by Winter Pennington. Preternatural Private Investigator (and closeted werewolf) Kassandra Lyall needs to solve a murder and protect her Vampire lover Lenorre, Countess Vampire of Oklahoma—all while fending off the advances of the local werewolf alpha female. (978-1-60282-182-8)

The Devil be Damned by Ali Vali. The fourth book in the best-selling Cain Casey Devil series. (978-1-60282-159-0)

Descent by Julie Cannon. Shannon Roberts and Caroline Davis compete in the world of world-class bike racing and pretend that the fire between them is just professional rivalry, not desire. (978-1-60282-160-6)

Kiss of Noir by Clara Nipper. Nora Delaney is a hard-living, sweet talking woman who can't say no to a beautiful babe or a friend in danger—a darkly humorous homage to a bygone era of tough broads and murder in steamy New Orleans. (978-1-60282-161-3)

Under Her Skin by Lea Santos Supermodel Lilly Lujan hasn't a care in the world, except life is lonely in the spotlight—until Mexican gardener Torien Pacias sees through Lilly's facade and offers gentle understanding and friendship when Lilly most needs it. (978-1-60282-162-0)